TOWER FICTION

THE SILVER STAR

By Jackson Gregory

WOLF BREED
THE OUTLAW
LADYFINGERS
MAN TO MAN
TIMBER WOLF
SIX FEET FOUR
DESERT VALLEY
THE SHORT CUT
EMERALD TRAILS
UNDER HANDICAP
CAPTAIN CAVALIER
THE SILVER STAR
REDWOOD AND GOLD
DAUGHTER OF THE SUN
THE BELLS OF SAN JUAN
THE TRAIL TO PARADISE
MAID OF THE MOUNTAIN
SENTINEL OF THE DESERT
THE EVERLASTING WHISPER
THE DESERT THOROUGHBRED
THE JOYOUS TROUBLE MAKER
JUDITH OF BLUE LAKE RANCH
MYSTERY AT SPANISH HACIENDA
THE SHADOW ON THE MESA

THE SILVER STAR ✳

BY JACKSON GREGORY

CLEVELAND AND NEW YORK

THE WORLD PUBLISHING COMPANY

Published by THE WORLD PUBLISHING COMPANY

2231 WEST 110TH STREET · CLEVELAND · OHIO

By arrangement with Dodd, Mead & Company

TOWER BOOKS EDITION

FIRST PRINTING SEPTEMBER 1943

THE SILVER STAR.

CHAPTER I

THE gambler, preparing to ride to High Town, stood in front of a mirror which looked oddly out of place against the rough-hewn log wall of his solitary mountain cabin. As a rule a mountain man has little use for such accessories, being amply content with a glass big enough to shave in, and here was an affair flauntingly new and nearly a yard wide.

Given a man tarrying in front of a glass like this, the natural inference would find expression in the single word Vanity. What else do mirrors connote? It is certain that there would be far fewer of them in this complacent old world if there were in its inhabitants a degree less of self-satisfaction. Mirrors, it will be remembered, find their conspicuous places not alone among all the elegancies but as well in the most sordid of barrooms where the dregs of earth, the most unlovely sweepings of humanity congregate, and into them men with broken noses, drooping eyelids and crooked mouths peer without a twinge. Many a mirror, fine enough to reflect a lovely lady's bower and the lovely lady herself, has been shattered by a flying beer bottle or drilled by a bullet.

What the gambler would have seen had he been concerned merely with his own appearance was a thin dark face, cameo-like for still regular features and a pair of almost jet-black eyes just now fixed and expressionless

1

and cold, the watchful, tell-nothing eyes of the professional gambler. His hat, broad-brimmed and as black as his hair and eyes, was pulled forward and down, hiding the high forehead, shadowing the eyes.

As the incongruous presence here of his mirror raised a question, so did his dress. He wore a soft white silk shirt; the almost inevitable diamond, which is at once hallmark of his trade and a sort of concentrated reserve funds, shone in his black tie—and his coat was old, disreputable, torn, a thing of tatters. But his glance tarried neither with his own face nor with his clothing; rather it was fixed on that portion of the wall which, though at his back, reflected itself before him. So large was the mirror that from where he stood he could see the greater part of one side of the room, with its door in the middle, with a tin pie pan nailed at one side of the door and an old hat hung at the other side.

He slipped his hand under his coat, up under the left armpit. Without turning, without removing the weapon from its hidden shoulder harness or withdrawing his eyes from the glass, he fired twice. His revolver nosed the back of his tattered coat through which the bullets drilled two new holes. The tin disc fell clattering at the first shot and at the second the old hat stirred gently.

He took off his coat then and tossed it to a chair; he withdrew the short-barrelled revolver from the ingeniously contrived strap which held it and cleaned and reloaded it; from a convenient peg he took down a loose black leather coat and slipped into it. He had buttoned the coat and was drawing on a pair of riding gauntlets, sensing that already the late October afternoon had put a sting

into the outside air, when someone knocked at his door
and a voice called drawlingly:

" Hey, Steve! Is it safe to come in? What's all the
fireworks about? "

The gambler made no answer. Instead he stood motionless, thoughtful, bent on answering his own question:
" Who's that? " The voice was familiar; it was only that
he had not heard it for a long time. It was characteristic
of him that he did not give instant voice to the question;
he liked answering things for himself. In another moment he had it: Laribee. Yes, it had been a long time.
Not that Laribee had left the country; only that an old
friendship, begun in boyhood, had gone onto the rocks.
He crossed the room, lifted the heavy bar out of the iron
sockets and opened the door.

" Hello, Steve," said his caller offhandedly, quite as
though the two had parted yesterday. " Going somewhere? "

" Hello, Laribee," the gambler returned.

The two looked deep into each other's eyes, perhaps
hunting shadows where there were no shadows, Laribee
frank and a little eager in his interest, Steve habitually
inscrutable. Neither offered to shake hands. They were
much alike in some externals, so different in others that
inwardly they must be wide worlds apart. Two tall rangy
fellows, both outdoor men to begin with, Laribee still
brown and hardy while his former friend showed a pallor
under the dark skin which did not go with open air.
Whereas Laribee, who was far more of a dreamer of
dreams than most men ever guessed, had the look of a
hard-fisted, matter-of-fact young mountain rancher, the

gambler was of that rare type whom dissipation merely gives an appearance of spirituality.

Their eyes drifted apart. Laribee half turned and looked back over the way he had ridden, a winding trail leading among cliffs and steep ravines into this rarely beautiful mountain valley; having none of a gambler's instincts, Laribee had never acquired the trick of a blank and expressionless face. What he saw pained him, and he did not even think to mask his thought: This ranch had at one time been a rancher's ideal, spick and span, groomed to the last blade of grass, and was now as shoddy and down at the heel as though long abandoned. Well, a man couldn't run a ranch and live the life that was Steve Cody's.

" Got a letter for you," said Laribee abruptly. " Guess you were wondering what brought me up this way."

Steve had tucked his gauntlets under his arm and was rolling a thin brown cigarette. He completed his labor and then, with no sign of curiosity and in fact none even of interest, took the folded paper which his friend of long ago was proffering.

" Better read it," said Laribee, suddenly impatient and now obviously anxious to be gone, sorry that he had come at all. " I was to take back the answer."

His horse was standing close by; he went to the dragging reins, threw them up over the high head and swung up into the saddle. The gambler shot a swift, bright look after him, but when Laribee, mounted, faced about he was reading the brief message.

" Dear Mr. Steve Cody: I don't know how to write

this—it's to ask a favor—more than any favor. Will you come to see me for just a few minutes? It will not be far out of your way when you're riding to High Town. *I've got to see you.* There is something —— I wouldn't ask you if I could come myself. Please.

Corinna Lee."

" Answer? " asked Laribee. Perhaps, idealist and dreamer that he was deep down under the skin, he had clung to the contention that once a friend was always a friend; perhaps, with a reasonable excuse for coming, he had hoped that an old bed of coals might glow again and that from a living spark the aforetime cheery blaze of friendship might once more come into being.

Steve Cody, without looking up, sent a pencil of blue smoke stabbing down at the paper in his hand.

" Who is Corinna Lee? " he asked.

Laribee stared incredulously.

" Good Lord, man, where've you been? You don't know Corinna Lee? Don't even know about her? " Well, that was what cards did to a man! They spread out before a man's eyes; they extended into the vastness of a Chinese wall that excluded pretty nearly everything worth while on earth. Laribee, being outspoken, might have said all that and more, yet it chanced that he did not care to speak at length of Corinna Lee to any man. He merely said curtly:

" She is Tad Harper's sister. Half sister, of course. The Lees have bought the old Byron Motley ranch —— "

" Tad's sister? She doesn't say what she wants, Laribee."

" It might be—about Tad," said Laribee hesitantly.

"Yes? Anything wrong with the kid?"

"Nothing more than usual," retorted Laribee. "At least as far as I know."

The gambler folded the note back on its original lines and then tore it to shreds.

"Answer?" demanded Laribee the second time.

"No answer, Dave," said Steve.

Laribee's face flushed with quick anger. Then he straightened in the saddle and rode off. After all, this was no affair of his nor had anyone invited him to make it so. He was the queen's messenger, that was all, empowered to carry messages only when there were messages to carry. He struck into a gallop down across the unkempt meadow, swung into a cañon trail and vanished among the cedars.

The gambler, very erect and still, his head lifted and the lids half-drooping over his keen dark eyes, watched his former friend across the meadow lands. Then he withdrew his gaze and, quite as though Laribee had been outspoken in his criticism, let it wander across what was to be seen from here of his mountain ranch. The seal of neglect was upon it. He regarded it at first stonily, then whimsically. A fine gift it had been one birthday morning when his father, meaning to set his son's feet in a sober path, had ridden here with him and handed him the deed. The fences then were new or newly repaired, the low lands under cultivation, the orchard ploughed and pruned, the outbuildings models of all that ranch buildings should be. And the live stock was of the best.

"You always were interested in good horses, Steve,"

the elder Cody had said. "I've given you a start here in some Kentucky blue blood."

But that had been long ago, as far away now in the past as the days of friendship with David Laribee. Twice during those years the ranch had been pledged at poker; during that time storms had torn at roofs and battered at doors and walls with none to repair where they had ravaged; the surrounding wilderness crept steadily and stealthily in; fences sagged; weeds and thistles thrived. Only some of the original fine horseflesh, perpetuated in younger stock, remained of an earlier glory. For it was said of Steve Cody that there were two things and two only that he loved: Cards and horses.

He made his serene appraisal of the general untidy condition of things, whistling softly the while, then passed around his cabin and strolled unhurryingly out to the old stable, where he came upon the one ranch hand who took his pay, a gaunt, swarthy, limpid-eyed young Indian. The Indian squatted on his heels, his hands clasped loosely, a cigarette dangling from his full lips, his eyes giving the impression that his soul wandered afar. Thus he would squat by the hour.

"Saddle Blue Boy," said Cody.

The Indian came lithely to his feet, turned without haste and went into the stable. Presently he returned leading a saddled horse, a tall, rangy blue roan with a superb head held high on a proudly graceful neck. The gambler stood a moment, looking his mount over from high crest to gleaming hoof; there was not a hair out of place, not a fleck of dust or an adhering straw to make a blemish upon a smooth satiny skin. Cody went up into his saddle

and, as the eager horse whirled, he tossed a silver half
dollar to the Indian, who caught and pocketed it silently
and then dropped down on his heels, brooding.

The red sun slipped down behind the purple barrier of
the western mountains and the stinging crispness of a
late October day became a biting chill. Horse and rider
dwindled into a shadow shape at the lower end of the
meadows and were absorbed in the black blot of the
cañon into which the trail wound. But the first stars flaring out in the blue-black sky found them out where they
forded the upper tributary to Wild River, splashing water
gleaming like meshes of silver, and watched them strike
at last into the rutty county road. A little further was
a forking of the way, a narrow wagon track turning off
toward what had been known for years as the Byron
Motley ranch, the Lee ranch now. Blue Boy knew that
his master could have no business there, and kept straight
on.

In due course, which was something over an hour
after leaving the home stable, the few twinkling lights of
a tiny mountain village burst out into sudden cheery
being. The gambler had ridden around a sharp bend in
a rocky trail and abruptly the lights of High Town
flashed upon him. He drew rein and for a moment sat
thoughtfully regarding the oddity of a feverish community perched high upon a mountain flank. Only two
years ago a man might have passed this way and been
many miles from any more populous community than
that of a sprawling ranch. Then an unlucky devil, at the
moment holding himself the luckiest of men, had un-
covered a rich quartz ledge. For a few hectic weeks he

was in glory, his pockets heavy with money, his veins full of such corn whisky as came gushing in the wake of a new mining camp. Then he was dead, wiped out in a brawl in the Vargas road house, the victim of his own brief importance. For it was his discovery which sowed the seeds out of which sprang up such a crop of men as have made countless mining camps what the very word connotes. Into an almost depopulated corner of the California mountains had come surging individuals with little to lose and everything to gain, a hard and reckless lot. And so High Town was born, and already, only two years old, it had become a serious problem to a county which had long been at least as law-abiding as most.

Back into the mountains came Vargas as the first word reached him; he had been running a disreputable dance hall and gaming place on the Mexican border for some years, but was among the first to return. Back came Steve Cody who, having found the home mountains tame and unprofitable, had been plying his trade along that same border which had attracted Vargas. It was such as they who made the new town, and they made it wide open, a menace and a challenge to that steadfast, sober element which had so long dominated the county.

Had High Town been the only burning red spot on the local map it might have gone its rollicking, youthful way without more than a passing interest from the rest of the county. For it was after all but a devil's stewpot of humanity, set far back in the sparsely peopled mountains, and did not greatly matter one way or another to any save its own denizens. But fresh mining interest awoke in a region long given over to pastoral peace; errant prospectors swarmed in; a forty-years abandoned shaft in Chinese Gully was cleaned out, new-timbered and began to disgorge more or less profitable pay dirt; dredges were talked of for a gravelly sweep of Wild River; not ten miles from High Town the Connely-Prentiss interests started work and a newer camp, lusty rival to High Town, was already emitting the first strident birth-cry. Thus in an incredibly short time the country was being made over, and not to reflect God's image.

For so many years had a sort of dreamful ease and peace brooded over this aloof region that now this sudden change from drowsy placidity to hectic turbulence had found none of the old inhabitants ready to cope with it. Clay Hasbrook was sheriff; he had been a good and faithful officer; witness his re-election term after term ever since the young men of the county could remember. But Hasbrook was no longer as young as he had been twenty-four years before when he won his first election. Of late a troubled, perplexed look came into his eyes. "No, I ain't runnin' this year, boys," he began to say. "I'm glad to step out. Too old, I guess, for this fast pace. I'll try to keep the works from blowing up if I can for as long as takes you to get the right man. Most likely," he added whimsically, "if something like this hadn't happened I'd be running for sheriff when I was ninety!"

It had grown to be habit with Steve Cody, riding to High Town, to stop where he now sat his horse in the trail, and musingly regard the cluster of lights. He sat motionless so long tonight that Blue Boy grew fretfully restive, fighting the bit, pawing impatiently, striking sparks from granite with shod hoofs. Extended before Cody lay his playground or battle field, as one chose to regard the matter. He was a gambler and no true gambler ever lived who did not have his superstitions; he knew that there was such a thing as luck, a Something never as yet scientifically charted; he knew a man had his lucky and his unlucky days; there was no shadow of doubt within him that " hunches " were flashes of pure white light, true inspiration. Sometimes as he sat here and brooded " hunches " came to him.

But tonight, after he had waited a long while, none came. Then from the lights of the mining camp his eyes were drawn to the loftier lights of the stars shining in silver-white glory above the black wilderness. Of the stars one in particular caught his eye and held his interest. He stared at it fixedly; his upturned face in the starlight was more cameo-like than ever. He began to frown. The star drew and held him; he could not understand why; what significance for Steve Cody lay in a star?

" There's something coming up," he said wonderingly. " Something about a star.—I don't get it, though." He puzzled over the matter for some moments but in the end shook his head. " I don't get it.—All right, Blue Boy; shake a foot," he broke off, and pulled his hat down so that again his vision concerned itself only with the glitter of High Town's scattered lights.

CHAPTER II

THAT community is sadly bankrupt of human interest that does not have its genuine mystery or two, and the outstanding and baffling mystery of the environs of High Town was: " Why does the Judge always ride a mule? " Could any man have discovered the true answer to that burning question he might have burst without apology upon any of his fellows, no matter how busily occupied, and held undisputed center stage.

An hour or so before Steve Cody's arrival the Judge— to give him that title which he wore somehow flippantly like an old hat, and somebody else's hat, at that—rode his mule into the roadway which here served High Town as Main Street. A man of substance in the county was the Judge, physically no less than influentially and financially; he filled a saddle to overflowing, seeming to rest a compact and rotund burden on the horn; he was ruddy and nearly always smiling out of a pair of blue and childishly innocent eyes which had brought about the downfall of more than one gullible stranger who had failed until too late to realize that behind the baby-blue eyes was a brain of pure craft. At his sixtieth birthday, recently achieved, he had remarked: " Three score down an' ten to go. Let's make 'em good snappy ones, huh, boys? " Altogether he was likable and popular. In the main he was understandable. But the startling fact remained: He did ride a mule. Summer and winter, work

12

days and holidays, Sundays included, the Judge rode a mule.

The animal he bestrode today, a sleek, black, slim-legged, quick and sure-footed offspring of misfit parents, held one ear stiffly erect as though it had been well starched, while allowing the other to hang sharply downward and dangle and flop as though it had been broken. The Judge, ambling into town, regarded this eccentricity while singing softly:

> " Oh, she's the apple of my eye,
> An' me, I'm fond o' apple pie."

He greeted men to right and left with a hearty, " Hello, Bill," " Hello, Charlie," " Hello, Chuck," " Hello, Vargas." He knew every man-jack of them, including the latest arrival; and they all knew him. " Hello, Judge," he was greeted as he went rocking along to the newest new building in High Town.

It was a small square building of red bricks that had been hauled in on freight wagons from the sixty-mile distant railroad; it still smelled of green paint around the windows and fresh plaster inside. Over the single front door was a sign, gold on a blue background: " William Henry Bull." That was the Judge's name.

Dismounting agilely and lightly, handling his rotundity with the ease of a juggler and making nothing of it, he stooped with a first hint of difficulty and removed his spurs. His mule, alive to opportunity, made a swift gesture with bared teeth toward the seat of the Judge's trousers, but the Judge danced nimbly out of the way and went into the brick building.

" Evenin', Tim," he said affably.

A burly young man in shirt sleeves writing at a type-writer on a desk littered with papers, quartz specimens and small pasteboard boxes with labels neatly typed, looked over his shoulder.

" Hello, Judge," he answered, and humped back over his machine.

" Anybody been in the last hour or so? " asked the Judge carelessly.

Now there was no earthly reason for his not asking definitely if a certain particular individual had called, and Tim knew it and grunted somewhat disgustedly. For the young man was tired and hungry and of the proper mood for grunts. He kept pounding away with two calloused forefingers, and if he had spoken his thought it would have been to say acidly: " You know damn' well, Judge, that you can't get close to anything without creeping all around it and sneaking up on it from behind."

" Nobody, huh? " said the Judge. " All right, Tim, my boy. I wasn't lookin' for anybody. Now here's something I want you to do for me ——"

" Damn it, Judge," said Tim, striking a dozen keys forcefully, then pausing a moment to screw his head around and glare, " I got to get these letters ready and you know it. They go out on the stage the first thing in the morning. You better start signing what I've already written."

" Uhuh," said the Judge evenly. " But this here is all-fired urgent, Tim, old horse. Stop where you are."

Tim let his hands drop from the keys and swung about in his swivel chair. " Urgent, Tim. Get me? "

Tim appeared to know what was coming. He reached for his coat hanging from a hook over his desk and wriggled into it as he got to his feet.

" Yeah, I got you," he said out of a corner of his mouth.

The Judge's eyes twinkled.

" Bright kid you are, Tim," he chuckled. " If I don't fire you next month I'll raise your wages. What I wanted was for you to get Washington, D. C., on the wire, locate the President and tell him that the Prince of Wales ——"

" G' night," said Tim, on his way. But from the door he called back doggedly: " If those letters don't get off to Granite Gap on the morning stage, they'll be too late to do any good. If you've forgotten it, election's next Tuesday."

He closed the door emphatically and was on his way to a lunch counter. The Judge sat in one of the two arm-chairs in the room, shoved his hat back, put his thumbs into the armholes of his vest and his feet on the littered table. Thus he was in a strategic position to look across the table and out upon the road. But his eyes, at the very beginning of their journey, stopped a moment to tarry complacently at his boots. They always did. A generally untidier man than Judge William Henry Bull it would be hard to locate on short notice, yet all untidiness stopped abruptly at his boot tops. Small boots they were, squeezing his feet; black and shiny and high heeled; the exact replicas, in fact, of the boots of other days. The Judge liked to look at them and think of those other days. In the end he sighed comfortably and took stock of what lay beyond the confines of his office.

He saw a segment of a raw, brand-new town of crass unpainted frame buildings with freshly painted signs inviting to lunch room and " hotel " and hardware. It was at the moment a quiet street with a few saddle horses at hitching rails, with now and then a man or a couple of men, rough-garbed, heavy-booted fellows, appearing and disappearing. Diagonally opposite the Judge's vantage point, barely coming within the frame of his window, was the most popular place in town; the sign thrusting out over the side-trail which served as sidewalk announced merely, " Vargas's Place," and left to the imagination what was to be found within.

The Judge, never stirring, watched dusk fade into early dark. Lights came on, not street lights for there were none as yet in High Town, but lamps lighted in various buildings and shining out through shutterless and curtainless windows. More men appeared; the Glory Girl mine was running full blast, with day and night shifts, and there were the resultant ebb and flow of mine workers. The paths of most, going and coming, led logically through Vargas's Place.

It grew pitch dark in the room where the watcher sat, yet all the better could he observe the section of street wanly lighted by the stars and cut across here and there by paths of yellow light from kerosene and gasoline lamps. He chewed but did not light his cigar. He saw Steve Cody ride into town, pass out of sight on his way to the stable, return on foot and turn in at the door under the Vargas sign.

"It's a mess," murmured the Judge. "An unholy mess. It sure is."

It was but a few minutes later when a light buckboard drawn by two skittish horses came swinging into town. The man driving pulled up, handed the reins to his seat companion and got down in front of the Judge's door. The buckboard passed out of sight; the Judge pulled his feet down and stood up as he heard a hand at his door knob.

"Come ahead, Stephen," he called out cheerily. "I'm just gettin' a lamp lit."

The door opened, a stalwart form was briefly silhouetted against the outer night, then blotted out as the door was closed again.

"What on earth are you up to now, Judge?" demanded a deep, resonant voice, habitually grave and stern. "What are you sitting in the dark for?"

"Me?" countered the Judge innocently. "I tell you I'm just lightin' a lamp. Wait a shake."

First of all he drew down the window shade. Then a match flickered and a swinging lamp was lighted. The Judge, head cocked to one side, regarded his visitor interestedly.

"Look like you'd been goin' some, Stephen," he remarked mildly.

"Night and day," returned the other, rather grim about the mouth. "Thank God the end is in sight."

"Which end?" grunted the Judge. "The front end, maybe; just the beginnin' of the front end, too, ol'-timer. Squat."

The other shoved back his wide gray Stetson and

lowered himself into a chair with a long sigh. He was a big man, several inches taller than his companion, broad at the shoulders, but lean-flanked and trim for a man of his age. But a couple of years younger than the Judge, he had not run to fat about the middle; his face was lean and hard, strong-jawed and deep-browed. Under heavy brows merely sprinkled with gray a pair of wide-spaced eyes, very dark and very keen, looked sternly straight ahead of him. He was well dressed in a dark serge suit; he wore his clothes well; he gave the altogether correct impression of a man of power, of direct ways, of tremendous initiative—and of an utter lack of humor. There were no merry wrinkles about his eyes; no smile-creases about his large, firm mouth.

" What reports, Judge? " he asked curtly.

" Mixed, mos'ly. Good an' bad." The Judge sat on the corner of his table, swinging his small polished boots. " But you look to me like the nex' sheriff, Steve."

The big man nodded thoughtfully.

" It's going to be close," he said, " but I think we've got it. With less than a week left us, we've a lot to do.— How about Granite Gap? You still think I should go up there? "

The Judge waved to the pile of letters by the typewriter.

" My first hunch was we could round those boys up by letter. But it was a punk hunch. You start up that way in the mornin', Steve, and pull off a little round-up all your own. See ol' Matthews an' Ike Talbot an' the Poke boys an' the hull darned outfit. Like you say, it's goin' to be nip an' tuck, with every vote countin', an' it's my favorite bet that the game's goin' to be won up Granite way. You make yourse'f a nice snug solid delegation up that-away, an' it'll be you that's the man who gits the butter on his bread."

"I didn't come into this thing because my bread needed buttering, and you know that, Judge."

"Oh shucks, sure I know it. It's only a manner o' speakin', as the feller says. You're kind o' waspish tonight, strikes me, ol'-timer. Not a man in the county thinks you're goin' into this for what you can rake out'n the coals for yourse'f; you're too big a man to want to fool aroun' for any dinky sheriff-pay. But we need the bigges' man we can git, ol' horse, an' you're it."

"Never mind that part of it," returned the other crisply. "I am in it, and if the voters will give me the chance I'm going to sweep this county clean of riff-raff from end to end." His face flushed and his tired eyes brightened. "It's a tough crowd that's piled in on us the last couple of years, Bull; and I didn't realize half how strong they were until we began to check up votes. If this influx of bootleggers, card sharps and con men generally keeps up a little longer before we elect a ticket, they'll snow us under before we can ever get ready for a second try."

"That's account of Vargas," nodded the Judge, and made a face as of a bad taste. "He's lined 'em up; he's the one that made sure from the jump that the whole rag-tag an' bob-tail had registered. Either we down him good an' hard this trip, or he'll get his heel so solid on our necks we won't be able to wiggle our ears."

"I don't like to think of what conditions are sure to

be if we don't down him next Tuesday, that's all. This crowd that's flocking to the mining camps is going to come close to being the ruination of the whole county."

" They're a lot of *muy malo hombres*, I reckon," conceded the Judge. " But, in the end, they ain't goin' to do the country any hurt, m' son. They're runnin' wild just now an' they're full of oats and they need bein' halter-broke; but when things settle down, it's goin' to be a good thing for this end o' the state. Things was too smooth an' quiet with us, you know it, Steve; we was runnin' fast to seed an' squirrel grass. This used to be a minin' country, long ago, didn't it? Mining an' stock. Sort of gradual it eased off; 'stead of growin', it drivvled. The bottom fell out of stock prices, things got a bad case o' static; young fellers up an' went off; not too many babies got born an' a lot of ol'-timers up and died. We los' population in a steady leak, an' land prices dropped an' there was a bad complaint generally of no money. Now it's diff'rent ——"

" I'll say it's different! " snapped the other.

" Well, variety's the seasonin' that peps up the mulligan, ain't it? Our population in these here hills is well on the way to doublin'. As to money, we're goin' to be plastered with it. Money brings folks, too. We're goin' to creep back on the map, give us time; ranches that's run down now will perk up an' stage a comeback. After you're sheriff, an' clean up on the worst o' the Vargas outfit, there'll be a lot of good stuff lef'. Stuff that's jus' sort o' wild and—well, young, mos'ly. That's what's ailin' a sight of 'em." The Judge regarded his swinging boots and shook his head and sighed. "Me, I was a young feller once myse'f," he concluded downright wistfully.

"*Very* young," said the candidate for sheriff sarcastically.

The Judge cocked a bright blue eye at him.

"Yeah? An' how about yourse'f, Mr. Cody?" he asked pertly. "I seem to rec'lec' a certain time down to Halcyon ——"

"Never mind," cut in Cody shortly. Obviously he had no wish to go lifting dropped veils and peering back across the dead years. "Those were other days. There was no law in these mountains except the law which we made ——"

"——which, remarks Mr. William Henery Bull, formerly known as Buck Bull, now as the Jedge, was damn' lucky for me an' you, speakin' to Mr. Stephen Randall Cody, formerly known far an' wide as Curly Cody."

The heavy black brows gathered angrily.

"I tell you, those were other days ——"

But the Judge was reminiscent, and with some purpose of his own to be served, was not easily to be turned aside.

"I been called the Jedge quite some time, Stephen; so long, in fac', that I'd gamble mos' anything against nothin' a-tall that you, you short-memoried he-goat, can't remember when an' where an' why an' how I got that title of respec' an' admiration wished onto me."

"You were justice of the peace once ——"

"Rats. Long afore that, Steve, I was the Jedge. How'd it start?" He hitched closer, inching along the table top, and made a mystery of his very intonation. "It was when half a dozen of us boys 'bout twenty-five year ago, over Halcyon-way, caught Charlie de Vine an' Joe Vargas—which was this Vargas's grand ol' man, if you'll rec'lec'—an' hung 'em higher'n Jericho's kite. Now, wait a minute! We was all reg'lar an' proper; we made ourselves a sort o' court, rough an' very ready—an' I been the Jedge ever since."

Cody got up and moved restlessly about the room, keeping silent with an effort, hearing his old friend through, then for the third time making very clear that times had changed. Every human act must be judged by the period in which it was performed; what was criminal in one age might be common justice in another. Suddenly, aware that the circuitous Judge was shooting at some mark invisible to any other eye than his own, Cody swung about and demanded:

" What are you driving at, Bill? "

" Mos'ly nothin'.—By the way, I jus' saw your Steve goin' into Vargas's place. Funny, ain't it? A Cody son an' a Vargas son runnin' in double harness! "

Cody's large mouth clamped tight and made the watchful Judge think of a relentless steel trap, but at the same time a pained look, bleak and anxious, came into the dark eyes.

" I've told Steve to keep away from that place ——"

" Yeah, you're good at that. Tellin' people what to do an' what to leave alone. Not askin' 'em favors, not sayin' pretty please, just sayin', ' You do thus-an'-such or I'll knock your damned head off.' That's you, all right, old Blazes; only you picked the wrong man when you picked

young Steve.—Ever hear the expression used, ' Chip off
the ol' block' ? "

" Let be, Bull; let be," said Cody and looked wearier
than when he had slumped down in his chair. " I've
done the best for him that I knew how. If I've been
wrong ——"

" Leave out the ' If '," grunted the Judge mercilessly.
" That boy sure lost a lot when he lost his mother. Well,
I wouldn't rub it in if I didn't think he had it in him
yet ——"

" Let's not talk about him, Bull."

" I got to," contended the Judge. " Not all night,
though; jus' to ask a question: Is your Steve backin'
you? Or is he votin' for Vargas? "

Cody stared at him stonily. For a moment his face
was as inscrutable as ever was his son's. In the end he
threw out his hands in a wide gesture.

" I don't know, Bill," he said very simply.

" You haven't asked him? "

" No. I haven't seen him for over a month."

" You're not goin' to ask him? Before Tuesday? For
his vote? "

Cody's jaw hardened again.

" Do you want me to go to my own son, to ask him—
as a favor!—to vote for me? "

" Oh, hell," said the Judge spiritlessly, and looked
weary himself. But immediately he perked up again.
" Things keep a-boilin' up in my bean tonight, sort of.
Speakin' of them good ol' days an' the time when we
hung a couple fellers ——"

" What's got into you, man! "

" You'll maybe rec'lec'," continued the Judge equably
and a thought dreamily, " how one of our crowd was
a ratty little guy name of Spike Freedom? "

" What of him? He's dead long ago. You're just rob-
bing graves."

" Nope, Spike Freedom ain't dead. Nary. Ought to be,
yep. Ain't, though. You didn't see him las' time he blew
in an' out o' this neck-o'-the-woods, did you? I did." He
made a wry face. " Seven-eight your ago it was, as I
ought to know. Done me a low an' otherwise dirty trick,
too. Well, let bygones be bygones until chances come.
Now this: Me an' this ornery Spike Freedom seven-
eight year ago got together an', jus' for the sake of ol'
times, got pie-eyed out'n the same bottle. An' he, gettin'
loose-jawed an' wobble-kneed, let his foot slip once an'
spoke out o' time. I learned something from him that
I'd sort of had a hunch of already. When we swung Joe
Vargas off in the gen'ral direction o' the deep blue sky
we mos' likely did a good deed, but jus' the same we
got our rope on the wrong man. Happens it ought to
been Spike Freedom we dangled from the ol' oak tree."

Cody heard him out, at first incredulous, then frowning and at sea.

" You wonder why I'm turnin' back amongst the days
which are no more, huh? " said the Judge swiftly. " Well,
I sort of think out loud an' straight to the point when
I'm chinnin' with you, ol' timer." And though Cody
looked at him scathingly he continued unruffled: " Like
I said, las' time Spike Freedom showed up aroun' here
he popped in an' popped out like he was playin' tag with
the devil an' Spike was it. For reasons purely personal,

private an' unchristian, I been hopin' to see him ever since. Well, a feller tol' me this mornin' that Spike Freedom was back. Makin' split-hoofed tracks aroun' Halcyon. H'm."

Cody considered the news soberly but made little enough of it. He darted a shrewd appraising glance at his old friend's face but got no further along toward understanding what might be festering in the Judge's active brain. He did realize, however, that no questionnaire ever devised could corkscrew a direct statement from William Henry Bull when that gentleman was determined to remain evasive, and so made no attempt.

"One more thing," said the Judge, his attention abruptly seeming riveted upon his boots. "You heard, I guess, about the killin' over to Halcyon las' night?"

"Yes. And I'd say, not knowing any of the parties thereto, that whoever did the job saved the county an expense bill. The bird that he rubbed out was the man who robbed the down-stage last week, wasn't he, Bill?"

"Mebbe," said the Judge. "Anyhow, he ought to been killed—Heard who killed him, Steve?"

"No. Some fellow he was playing cards with, I heard."

"A feller hears lots of talk, don't he? What I been hearin'—oh, two-three blab-mouths tol' me—was that it was your Steve that saved the county that expense bill you was talkin' about."

When, in the silence that followed, he lifted his eyes from the gleam of his boots it was to mark how Stephen Cody had shoved his hat back and was wiping his forehead with a clean white handkerchief. Cody then pulled his hat far forward, shadowing his eyes, and returned the handkerchief to his pocket.

"Good night, Bill," he said quietly. "I'm off to a room. Got some work to do yet tonight, and I want an early start to Granite Gap."

"Night, ol' he-goat," said the Judge softly. "Keep a-ramblin', ol' kid."

CHAPTER III

By way of giving the devil a part of his due let it be conceded that Vargas's Place was characterized by a certain rough-and-ready honesty; it was openly what it was, and made no hypocritical pretence of being anything else. It was a saloon and dance-hall flagrantly defying the law, a new and slightly revised edition of the Mexican border dive which Vargas had sold in order to establish himself in High Town. Entrance into the main room from the street was through old-fashioned barroom swinging doors. Those doors were at once a promise and a defiance.

One naturally opens such doors by shoving them inward, perhaps with his shoulder. Steve Cody, however, observed another method. He pulled one of the swinging panels outward; thus before he stepped into the room he had the advantage of a swift moment of taking stock of those inside before his own person was more than dimly revealed. He did not appear to hesitate; he merely made an entrance which smacked of leisureliness. But his eyes were trained to observe in a flash and accurately.

Several voices greeted him. It was, " Hello, Steve," and " Hey there, Cody; just in time for a drink." He nodded in a curt fashion he had, but did not speak and did not smile. The pallor of his face was accentuated by the black tie and hat and coat which he wore; his

27

hat was thrust back a little so that a forelock of black hair escaped and had the effect of increasing the whiteness of his forehead; his eyes shone as black as two pools of jet ink and gave the one almost eerie impression of flashing, leaping life to a face which might have been cold marble.

He had unbuttoned his leather coat before entering, as though the short walk from the stable had warmed him; his gauntlets were in his left hand. He proceeded straight down the middle of the big room; it was kept clear for dancing, the small round tables of the place being set back against the walls. At the far end was the bar, and this the gambler approached, seeing his own image marching to meet him in the long mirror on the rear wall.

It was too early for more than a sprinkling of patrons at Vargas's Place; a half dozen men at the tables were buying commission drinks for a couple of Vargas's entertainers, importations from the south; a flabby anæmic looking youth seated at a piano was playing softly and listlessly and rather well, a dead cigarette hanging straight down from a loose lip; the three or four men at the bar, served by a white-coated gloomy-faced bartender, completed the toll.

" What'll it be, Steve? " asked one of the latter hospitably.

" Where's Vargas? " inquired the gambler of the man in the white coat. The latter jerked his head to indicate the rear of the house and the gambler passed about the end of the bar and disappeared through a narrow door.

" Friendly sort of icicle, ain't he? " grunted the man who had offered the drink.

"Know him? Or just know who he is? He looked like it was the first time he ever saw you."

"Know Steve Cody?" He snorted as much as if to say, "Who's asking fool questions now?" And after the snort he began what, if his hearers had been sympathetic, would have been a long harangue making clear that he and Steve Cody had known each other for years, had played more than one big game together and were, in their cool dare-devil qualities, brothers under their skins. Steve Cody walked to the end of a stuffy hallway. There were closed doors on each hand, a closed door directiy ahead at the end of the hall. It was from behind the latter that a quick, low-toned voice reached him. He put his hand to the knob and found the door locked.

"Who's that?" asked the voice.

"Cody."

The silence which followed was so brief as to be, to most men, unnoticeable. Almost the same voice, but louder now and less urgently quick and markedly hearty, called out, "Fine. Come ahead, Steve," and the door was plucked open.

There were seven men in the room and Cody entering looked them all over coolly. Vargas first of all, who had opened the door for him; Vargas who was the biggest prime factor in the new order of things in the mountains; Vargas who had the cool assurance to ask to be sheriff. In the man as in that house which he ran there was the same bold contempt of pretence. He in his own turn was what he was and made no bones about it. "To hell with the law," said Vargas's hard, fearless reddish brown eyes; "men make it an' I'll break it." In another age he would have been a freebooter; he was man enough for it and sufficiently unscrupulous. Its nearest approach he had found in the activities of a bootlegger, a border smuggler, a captain in various unlawful ventures. He had the trick of command; he had ability; he had a fine high courage. At thirty-five he was content with himself and with his lot; he inclined to a swaggering conceit. His big muscular body was pliant with youthful vigor; his ambitions stood sturdily on his achievements and still leaped; he was full-blooded and strikingly handsome in the way of coarse animalism.

The men with him were as well known to Cody as Vargas himself. They were all Vargas men; some had come with him from the border; the rest had flocked to him as naturally as any rabble of banditry to a bandit leader.

" We were just holdin' a little political caucus, Steve," laughed Vargas easily. " Accordin' to the way we dope it out, I'm your nex' sheriff."

" You're not as big a man as you think you are, Vargas," said Cody coolly.

" What do you mean by that? " demanded Vargas, though his grin remained like a good-humored afterglow of his laugh. " Mean I'm foolin' myself about the election Tuesday? "

" No. We'll know about that Tuesday night. You do too much explaining, that's all."

Vargas looked blankly at the faces of his men, then cried out half angrily:

" What in hell have I been explainin' now? "

" Why you happened to have the door locked. What

you were talking about. How pleased you are to have me drop in."

"Look here, Steve Cody! " Vargas thrust his face forward and his eyes narrowed. " We're friends, you an' me, or we ain't. It's been my idea we are. How about it? "

The gambler drew a step backward. The gesture was one of pure fastidiousness; Vargas's breath was hot in his face.

" I haven't any friends, Vargas," he said coldly.

" I've taken it for granted you're votin' for me."

" I don't think you have."

" Why not? "

" Because you don't take things for granted."

" Look here, kid ——" But again he grinned and once more reflected only untroubled good humor. He had been about to take an attitude of forcing an issue and common sanity said that this was the wrong man to seek to force. " Shucks, Steve. If you an' me ain't friends, nobody is. You got to vote for me or vote for your ol' man—an' I guess you got a good idea what'll happen to you if the county made a mistake and had Stephen Randall Cody for sheriff. I'll take a chance," and he winked broadly at his following and for full measure of camaraderie clapped the gambler friendliwise on the shoulder. " Might make you my deputy later on; been thinkin' about it. Where was you las' night, Steve? " he concluded after the fashion of a man who closes a business discussion and opens a casual chat.

" At Halcyon."

Vargas, and not Vargas alone, stared at him, astonished. Whether the surprise was at the fact or at the bald admission of the fact, did not appear.

" That's funny," said Vargas soberly. " There was a killin' over there las' night, you know."

" What of it? "

" Nothin', far as I'm concerned," said Vargas bluntly. " Know who got killed, don't you? "

" Yes. One of a pair of men that needed killing. Boney Marks. Maybe you'll remember," and the gambler's eyes under lids which were lowered just a trifle stared insolently into Vargas's, " that I had a little run-in with the two of them about a week ago? Whitey Robbins was the other. Seen him anywhere tonight? "

Vargas shook his head. One of the other men, a swarthy, thick-necked, small-eyed, crooked-mouthed and generally unspeakably vicious looking brute of the type that brews venom in the slums of the world, spoke up sharply and for the first time. He had shuffled his feet while Cody was talking; he now mouthed out his words in a sort of half articulate whimper:

" The guy wot bumped Marks off better look out f'r his pal. Whitey's bad med'cine, I sez it."

" Talking to me, Mush Mouth? " inquired Cody with the slighest elevation of his brows.

The man of the crooked mouth and mumbling articulation shuffled again.

" All I sez is ——"

" Anybody seen Whitey? " the gambler asked the second time.

No one, it appeared, had. Cody set his hand on the doorknob.

"I'll be around, Vargas, if there's a game," he said, and turned to go out. But at that moment rushing footsteps were heard along the hallway, the door was flung open and the sad-looking bartender burst into the room and treated them to the astonishing sight of his melancholy visage convulsed with laughter.

"What the devil!" exclaimed Vargas.

The man choked on his words and seemed caught in merry throes of mirth as finally he gave birth to his speech.

"Cripes! It's a girl! Y'oughta see her. Come knockin' at the door like it was a house! Cripes!" He goggled and choked; than knocking at the door of a saloon this man had never dreamed of anything funnier in an existence of many experiences. "Stan's outside, I tell yuh, an' knocks at the door! Kin you beat it? Fellers look aroun', wonderin' what the blazes. The girls looks up an' looks aroun' an' somebody says, 'Say, it's somebody knockin' at the door!' Beat that, will yuh? Me, I'm wonderin' what kind o' new shennanigan this is, an', bein' cautious by nature, I reaches under the bar an' gits my hand on a gat. An' I yells out, 'What the hell? Come in, why don't yuh?' An' in comes a—a girl!" He wiped the tears from his eyes, using his bar apron, and a new look dawned on his face. "Aw, you suckers, I mean she's a real girl. No doll-baby, no cabaret queen. Just a girl. An' awful pretty. Innocent kind, get me? Looks like—looks like—like dew was on her. Get me? An' scared? Scared pink. Ah. Scared pink an' white, that's what! Say, y'oughta seen her face when she looked aroun', when she piped the girls at the tables! An' y'oughta seen their lamps, too! Gee, it was funny, all right. A girl like her—I tell yuh, kinda like she had dew on her ——"

" You're crazy," said Vargas at last. And then he asked curtly: " Well? What's she want? "

The white-coated man's face straightened. He turned from Vargas and looked curiously at Steve Cody.

" Him," he answered and continued to study the gambler as though looking on him for the first time. " She asked for him."

No one had heard her steps in the hallway, light quick steps drowned by the clamorous voice of the man telling of her. And no one noticed her until she stood close to the door, looking in on them.

" Is—one of you—Mr. Steve Cody? " she asked, her voice sounding faint and far away, her speech broken by little breathless pauses.

She was looking all the while from face to face, anxious, eager, and was like some timid wild thing which had come to the edge of a man's camp, with eyes like a young deer's that might come closer to a friendly hand or, at a move, might whirl and run. She wore a fur jacket with a high collar turned up, and riding breeches; spurs were still on her boots; her head was bare; she had ridden into High Town and the night air had blown her hair about. A pair of gray eyes—they looked blue in the night-light—it was from them that the bartender must have caught his impression of dew—were big with her emotion of excited eagerness. They flashed across the hard faces turned toward her and then came to rest, at once shy and beseeching, upon the gambler's.

" You are—Mr. Steve Cody? "

He nodded curtly, staring at her, waiting for her to go on.

"I—I want to talk with you. It's important. Just a minute."

He nodded more curtly than before.

"I'm listening," he said.

"Oh!—But ——" Again she looked at the other faces bent so watchfully on her. "What I had to say—I wanted to say to just you."

A man nudged his nearest neighbor and the two laughed. Vargas started as from a deep reverie; his red-brown eyes had been fixed with burning intensity on the girl's face. He had been looking at her as a man might have looked if he had never seen a girl before.

"Come ahead, boys," he said bruskly. "We're through here. Let Steve an' the girl talk."

She stepped hastily aside, back into the hall, for Vargas to pass. He went out and the others followed; she drew even further away as man after man of them, each after his own fashion, availed himself of the improved opportunity of seeking her eyes with his own as they went by. One of them called back, "Luck, Steve." She came hastily into the card room and closed the door.

"I had to see you.—You wouldn't come to me and—and so I am here. I had to talk with you."

She had clasped her hands together, squeezing them tight to keep them from trembling visibly. She glanced swiftly over her shoulder at the door she herself had closed; it had been impulse, to shut out those other men; it was far less simple a matter to shut their faces out of her over-stimulated mind. Only now did she realize how the shutting of the door against them had served to immure her with the gambler. Obviously she was frightened; in a sudden panicky flurry she came very close to the sudden abandonment of her errand. With an effort she held herself back from headlong flight.

Again she looked straight, deeply searching, into Steve Cody's eyes. They told her nothing. They were watchful; they took in but did not give out save that it seemed to her, so darkly brilliant did they gleam from the mask of his pale face, that they radiated black light. She had imaged the man vaguely from careless descriptions; what she saw or thought that she saw in him startled her. He was so still, so coldly reserved, that he frightened her and she shrank from him as from something deadly. On the other hand, he fascinated her. She sensed an utter loneliness in him. He was one of those restless spirits who moved among other men, always in the thick of them, yet who was always alone. More troublesome to her preconceptions of him was that queer, haunting sense of spirituality; it was as though long dissipation had been a white flame which in the end had purified, consuming all gross materialism, leaving behind white ash and deathless spirit. Saintlike!—His eyes flashed malignantly. She felt that he had read her thought and grew angry at her for her prying fancies.

She grew aware of the long heavy silence. He was waiting for her and now her errand grew a thousandfold more difficult than before. He was a stranger inhabiting a world of which she knew nothing; it was almost as though they spoke different tongues. She had come to plead with him, and suddenly she felt as though a devotee might plead with equal chance of result before an idol. He had no interest in her or in what she might say; no curiosity. He merely waited that she might get through with what brought her and then go.

She began speaking swiftly, yet from the first she was hopeless. Her hope would have been higher had it not been Steve Cody but any one of those other men with whom she pleaded. Coarser clay, those others, and unspeakably repellent, yet somehow more human.

"I came to speak to you of my brother, Tad Harper. You are his friend."

He lifted the black line of his brows at her. It was a slanting line, the left eyebrow raised perceptibly higher than the other. All the expression to be read in his face was the speech of that slanting line. He corrected her as dispassionately as he had spoken to Vargas, and in the same words:

"I haven't any friends."

She glimpsed much of the man and something of his code, if code is the right word, in his rejoinder. He stood or fell by his own act. He asked no odds and gave none. What he did was done by Steve Cody. What he won was Steve Cody's winnings. What he lost, Steve Cody's loss. He shifted none of his responsibility to shoulders other than his own and he took upon them no other man's responsibility. At some time or another in his life friendship must have meant much to him, so emphatic was he now in abjuring it. . . .

She had to seek a new beginning.

"Tad is, after all, only a boy. You know what he is like, good-hearted and sincere and earnest and loyal." A

warmer flush came into her cheeks and her eyes brightened as she spoke of the boy who had been her hero and
about whom, as both grew into maturity, she had come
to cast a fuller, richer love that was almost motherly in
its protective instincts. " He is almost at the top of what
my father calls ' Fools' Hill.' Until we moved here Tad
was—was different. I am afraid for him! You know what
I mean, you who are older and have had so much more
experience. Tad is ——" She bit her lip and hesitated over
the actual admission; she had used the word "loyal "
just now and it meant so much to her. To go on was
almost to be guilty of disloyalty to her half brother. Yet
complete loyalty demanded the seeming disloyalty of her
charge: " Tad is changing so fast that he is no longer the
old Tad at all. It was little things at first; it is bigger
things now. He has begun to drink; he has taken to
gambling. We hardly ever see him. When he does come
back to us you can tell by his eyes that he is in a sort
of fever inside. He is slipping; slipping terribly! Oh, I
am afraid! "

Her tightly clasped hands came up before her breast
in a gesture that was involuntary supplication.

"You know what I mean! You know what Tad is
headed for unless something happens to stop him. Oh,
Mr. Cody, for God's sake——"

Even then he would not help her. He kept his silence,
waiting.

" I wish we had never come here! " she burst out passionately. " There is so much evil here; there seem to be
only lawless men. There is always gambling and drink-
ing; men laugh at stage robbery; a man was killed last

night over a card game. Tad has taken to carrying a pistol. He goes off by himself when he is at home, into the woods. I hear him shooting, practising.—Oh, haven't you any pity? Won't you help me? "

Asked a direct question he answered crisply.

" This is no business of mine."

" You could so easily make it so! "

" I don't interfere in other men's affairs."

" That is what Cain said ———" Again she caught her lip between her teeth, regretful of the words. But he did not appear in any way affected by them.

Baffled, she did not yet give up.

" Do you know why I have come to you? "

" You have told me that you made the mistake of thinking that I was Tad's friend."

" You are more than that! You are his hero! Do you realize that? And you are even more than a hero to Tad—you are more like his god! He would give his soul to be like you."

The gambler smiled cynically.

" You musn't sneer at what I say! " she cried tragically. " It is true. For Tad you have some sort of a terrible glamour; he is always talking of you; what you do and how you do it seem to him perfection. He is going wrong, all wrong, and no power on earth can sway him but you. You could turn him aside; you could turn him back. Back to his father and to his old, sweet life and back to me! "

" I am afraid I can do nothing of the kind," Cody told her impassively.

Still warmer grew the color in her cheeks and brighter her eyes.

" I know what is going to happen, for I know Tad so well. He is going to get into trouble, serious trouble. And in the end—he is going to be killed or to kill. You don't want that to happen, do you? It will be on your shoulders. You could do anything you wanted with him; you could make him a fine, good man or a bad. You can do more with him than a doctor can do with a patient he has hypnotized."

Tears of sheer hopelessness welled up in her eyes while she spoke and at the end she drooped despondently. The bartender was quite right; her loveliness was that of a dewy flower. But Steve Cody, whose love had been given to cards and horses gave no hint of being touched by either her loveliness or her poignant distress. He understood as she drooped before him that the interview was at an end, and opened the door for her. But it remained for him to see her in another guise before she went. The unshed tears dried and her eyes grew flamingly bright with anger.

" I think you have been more wicked tonight than even you ever were before," she cried swiftly and hotly. " And if there is any justice on earth God will punish you.—I hope He will! "

She slipped by him, drawing as far from him as she could, and passed through the door he held open for her. As she went down the hall she heard him following and came close to obeying an impulse to stop, to go back to him, to plead again with him. But the memory of his eyes checked her and she went on.

She passed through the large front room, looking straight ahead, conscious of all eyes upon her, hearing subdued voices, crimsoning under them. She felt rather than saw that there were men and women at the tables; the center of the floor was empty and she felt it to be endlessly long, a stretch like eternity between her and the front door.

But at last she gained the swinging doors, pushed one of them back and stepped out into the fresh night air, under the welcome stars. A quick deep breath of relief was checked abruptly at the sight of a man standing just outside the door. The light flooding out while she was yet on the threshold showed her a face which terrified her. It was a cruel, bleak, pasty-white face out of which peered cold, bleak eyes which were almost devoid of color. The man was young yet his hair and brows were white; his face was distorted by some governing emotion and she felt instinctively what it was even before she saw the weapon gleaming in his hand.

She tried to scream out and could not make a sound. She saw him raise his weapon; she whirled and looked back into the barroom. At the bar was one man. It was the gambler and she could see his reflection in the big mirror. He was raising a glass to his mouth. The albino was going to shoot him in the back.

Though it all happened in a flash, there was time in that overcharged moment for her to remember her own words; they had been a prayer to God for Steve Cody's destruction. How swiftly the answer was coming!

Fascinated, unable to stir, powerless to withdraw her unwilling eyes from the gambler, she watched to see him

drop under a hail of bullets. What she saw she did not at
once understand. What dropped was the glass in his hand;
his hand vanished under his coat; he did not turn, but
as the roar of a pistol-shot at her side burst against her
eardrums there were two other shots from somewhere
else. The man who sagged, his gun clattering to the floor,
and who then pitched forward to lie across it, was the
albino.

There was a clamor of voices. The released door swung
shut. She could no longer see within. But there remained
before her inner vision, like a vivid picture on a screen,
the image of the gambler, never turning, putting out his
hand to take up the glass which he had dropped to the
bar. . . . .

CHAPTER IV

MEN gathered in groups at various news-centers in the mountains to hear the election returns. One of the liveliest of these gatherings was at Vargas's Place in High Town; the big main room was filled to overflowing shortly after dark. As the first of the reports began to trickle in and the tally-man at the blackboard over the bar called them out and chalked them down they were greeted by shouts of approval or jeers of dissatisfaction. Vargas had engaged extra bartenders for the occasion.

Fewer in number, though no less tense and eager, were those who assembled at the old Byron Motley ranch. In the golden dusk of a day which had been like a shaft of Indian summer projected into the proper domain of winter a man riding a sleek and nimble mule pulled up at the steps of the deep porch which ran about three sides of the rambling old house. Of the two persons seated on the porch one rose swiftly and came to the top of the steps.

" Evenin', Miss Corinna," sang out the newcomer cheerily. " My, but you look sweeter'n any picter."

" Judge," laughed Corinna, " if they were electing a chief humbug today you'd win by—what do they call it?—a handsome majority. You know that you can't see what I look like in the shadows here! "

" Don't need to see," chuckled the Judge, and swung

43

skillfully from the saddle to the porch at her side. "What'll I do with Bucephalus? I've come for supper, y'know."

"It's good of you to come," said the girl, and her voice sounded grateful. She squeezed the hand he gave her and the warm friendly pressure was returned with interest.

"Good o' me, huh?" chuckled the Judge. "T' invite myse'f to biscuits with brown crisp shells on 'em, an' sech gravy as is made in heaven!—Cake, mebbe, too?"

"The kind you like best! How did you guess it?" smiled Corinna.

The Judge tipped his head to one side.

"I c'n see you fine now," he nodded at her. "I was right, too. An' you figgered on me comin', eh?"

"We hoped you might. Now never mind about Bucephalus; one of the men will put him in the barn."

The Judge moved along the porch to the side of the man who had not risen.

"Hello, Charlie," he said genially. "Feelin' pretty perky, huh?"

"Right as rain, Judge," he said in a hearty voice, and a hearty grip of the hand accompanied his words. "Take off your spurs, hang up your hat and rest a while."

The Judge stood looking down at him approvingly. Corinna's father, a long lean specimen of humanity, lay back in a big armchair with cushions piled about him, his right leg extended on a low bench. In the shadows not much was to be made of his face excepting that, like himself, it was lean and long, that the generous mouth was smiling, that his dark eyes glowed.

" What's the doctor's last report, Charlie? " asked the Judge casually.

" I fired him," said Lee.

" H'm! Bad as that? Well, I'm with you, m' son; me, I'd rather fire one o' them gents any day'n the week than hire him. It's a good sign, too, ain't it, Miss Corinna, when a man casts off his crutches, doctors an' things —— Where'd that girl go to, anyhow? "

" In the house, I guess, to order the biscuits in the oven ——"

" You can't fool me! She's takin' chances with that mule o' mine! "

" If she is she can handle him all right. And one of the boys at the bunk house will take him off her hands.— Look here, Judge, I've known you only a few months, not long enough for a man to be getting noseily personal. But I warn you that when I know you a little better the first thing I'm going to want to know is why a man like you rides a mule."

" Now, sir! " said the Judge. He sat down, stooped breathlessly for the brief battle with his spurs, put them inside his hat and the hat on the floor by the wall. " Now, sir! When you know me better, says you, you hungry lookin' houn', you're sot on gettin' personal. So be it; the gate's down an' decency is at an end. I take up the ga'ntlet an' I nose in right off among your heartstrings. Answer me this: How's it happen you're laid up right this minute like a broken soldier home from the war! "

" You know well enough, you old devil ——"

" Bein' as there's no ladies present," nodded the Judge, " speak freely! "

"I'm lucky to be alive. When my horse got his foot in a squirrel hole and ——"

"Whoa!" The Judge threw up a commanding hand. "You said it. When your horse—horse, mind you!—socked his fool foot down a squirrel hole an' shot you over his head like a cannon ball, you ought to made up your mind right then! A mule, sir," said the Judge forensically, "is the nobles' of created beasts. He's the only mount for a man as is endowed with any o' the instinks of a gentleman, sir! Take it from me. A man that takes pains about such things as his honor an' his underclo'es, that man ought to be jus' as partic'lar about what's under the saddle he straddles. A mule wouldn't of fell with you an' slung you over his head, an' rolled on you an' stomped on you an' savaged you with the saddle-horn. A mule's sure-footed; when bred as my mules are bred, he's quick-footed, too. He has noble qualities. An' he's faithful; he's like a one-man dog, that's what he is. He's been misjudged an' gossiped about long enough; it's time he was a-comin' into his own. Me, I'm for a gallant steed like Bucephalus firs', las' an' all the time."

A soft clapping of hands behind him advised him that Corinna had returned safely and was listening in delight. Charlie Lee laughed softly.

"Judge, you old pirate, of all the liars ——"

"Sh!" commanded the Judge. "We're no longer alone. There's a lady present—which is the final argument! You've got optical evidence that my Bucephalus, lef' alone with her, didn't either raise her to glory on his rear hoofs nor yet tear her to bits with his front teeth ——"

"He tried both," laughed Corinna, "but I carried a long stick and fought him off."

"Better go see about the biscuits, hadn't you?" queried the Judge. "Blasphemin' my mule! Pshaw!"

But she came and sat down at her father's side; her hand began a soft patting and fondling of the lean brown hand on the arm of his chair. The Judge's shrewd eyes watched them covertly. Close together, those two. Well, the ups and downs of life, the downs in particular, had tightened the bond between them. The Judge had known them for but a little more than six months; it was only last spring that Lee had bought the Byron Motley ranch and it was the Judge who had made the sale. He was always buying and selling, in his glory when swapping ranches or town lots or corner buildings or mining properties or horses, dogs, sheep or hogs. Witness his new brick building in High Town, his ownership of embryo town lots, his option on lands about and within the new camp, his shares in the Chinese Gully mine. He had snatched Charles Lee out from under the talons of a flock of real estate agents down in the county seat, had practically kidnapped him and had in a week's time taken his money and given him a deed to the ranch here. Now Charles Lee had the five thousand acres of land and the Judge had his money and the mortgage. The Lees, though not garrulous, were not secretive by nature, and the inquisitive Judge was not long in learning many things about them. They came from western Canada where they had lost Corinna's mother; this mother had obviously been a widow when Lee married her, and with them came the offspring of her first marriage, Tad Harper. Lee had been frank about his finances, and the Judge estimated that he would be holding the mortgage of fifteen thousand dollars for quite a spell. But the interest was at six per cent and the Judge was satisfied.

Then had come the accident; Lee, racing to head off a band of colts, had been thrown and brought to the house unconscious and, to all appearances, dying. For weeks he was despaired of; only recently had the man's grim determination shown signs of battle-winning; he had been injured internally and a leg, broken at the hip, obstinately refused to mend itself properly. As a result, all ranch responsibility had been thrown on young shoulders, those of Tad and his half sister. Corinna thrived under the new order of things; to her the sprawling ranch with its dimpled meadows, its flashing streams, its dense woods and deep, dusky ravines, was a bit of heaven on earth. She loved the place, she yearned to make it fully their own by making it prosper and thus throwing off the incubus of a mortgage. Young Tad Harper, too, at first was mightily absorbed in it and dreams of all that might be done with it. But of late had occurred that change in Tad.

The three on the porch sat a while in companionable silence, watching the light fade across the green fields threaded by the darkly flashing creek. From the bunk house, just out of sight among the pines, came little puffs of sound; men's voices, a harmonica in a sleepy rendition of " Over the Waves." The Judge whistled the old waltz softly, and his neat boots, patting time, gleamed softly in the dusk.

"It's getting dark," said Corinna. "Chilly, too. Shall we go in?"

Lee picked up his crutch, Corinna slipped an arm about him and they went into the house. A stout motherly woman in gingham apron, the housekeeper, Mrs. Hodges, but known by everybody as Aunt Mary, came bustling out of the kitchen and lighted the lamps for them.

"Howdy, Jedge," she greeted their visitor with a warm, moist grip of a capable hand. "Smelled the cookin' an' dropped in, did yuh? That's right. How's politics?"

"We'll all be knowin' right soon, Aunt Mary," responded the Judge cheerily. "If you've got any bets to place, I'll still take 'em. Cody's ticket wins."

"We all hope so," said Aunt Mary, and hastened back to her kitchen.

"You know I haven't a telephone line up yet, Judge?" said Lee from his couch.

"News'll trickle right out, jus' the same," the Judge promised him. "I got a hard-workin' sec'etary with nothin' much to do. Tim'll be pokin' out this-away off an' on all night—less'n you throw me out first."

"Laribee's coming to have dinner with us," Lee told him. "David Laribee, you know. He said that he'd keep us informed." He looked a little anxious as he added: "Think we're going to make the grade, Judge?"

"I think so. I'm bettin' on it. I almos' disremember at this partic'lar minute who's runnin' for president, but I do know that Stephen Randall Cody ought to be our nex' sheriff, an' John Bingham our nex' distric' attorney. Give us them two men in office an' we'll wiggle along. Don't know as the man in the White House matters so much;

leastways he don't cut so much ice in an' aroun' High Town.—So Dave Laribee's ridin' over, is he? Nice young feller. Think so, Miss Corinna? "

Corinna made a face at him.

" If you knew all the things you're dying to know, Judge Bull," she laughed at him, " you'd know all there is, wouldn't you? "

" Oh, Dave's all right," he rejoined smoothly. " I've known him since he was a pup; used to be one o' my boys, Dave did. Him an' young Steve Cody," he added thoughtfully.

Corinna, who had eyed him so steadily at his searching look when he had mentioned Laribee, moved restlessly about the room now, and at last set a lighted match to the prepared fuel in the fireplace, largely to be doing something. There were few secrets in this household, but she had kept from her father all knowledge of her ride into town a few nights before. He must not know and Tad must not know of her errand that had taken her there. Her back was turned when, taking up the cue, Lee gave expression to a thought which had suggested itself to many.

" If we elect Mr. Cody sheriff, looks as though he'd have an awkward job to do pretty close at home."

" Meanin' to get his rope over his own son's horns, first thing he does? " asked the Judge drily. " Well, he's man enough for the job, if it's got to be done."

" It's common talk that young Cody has shot two men during the week, Judge. One's dead; I haven't heard about the other."

Corinna leaned against the mantel, looking into the

quick bright flames and seeing Steve Cody's face in a barroom mirror, and a man falling to the floor at her side, sprawling horribly through a doorway ——

"Yep, one's dead, all right," chirped the Judge briskly. "That tin-horn card sharp that got his clock fixed over to Halcyon th' other night. Rumor says young Steve pinned the wings on him; dunno. Nobody has showed up yet an' said he saw the thing done. This other guy, the albino, Whitey, he's alive yet or was late this afternoon. Young Steve popped him over, there's no gainsayin' that; a dozen men, more or less, watched the how of it. That's no arrestin' matter, though, Charlie."

"Because the man hasn't died yet?"

"N-o. Mebbe he will. But the way it happened puts Steve in the clear. They say he was standin' up to the bar, takin' a drink. The man Whitey that was afraid of him stuck his gun in from the door an' started to drill him in the back. Steve was wearin' a gun under his lef' arm; he jus' let go his whisky glass, shoved his hand under his arm an' let drive, two shots, through the back of a nice new leather coat that must o' cost him fifty bucks. Kind o' fancy shootin', come to think of it; lookin' in a mirror and shootin' behind him. By rights," he added solemnly, "he could sue Whitey for his coat bein' spoiled, in case Whitey pulls through!—By golly, come to think of it, Whitey won't die, shot twice though he was! Not for seven years, anyhow!"

He began chuckling as though in high delight.

"Let's have the joke," demanded Lee. "I'm curious to know how even a hard-boiled old sinner like you can find anything funny in it."

" Why, it's this-away: Whitey's one bullet got away firs', didn't miss Steve Cody's head more'n a couple inches, an' drilled a hole dead center of Vargas's big new bar mirror. Know what Steve Cody said when the crowd began jabberin' all over the shop? He jus' said, ' Whitey should have remembered it's bad luck breaking mirrors!' "

Corinna at the fireplace shivered. The Judge cocked an eye at her, then rounded out what he had to say by remarking to Lee:

" Seven years' bad luck, they say, don't they? Well then! Here's the firs' instance, so to speak, I ever heard of where a man's playin' in luck to be unlucky. To make which clear to simple-minded folk, how c'n a man draw down seven years o' bad luck less'n he lives them seven years aforesaid? "

" There's someone coming," said Corinna and hurried to the door. She stood a moment listening eagerly to the drum of hoof beats, then went out to the porch, closing the door after her.

" Might be Laribee? " suggested the Judge.

" Laribee or Tad, I suppose," returned Lee.

" Tad, now," asked the Judge in all innocence; " how's the boy makin' out, Charlie? Takin' holt all right? Y' know, I like that boy a lot. Good stuff in the kid."

Lee smiled rather crookedly.

" And you ask a stepfather about him! You know what stepfathers are, Judge; mean and ornery and would rather say two mean things about a stepson than one good thing." He drew a long breath and stretched his arms high above his head. " Yes; you're right. There's a

lot of good in Tad. But you know as well as I do that
he has begun to run with the wrong crowd."

" Shucks, that's nothin'," was the cheery rejoinder.
" Me 'n' you, when pups, did the same thing, only later
on we outrun 'em an' turned out pretty nigh decent."
He tipped his head aside and listened to the subdued
voices outside. " Yep, Laribee, all right."

Laribee, looking fresh and eager and glowing, came in
presently with Corinna, the presentable prosperous young
rancher dressed in his newest best blue serge suit with
wine-red tie and shining tan shoes. He shook hands with
his host and greeted the Judge warmly. But while he
spoke with the two men he was obviously hard pressed
to keep his eyes from straying to Corinna; they were
honest, straightforward brown eyes, bright with eloquence
just now, and that eloquence had to do exclusively with
the intriguing picture Corinna made in a gay little dress
which Laribee could have described only as being " blue
and frothy and mighty sweet." He and Corinna withdrew
after a little while to a cozy corner where they talked in
hushed voices while the Judge and Lee concerned themselves with politics.

" It's goin' to be nip an' tuck, of course," said the
Judge, and for once in his life looked anxious. " I'm
bankin' a lot on what Granite Gap does. Cody's up there;
has been there four-five days, corrallin' votes. It's my bet
that he's winnin' or losin' the fight right up there." He
took out his old-fashioned gold watch, thick and cumbersome and faithful. " Reports'll start comin' in 'fore long
now."

Aunt Mary came in, shook hands with Laribee and an-

nounced that supper was ready. At table the Judge
revelled in crisp-crusted hot biscuits, roast chicken, rich
brown gravy, chocolate cake, innumerable cups of coffee
and conversation. He protested that though he had some
doubts concerning the election when he sat down, all
doubts fled before the second helpings, and that courage,
confidence and cheer were bred of such meals as Aunt
Mary had the knack of turning out. But they noted that
frequently he peeped at his old watch, and knew that
he was vastly more concerned than he gave out.

As he was picking birdlike at the last of the cake
crumbs on his plate a businesslike knock sounded at the
front door and the Judge surged up out of his chair and
cried out sharply, " Come in."

" That'll be my sec'etary, Tim," he told them, " with
the first precincts."

True enough, it was the burly young fellow who
pounded out picturesque letters at the Judge's dictation,
and who had ridden the half dozen miles from High Town
to give them their first inkling of how things were going.
He nodded in a queer machinelike way to all present,
beginning with Corinna and coming back to her in the
end, and promptly declared himself.

" Only scraps of news this early, of course," he told
them while unfolding a bit of note paper. " But the Judge,
there, was set on quick action tonight. Most likely before
day I'll wear out a saddle or two. A few precincts from
the biggest towns in the county ——"

But the Judge pounced on the memorandum and went
to work at it with a stub of pencil, sitting down again
and clearing a place among the dishes.

" We got two hundred ninety-seven votes, Vargas eighty-six," he announced with grim satisfaction.

" Here's High Town," said Tim, and handed him another slip of paper.

The Judge snatched it, sat looking at it a moment, plucking at his lower lip, and said quietly:

" High Town slid pretty solid for Vargas, huh? Gives him five hundred an' fourteen votes, Cody only forty! Well, they's forty white men lef' in High Town an' that's good news to me.—What'd you say about wearin' out saddles, Tim? "

But Corinna, abetted by Aunt Mary, would not hear of the young fellow dashing back to town without at least a slab of cake and a cup of coffee. He grinned defiantly at his employer and sat down.

" High Town belongs to Vargas tonight, if never before," he told them, his mouth full. " His place is jammed; he's cocky and full of swagger an' his own booze; he stood treat to the whole crowd when the High Town count was turned in. Already his place is getting what you might call lively."

" Let 'em eat, drink an' be merry," jeered the Judge.

Until now all anxiety had been kept under a surface mask, but from this point on until morning the little group at the Lee ranch grew frankly in tenseness, swung back and forth between quickened hope and fear. Early despair began to lift its head among them.

All night long riders between the ranch and town brought news. Laribee rode away with Tim; now one, now the other came hurrying back with the latest information. There were those inevitable surprises against which old campaigners like the Judge should be steeled, yet which again and again took them aback. The Judge began to perspire freely; at times he stamped and shouted like a boy, at other times he forgot that Corinna and Aunt Mary were at hand, and swore as not even he had sworn since the last election.

About midnight young Tad Harper came home. His face was flushed, not altogether with excitement, and his blue eyes were shining. Corinna ran to him eagerly, a great sigh of relief escaping her that he was at home again. Lee regarded him calmly, striving for tolerance. The boy, a man by the absurd measure of the twenty-first birthday past, was an engaging youngster intended by his own nature for sunny, frank ingenuousness but molded otherwise by recent environment. He thought to hide much man-stuff behind those clear eyes of his, but succeeded only in being pretty obvious.

"Hello, folks," he greeted them all breezily. "Great night, isn't it? Howdy, Judge. Hello, Laribee.—How's the game leg, Dad?"

They had thought it was Tim returning when they heard his horse in the yard, and the Judge spoke up eagerly:

"What's the lates', Tad? Us folks out here heard there was some sort of an election on. How's she goin' when you lef'?"

Bright as were Tad's eyes at the beginning they grew even brighter. Despite his effort his expression was one of high triumph. He was the one person here who had voted the Vargas ticket and—well, he didn't mean to

crow over them. So he spoke in a subdued fashion and
with an almost humorous attempt at indifference.

"It looks like Vargas, all right. Most of the biggest
precincts are in. Pretty close, at that, but I guess Vargas
is elected by a couple hundred votes. It—it's a big night
for him. He's standing treat to the whole town; I guess
it's cost him a thousand dollars already."

The Judge stood at the fireplace, his knuckles drumming on the mantel, his eyes narrowed.

"Granite Gap heard from yet?" he asked.

"Granite Gap? I don't know," said Tad. "Seems to
me—I think it is. Why, Judge?"

"Why, your eyebrow!" snapped the Judge. "If
Granite's in, an' we're behind, then we're sunk, that's all."

Tad grinned broadly, then with a heavy square hand
strove to wipe the grin away. Corinna stood looking at
him, a little pucker of distress between her brows.

Laribee departed and soon thereafter Tim came spur-
ring back. He looked gloomy and briefly confirmed what
Tad had said in the matter of figures: Vargas and his
running mate, George Epperley, candidate for district
attorney, were both leading Cody and Bingham, and it
began to look like a safe lead. High Town, at least, conceded the victory to the Vargas element. Granite Gap?
No. Granite Gap and some few other outlying districts
were not yet accounted for.

Whereupon the Judge drew a long breath and went
hunting black coffee.

"We'll lick 'em yet," he muttered. "Jus' you fellers
watch!"

The final, complete news came to them about two hours

later. It was brought by David Laribee. Even before he spoke it, even before he came into the room, they looked at one another with white faces. His tread on the steps and across the porch was the ponderous, dragging tread of a man who brought heavy tidings.

He stood in the door looking in at them, and his own face was white and drawn.

"Out with it!" shouted the Judge. "Out with it. Damn it man, out with it! We c'n take it standin' up, I guess. We're licked, are we?"

Laribee shook his head.

"No," he said, in a curious, strained voice. "That isn't it. Granite Gap came in solid and, as far as the election goes, we've won. A few other tardy districts make it sure. Even Vargas concedes it.—No, Judge, that isn't it——"

Mystified, the Judge stared at him. He started to open his mouth, then clamped it tight; his eyes were like gimlets. He did not speak again.

"It—it's bad news, Judge," said Laribee softly. "Hard on all of us; hardest on you, I guess. Cody—Cody's dead!"

He told them gravely all that he knew. At Vargas's Place, with a half-drunk crowd going crazy with excitement as the pendulum of votes swung back and forth all night, now toward Stephen Cody, now toward Vargas, there had been at the end an almost steady storm of Cody votes. Higher and higher climbed the Cody majority, until Vargas no longer swaggered but began to grow uneasy. Then Granite Gap; the crowd heard the tally-man out in silence, then broke into a storm of anger at the result. Cody was elected.

"A man had just come running from the telephone," said Laribee. "In the hell of an uproar no one would pay any attention to what he had to say; nothing else seemed to matter to anybody. I was shouldering my way out to get back to you on the run. Then someone caught what the man was yelling, and pretty soon it came up in a roar: 'Cody's dead! They found him up Granite Gap way. Somebody shot him.'"

The Judge took the news like a blow in the face. But, as after a savage blow, he stiffened. He opened his mouth to speak, then closed it wordlessly. No one but himself knew, though they partially understood, how close together throughout the long years the Judge and Stephen Cody had stood.

The Judge, stepping softly, crossed the room and went outside, closing the door quietly after him. They heard him go down the steps into the yard.

"He's gone without his hat," said Charles Lee.

Corinna, understanding more than the others, shook her head.

"He hasn't gone—he just wants to be alone a little while. He ——" She broke off, a catch in her voice, and hid her face in her hands.

The others spoke in hushed voices.

"We might have been on the lookout for it," said Lee drearily. "They meant to win either way. Here we elect a fine, decent man for sheriff and then they mow him down ——"

"No," said Laribee stonily. "It wasn't like that." His

weary face was haggard now and the clear eyes clouded with tears which he dashed away angrily; tears of rage, tears too of profound sorrow. For there had been the time when David Laribee had been almost like another son in Stephen Cody's house.

"I don't understand," said Lee after a moment.

"Wait," muttered Laribee. "Any coffee left, Corinna? The Judge will be back in a minute and he'll want to know. One telling will do for all."

Corinna, brimming with tender sympathy, went with him for the coffee.

The Judge returned almost immediately to glare at them out of red puckered eyes.

"Well?" he demanded curtly of Laribee. "You was sayin' something, young feller. Me, I thought I heard that damn' mule o' mine kickin' the side out'n the barn. 'S all right. Now, what's the story? We elec' a man an' them skunks up an' kill him, that it?"

"What we did, Judge, was elect a dead man," said Laribee. "They found him only a few hours ago but—they say he had been dead at least two days!"

"My God!" said the Judge. "Then—then——"

Lee, stiffening in his chair, put it into words:

"Then who is sheriff? If a man is elected—and he is dead while the votes are being cast—then what?"

Out of a heavy silence Laribee spoke again.

"All I can do is tell you what I know. The crowd at Vargas's Place went crazy again when the word was passed around. They yelled the same thing: 'Who's sheriff now?' Vargas's face was a study; all of a sudden he jumped upon a chair and yelled them down. 'I ran him a close second,' he yelled at them. 'Me, Vargas; I come close to bein' elected an' would have been but for crooked work. Anyhow, he's dead now an' I'm the county's nex' choice. Me, I'm sheriff by rights, an' by God, I'm a man to take my rights, too!'

"The drunk fools all around him began cheering and shouting that that was right; that Vargas was their sheriff. Then I saw Steve Cody. He stood looking around at them; just looking. What Steve was thinking or whether he had started at all, you couldn't tell. He just looked and kept quiet. And then pretty soon the mob got tired of yelling and Steve walked up to Vargas.

"'Look here, Vargas,' he said, cool as ice. 'You want to know who's sheriff, do you? Well, I'll tell you. I am.'

"Vargas stared at him, then hooted. But Steve, never batting an eye, went on. He said: 'The county elected Stephen Randall Cody. My father had been dead two days, they say, when the votes were cast. Just now I am the only Stephen Randall Cody on earth, so far as I know. And I'm sheriff. I mean that, Vargas.' And he went out, and men just stood back and looked at him, watching him go, and never said a word."

And in the matter of not saying a word the little gathering here at the Lee ranch emulated that mystified crowd at Vargas's Place. At last:

"It's an absurdly impossible situation," said Lee, frowning.

"Impossible be damned!" shouted the old Judge. "Where's my hat?"

"What are you going to do, man?"

But all that the Judge would say was, "Where's my

hat? " And when it was brought for him from the porch, his spurs still inside the crown, he took his departure without apology to his host or explanation to any. They heard him race townward on his mule, rushing by the house, swearing at every jump.

CHAPTER V

. . . AND on the first day of January, Steve Cody, gambler, took the oath of sheriff and pinned to his shirt, under the lapel of a new black leather coat, the shining badge of high authority.

An unprecedented, utterly unheard of condition of affairs had convulsed the county. Voters, at the moment they exulted over having elected Stephen Randall Cody, learned in dismay that there was but one Stephen Randall Cody among them, the gambler and consort of that very element they had thought to be taking the first step toward stamping out. And it was borne in upon them without delay that this man stood with stubborn firmness by his declaration that, like it or not, they had voted him into office.

When first that coolly delivered ultimatum was made there was not a man in the county who stood by him, not a man but laughed at the mad brazenness of it. There was the Vargas faction who hoped still that Vargas would find his way into office; the opposing faction that held Steve Cody to be no better than a Vargas man. Yet from the first the gambler had had no misgivings.

He had first of all sought out the Judge even while that worthy, riding a mule as hard as ever mule was ridden, was seeking him, and in an interview that lasted scarcely ten minutes put his cards on the table. Leaving the Judge to study and ponder, he had spent what was

63

left of the night riding to Granite Gap where the next morning the Judge joined him. The bullet-riddled body of the elder Cody made its last short journey, and together Cody's son and his best friend turned away, one face puckered and twitching, the other as blank as a whitewashed wall. A hundred men had gathered, bare-headed, stern, silent fellows, and now looked curiously after the two figures moving off toward the blue roan and the sleek mule tethered under a black oak. Such a hush pervaded the air that the dripping of last night's raindrops from leaves now glistening in the bright sunshine was like the thresh of fairy drums.

Steve buckled on his spurs and went up into the saddle.

"Hey there, Steve; wait a shake," said the Judge.

The gambler merely shook his head, dipped forward in the saddle and flashed away. It was forty miles down to the county courthouse in Madrone and he scarcely drew rein until he came before the double doors of the granite pile that housed the county's officers. Two minutes later he stood before John Bingham, newly elected district attorney, the elder Cody's running mate and friend. Bingham, a keen, nervous man, was haggard from weeks of stress capped by last night's sleepless strain, and flew into a passion the instant he glimpsed what was topmost in his visitor's mind. But Steve Cody had his way and made a full declaration of his purpose before he took his departure, and left a very thoughtful, perplexed and finally perturbed man behind him.

"Damn him," grumbled Bingham irritably, "he's got all the nerve of a gambler and the brain of a Philadelphia lawyer—and I'm hanged if I know whether he can get

away with it or not. If there is any law on the point,
I never heard of it; it's a thousand to one shot that no
decision has ever been handed down that will fit this
case. And there's going to be no shaking that hard-headed
young devil. Most emphatically, damn him."

He clamped his big, thin-lipped mouth shut and it was
hard to get a word out of him for several days. He saw
the Judge without stirring forth to seek him; the old
fellow invaded the office and there was a long conference. " I'm backin' Steve," said the Judge. " Backin' him
strong. He's the right man for this job an' I reckon
mebbe it's jes' the right job for him." Later Bingham
was visited by a delegation from Granite Gap; they came
trooping in on him, wanting to know the law. He laid his
ear to the ground and harkened to the rumble of public
opinion. Over the entire county swept a fresh ripple of
indignation; that ripple began swelling into the propor-
tions of an angry tidal wave. Men contended that it was
no private feud that had mowed down the outstanding
man they had chosen to sweep their mountains clean of
riffraff. And they began to say: " It was Steve Cody's
father, and Steve's got the first call to square the deal.
What's more, he can do it. If he stood for election right
now on that platform, he'd be elected."

Bingham also interviewed the supervisors, one at a
time, and learned from them that in case the courts
should decide a vacancy had been created after election,
they would without a doubt appoint the dead man's son
to the position. Bingham observed them narrowly and
kept his mouth shut; it was clear that Steve had seen
them, though it was not so clear what arguments he had

used. Money? Rank bribery? Bingham could only shrug; Steve Cody now, his father's sole heir, owner of some sixty thousand acres of ranch lands and timber, of a snug fortune in high-grade securities, could pay the price. And as time passed it grew quite obvious that the old Judge had been busy at a game that none understood better, that intriguing pastime known familiarly as wire-pulling.

Well, in one way and another, all devious no doubt, the thing was done. On the first of January when old officials made way for new and Bingham watched Steve Cody, sheriff, go down the courthouse steps to his horse, the district attorney's eyes were anything but serene. Very far from being a rich man, Bingham would have paid a thousand dollars at that moment for one good glimpse at what was going on inside young Cody's brain. One thing he did know, for Steve had told him: The sheriff's office here at the courthouse was to see little of the sheriff.

" You'll be looking in here oftener than I will," Steve had said; " it's only fair that I leave a man you can work with. Got anyone to suggest? " And when Bingham had leaped at the chance of suggesting his own brother, Steve had nodded and concluded indifferently: " Fine. We'll swear him in as a deputy and he will look out for office routine."

Then in the bright silver and blue morning of the new year he had ridden away. He was in no hurry; he could have taken a car as far as Oak Flats, the crossroads village at the foot of the mountains, but preferred Blue Boy. He abandoned the road for familiar trails; he succeeded in having the day almost uninterruptedly to himself. At noon, in a solitary spot among shivering poplars on the banks of a creek, he ate his sandwich while Blue Boy lipped up his handful of oats. Though the season was midwinter's and branches overhead were bare, still the sky was blue and the yellow sun genial; the man topped off his lunch with a cigarette, and the horse with short fragrant grass, and there was no haste.

When a man races, so does time; when he loiters his day loiters along with him. Steve Cody, with many things to think upon, found ample time for musing, and the stars were already trooping out and lamps were lighted before he came at last within sight of High Town. He stopped at the bend of the rocky trail where it was habit for him to pause a moment or two, and looked meditatively ahead. Long ago he had tried to make out for himself, as all men must, what life was and what its meaning, if any; life was admittedly a game and that had been the most he could say of it; ergo, he had chosen to be a gambler. This game had led him as far afield as the Mexican border; now it had brought him back to his boyhood's mountains and to High Town. Well, the essence of all games lay in chance, uncertainty, skill and possibilities. He looked up at the stars which always fascinated him, which always started those vast questions which roll eternally through the soul. He sighed as though with weariness and gave the impatient Blue Boy his head—and thereby chanced to postpone that final moment in which all questions are settled. For, at the instant he slackened the reins and leaned a little forward in the saddle there was a red flash, a report and the whine of a bullet cleaving the air close to his head.

Instinctively he slipped from the saddle, sending Blue Boy racing ahead of him with a sharp slap; to have remained on his horse's back, silhouetted against the starry sky, would have been to have stopped the second bullet which sped swiftly after the first.

Today, for the first time, beside the weapon under his arm, he wore in full sight a heavy Colt revolver at his hip; he had meant it to be the visible token and reminder that he was sheriff and intended to commit himself to a line of action which was only possible to a man who could back up his own play with the most unanswerable of all arguments. Now, as he lurched and stumbled among the rocks edging the trail, he unsheathed the heavy revolver, crouched in the shadows and awaited the third flash. The man who had shot at him had hidden on the mountainside where jagged granite spires broke the skyline, and it was a degree worse than useless to start returning his fire until something more definite in the way of a target was afforded. The one who sped the next bullet would be informing a watchful antagonist just where he stood.

But there was no third shot. Steve waited a moment, then edged off among boulders, making his way on toward High Town. To return, to quest his would-be assassin were only gigantic folly. And nothing was more likely than that the fellow, having in the first place made sure of a protected pathway of retreat, was already on his way. Steve doubled about a sharp turn in the trail and hurried on.

"Making habits is always dangerous business," he told himself in his cool, curt fashion. "To ride the same trails in the same way, to stop at the same place even to compare high lights and low, is to be a fool. Thanks for the tip, Stranger."

Blue Boy had gone straight to the stable, and here some twenty minutes later Steve found him. The horse was stirring restlessly, excited and nervous, in front of the closed door; Steve led him within, called the stable-tender down from the hayloft, and turned back along the street. At this early hour it was all but empty and he met no one before climbing the three steps of a square boxlike building which stood in neighborly proximity to the livery stable. A sign over the door announced, " Dr. Burton—Hospital." He opened the door and stepped in, to be met by a nurse in uniform coming down the narrow hall.

" You, Mr. Cody? " she said quickly, seeming mildly but only mildly surprised.

" I'd like a word with Whitey Robbins," Cody told her.

She hesitated.

" I don't know, Mr. Cody. You see, the doctor isn't here, and ——"

She saw the holstered weapon at his hip, bit her lip in brief perplexity, and then added briskly:

" No. I can't take the responsibility. You will have to see Dr. Burton."

He flipped back his coat, revealing his new badge of authority.

" A matter of the county's business, Mrs. McCall. I'll undertake not to be long and not to make your patient feverish. I understand he is out of danger? "

She shrugged her lean, capable shoulders.

" It's a funny thing —— All right, go ahead. Yes, he's doing nicely. Room 9."

She went about her business and Steve walked down the hall, looking at room numbers. The one he wanted was quite at the end of the hall. He opened the door and stepped in.

The albino lay on a narrow cot, propped up with pillows. He turned his head listlessly, then sat up quiveringly erect, a flash of fear in his eyes. He opened his mouth to cry out, when Steve cut him short with a lifted hand and a quick command for silence.

" I'm not here to hurt you, Whitey," he said quietly, as the man sank back on his pillows and stared wonderingly at him. " I want a few words with you, that's all."

The fear oozed out of Whitey's eyes and they grew sullen; his thin-lipped mouth set in an ugly line of defiance.

" Maybe you've heard I'm sheriff now, Whitey? " Whitey's sullen eyes all but hid themselves under his blue-veined lids but he said nothing. Steve with arms folded stood over the cot, looking down at him intently. " What about the stage holdup last October, Whitey? About a week before election? "

A very faint tinge of color seeped into the wounded man's pasty cheeks and a more obvious expression of surprise came into his pale eyes. But again he made no voluntary answer to a question.

" You were in that deal, Whitey," continued Steve, making his accusation quite casually. " You and Boney Marks. Marks, as we both know, pegged out the next night, getting taken apart in a card room at Halcyon. That's two of you pigeonholed. Now for the third man, who is he? "

At last Whitey spoke in a sharp, rasping voice, demanding:

" What third man? What're you drivin' at, Cody? "

" Had many visitors while you've been lying here? "

" What of it? "

" The third man, the guy that worked the holdup with you and Marks, has he sent flowers in? "

" You're crazy! " Whitey's glance bit deep but the glance he had in return bit even deeper, and Whitey's eyes roved away and his fingers began plucking nervously at his bed covers.

" I'll check up later and find out who has dropped in on you. Here's hoping your friend is a square guy; it would be tough on you if, with Marks out for good and you on your back for two months, he had decided that a whole pot is better than one split even two ways."

He knew from the working of the man's mouth that Whitey was far from feeling at his ease and made the most of that scant knowledge.

" All right, Mr. Robbins," Steve said coolly. " Keep a shut trap all you like; it's safest usually. Now, since you don't feel like giving out news bulletins, I'll do the broadcasting myself. I'm going to tell you something and when I'm gone I want you to chew on it: I am not the man that shot Boney Marks." He spoke the words slowly and so without altering his tone or lifting his voice achieved emphasis. He paused a moment, that what he had said might have still further impressiveness by being separated by a brief silence from other words. " What is more, I have a hunch as to who did the job. Later on, when it dawns on your stupid wits that I've told you the truth, come to me and we'll chat."

Quitting the hospital which, by the way, had originally been intended as a sort of adjunct to the Glory Girl mine, Steve made his way to the little board-and-battin house where the mine superintendent lived. It sat back a couple of hundred yards from the main street between two big pines, and lines of light were shining out along the edges of drawn shades. A sharp rap at the door brought a thick, heavy-jowled young man hastening in answer. A key turned, the door opened and Tom Grady, the superintendent of the Glory Girl, spoke as he discerned the tall figure on his porch.

" Come on in. I was wondering whether ——" He broke off, looked closer and demanded bruskly: " Who is it? Oh, it's you, Cody? Glad to see you. Step along in."

Steve nodded, then followed the other into the lighted room where two chairs were drawn up to a big table littered with odds and ends in a way reminiscent of the Judge's table.

" If you're expecting someone ——" Steve said with a sufficiently marked rising inflection to open the way for Grady, were he so disposed, to say who it was that he had expected.

But the mining man either did not note the opening or did not care to avail himself of it. Taking a chair and gesturing invitationally to the other, he took up his pipe and smiled across it at his visitor.

" Well, Sheriff," he chuckled, " glad to see you, as I

said. But I hope this isn't official? Haven't caught me at anything shady, have you? "

Ponderously affable, his alert eyes yet conceded the fact that he would be interested in knowing what brought his visitor. Steve did not take the proffered chair and did not keep him waiting.

" Official only in this: I am interested in the stage holdup that was pulled off just before election. The Glory Girl had some money on the stage, coming up? "

" Yes. Lord, man; that seems like ancient history now! You haven't got any idea, have you ——"

" How much? " asked Steve.

" Close to three thousand dollars."

" Since there's no bank yet in High Town the mine, of course, has to have currency sent in. You pay your men in cash, don't you? "

" Yes. As you say, there's no bank, and the men want their money in readily squanderable shape."

" Does the stage bring it in every week? "

Grady, though he still smiled, moved cautiously.

" I'm the big cheese right here on the job," he said presently, " but I don't own the mine, you know. I have my own orders and I try to carry 'em out." He began drumming on his table top. " Here's the idea, Cody: No, we don't have money shipments come in regularly. That would be too much like advertising to the world that on such and such a day there'd be nice pickings for a stick-up gent's party."

" You're not talking to an advertising agency right now," Steve reminded him. " If you care to tell me how and when your money comes up, I'll listen."

Grady's broad smile was replaced by a shadowy frown.

" Of course you're right. But as a mere matter of form, I'm tongue-tied. I'll get in touch with my boss right away."

" Good enough. And you might suggest that from now on the bank notes be marked."

" As to that —— Well, it does no harm to say that we always have 'em marked."

" The lot that was stolen? " And when Grady nodded, " Show me. Marked just how? "

With a dollar bill from his bill fold and a pencil from his table Grady demonstrated. A swift flick of the pencil left a scarcely discernible hair line against the dark background of one of the serial numbers.

" Ink? " asked Steve.

" Indelible pencil. A man wouldn't notice unless he was pretty definitely looking for it. Almost invisible unless in a certain light you catch the shine of the pencil mark. If a man should moisten it," as he proceeded to do with a thick finger tip, " of course you get a purple smudge."

" Why should a man moisten a bank note? "

" Oh, sometimes one gets plunked down on a wet bar, you know."

" You've got men on the lookout, of course? And nothing has showed up yet? "

" Nothing. Sort of funny, too, after all this while— unless the jasper that made the haul tumbled to the markings. Or maybe he has moseyed on to parts remote. Got any sort of line on the thing, Cody? "

" When you hear from your higher-ups," said Cody,

going to the door, " in case you have anything more to tell me I'll not be hard to locate."

He went out, down the steps and into the black shadow of one of the pines. Here he stood a moment, looking down upon the rutty road which served High Town as its one thoroughfare. At this early hour there was little activity on the street, an occasional blurred form moving along, now and then the swing doors of Vargas's Place shoved back to a man's entrance. He struck a match and looked at his watch; only seven minutes had been consumed in making his two visits. Hardly time, he estimated, for the man who had shot at him to have made his way back to town, for even though he did not doubt that his assailant had had a horse at hand, he would have been forced to avoid the road and make a detour in order not to have been seen by his intended victim.

Steve Cody, watchful at every step though appearing to be concerned with nothing weightier than the gay little tune he was whistling softly, made his way to Vargas's Place.

CHAPTER VI

VARGAS, experiencing at times a desire for a high degree of privacy, had had constructed in his own back yard and a score of paces from the main building, a second small, compact edifice of two rooms. It was a stocky and sturdy affair, constructed like the Judge's office of red bricks, with heavy oak door at front and rear and small, shuttered windows. To this place came Steve Cody, after a few minutes spent in the barroom during which his eyes had flitted from face to face, recording for possible future reference the presence of men in whom he felt any interest, the absence of others.

At Cody's knock Vargas's voice sang out, " Come in," and a moment later Vargas, seeing who his visitor was, greeted him cordially, exclaiming:

" Hello, it's Steve. Shut the door, pull your hat, squat and put your hoofs on the table.—Whew! Look at the artillery! Lion huntin', Mr. Cody? "

One would never have guessed without tracking Vargas to his own particular lair that the man had a taste for the elegancies. The walls were plastered, then tastefully papered; there was a decent rug on the floor; the oak furniture was good and, striking the clearest note of all, there was a small bookcase beside Vargas's chair. Vargas a reader of books? Of one kind only, as a glance at the titles of his snug little library would have disclosed, and not at all the type of thing which might have

76

been anticipated by one who knew the man only super-
ficially. Here were biographies only; the lives of men
who, as one pondered the matter, were alike with regard
to strong human achievement, the cleaving of a high path
among difficulties, the brushing aside of obstacles. There
were Cæsar, Napoleon, Columbus, Cortez; there was
Lawrence of Arabia; there was Cecil Rhodes; Captain
Kidd was of the number. Two women only commingled
with this strong company, Queen Elizabeth and Cleo-
patra.

One book lay open, face down, on the table where
Vargas had put it as he called out his invitation to come
in. And Vargas was not alone; three of his following,
typical of one order of men in whom the saloon-keeper
was keenly interested and who were frequently with him,
had been listening to Vargas expounding theories. Young
fellows all three of them, only one of them above twenty-
two, and that one Tad Harper. Of the other two one was
a wolfish-faced, lanky youth with pale plastered hair, too
prominent teeth and small hard blue eyes, a high-strung,
tense and nervous looking animal who fancied himself as
a flashy sport and went under the name of Slim Brilliant.
Brilliant? " Sure, it's a monniker," he had a way of admitting boastfully. " Picked it out meself, an' what I
pick's a winner! Say, if you bos knew my real name,
you'd be f'r turnin' me in f'r the big bounty that's on
me hide! See? " At Slim Brilliant's elbow sat the other
youth, Connie Miner, swarthy, thick-lipped, greasy, a
misbred unfit who had followed along from the border.

" Teaching night school, Vargas? " asked Steve gravely.
Vargas laughed.

" The boys felt like a little game; just a sociable af-fair, you know. We're waitin' for Chink Johnson an' Bird Galloway; they're due about now."

Steve glanced about the room casually before taking a chair. With doors and windows closed it would have been unendurably close here were it not for the deep-throated chimney and the draft-creating fire on the brick hearth. The men had been smoking; bottles and glasses stood on the table. Besides the door through which he had entered there was another across the room, leading to Vargas's bedroom. It was closed. Steve took a chair where he could see both doors; he moved it a couple of feet so that not even a window was at his back.

A flash came and went in Vargas's eyes and he ob-served jestingly:

" Anyways huntin' corners, Steve? "

" Steve's sheriff now, don't forget that, Vargas," said the thick-lipped youth, Connie Miner. He licked his lips and concluded: " Maybe he's goin' to raid the works! Pull the crowd for breakin' the law with booze an' a poker game! "

" This is my first day in office," returned Cody equably. " I thought I might start in right by putting you tough guys afoot. If you've got a game on, I've got chips."

Tad Harper, who had looked dubious, brightened. One never knew in advance what a man like Steve Cody was going to do, and it was a relief to be assured that he had not altogether turned his coat overnight. In Tad's eyes there were two resplendent figures bestriding the world, and they were Steve Cody and Vargas. He had wondered at times which side he himself would take if those two flew at each other's throats. Two months previous there would have been no question; he was Steve Cody's man. But two months had worked changes in a soul in turmoil; he had seen little of Cody and much of Vargas. He poured himself a drink and gulped it down.

" Good man, Steve! " he cried warmly, and looked flushed and excited. He lurched to his feet and demanded of Vargas: " Will I shove this table out o' the way an' get the poker table? Let's go."

Vargas nodded.

" Get the table, but we'll wait a shake yet." He turned to the wolfish Slim Brilliant. " The other boys ought to be here any minute, oughtn't they, Slim? "

" Sure. I seen 'em over at Halcyon jus' before I lef'. They said they had to see a guy they'd get some coin off'n, an' would be here about now."

Meanwhile it did no harm to shift furniture, to get the poker table in place and the cards ready.

" Well, Steve," said Vargas good-naturedly, legs thrust out, hands clasped behind his head, " you made the grade O. K., didn't you? Sheriff now, huh? My job, grabbed right out o' my hand, too! I guess it's just as well, though. Me, I'm busy enough an' goin' strong as things are. Just the same, between friends, I did hanker to wear what you're wearin' now. I'm no office-seeker an' I'm not thinkin' about the measly salary that goes with the job. But, sheriff!—Well it's you, an' here's luck! "

" Luck," said Steve and drank with him.

And understood more clearly than any other, Vargas himself excepted, why he had been so heart-set on this particular office. You never quite knew Vargas, perhaps

not any other man, until you knew the books he read.
In his secret soul he was far more than bootlegger,
saloon-keeper and petty lawbreaker. He was in his own
eyes a sort of superman, toweringly ambitious, swollen
with ego and the confidence that goes with it. In another age he might have made himself a tribal chieftain;
uncontent with that, he would have banded tribes together and been a barbaric king over them. He had imagination and he let it fly untrammelled; therefore he was,
no doubt, a little mad. He read his books and, like his
heroes, he put his bootheel on many a human neck.

With the sheriff's office went a sense of power. Better
today than ever before did Steve Cody understand that.
That sense was stirring in him; he had the right at this
moment, a right backed up by the county machinery, to
stretch out his hand to any man present and cast him
into the modern equivalent of an ancient feudal dungeon.
A charge was easily enough formulated: vagrancy, carrying concealed weapons, illicit liquor selling. More serious
charges lurked around the corner. The sheriff's hand was
on the lever. Give that lever into Vargas's clutch and
what happened?

" Here they come," announced Tad Harper, who alone
of them all had caught the faint sound of footsteps.

Chink Johnson and Bird Galloway entered without the
formality of knocking. Here again were young men, Chink
with a flat Oriental face and crafty eyes but an ingenuous
grin on his wide mouth, Bird Galloway in the last of his
teens, Chink's shadow and admirer, large-handed, awkward and shambling, yet with sharp face and birdlike
round bright eyes bespeaking an alert if warped brain.

Steve regarded them casually; they greeted the gathering breezily as a whole.

" Gosh, I'm glad to look that bottle in the face, Vargas," grinned Bird Galloway, and helped himself. " Just rode in from Halcyon an' got a lot o' cold air in my throat."

" Let's get goin'," said Tad eagerly. " We've been waitin' for you guys."

" And of such as these," mused the new sheriff, " Vargas is building his kingdom! "

Well, why not? Youth was hasty and made its blunders, yet it remained that youth was fearless and reckless and that, given its leader, it followed that leader blindly, even worshipfully. Vargas had but to flatter, and there was the subtlest and most efficacious of all flattery in the bald fact that he consorted with them. Tonight's gathering was no novel occasion; harking back a short two months Steve recalled that all of these hot-eyed young men, with the single exception of Tad Harper, had been with Vargas that day shortly before election when Steve came on them behind a locked door.

" Seven men crowding around a poker table? " he said, lifting his brows.

" Me, I'm out," grinned Chink. " Thought I c'd raise some money off'n a guy, an' missed the boat. I'll watch you guys a while."

" Same here," said Bird Galloway.

" I'll stake you two boys," proffered Vargas, and reached into his pocket. " You can get square with me later."

They looked at each other, then shook their heads. They'd just watch a while.

So it was Steve and Vargas, Slim Brilliant, Connie Miner and Tad Harper who sat in at the game. From the first hand dealt the game leaped. They played with money, not chips, and the younger eyes brightened at the sight of thin sheaves of currency.

" I'm goin' to make a killing," laughed Tad. " I can feel it in my bones."

" Yeah? " drawled Slim.

With the play hard and fast and the room soon grown quiet save for the shuffle of cards and flutter of bank notes, with the occasional clink of glass and a rarer exclamation, Fortune at first smiled or frowned in her random way, choosing no favorites. Within fifteen minutes Vargas, a man who saw most things that went on, noted something which caused him to look penetratingly into Cody's face, wondering if after all the gambler was beginning to have " nerves." At the poker table Steve was habitually quiet, every muscle even to those of his little finger under control, looking merely profoundly thoughtful with no waste motion of any kind. Tonight his hands seemed restless. His fingers toyed almost unceasingly with his own stack of bank notes, rearranging, slipping one under another, doubling them over, smoothing them out. It was a small thing; others at the table shifted or drummed with their fingers or in other ways betrayed a tense interest. A small thing surely, but in Steve Cody it was enough to set Vargas wondering.

But in his play Steve was the same swift, inscrutable gambler he had always been. He won and lost with no glint of the eye, no shadow between the placid brows. But when he lost his fingers went back to his diminished bills; when he won they toyed similarly with his increased stake.

In varying ways and degrees the others gave outward sign of inner reaction to those tenser moments which besprinkle a poker game. Tad, whom nature never meant to run in the company into which he had of late found his way, essentially anything but a gambler, grew flushed and feverish; his hands shook and his voice was sharp and fretful. Slim Brilliant over-assumed nonchalance every time he was out on a limb; if he bluffed, Steve knew it the moment Slim made up his mind. Much like him was his shadow, Connie Miner; boys playing at manhood; lambs running with the wolf pack.

And Vargas? Any sign from Vargas, an old hand, hard-bitted, whose education had been absorbed in gaming dens? His eyes were as steady and blank as though carved from some reddish brown stone; his half-smile never changed, a queer characteristic smile in which the corners of his mouth never lifted, always sagging just the faintest bit; his hands were sure and steady; the pulse-beat in his wrist never hastened; his breathing was regular, unforced, natural. And yet, when the time came when Steve wanted from Vargas an answer to a fateful question, Vargas all unconsciously gave it to him, and that answer was, " Yes. I know."

It was when Tad, going from bad to worse, began to lose heavily. He and Vargas were contending for a jack pot of about forty dollars. Steve had regarded his own hand thoughtfully, then put it down—quite at the edge of the table. One of the cards fell; he leaned far out for it and for an instant commanded a view of several pairs of legs. It was from them that he got his answer.

Mere chance some years before had given Steve Cody a choice bit of information. At that time he and Vargas and some border gamblers were playing a game which ran into big figures, a stiff game even for seasoned old hands. Steve, really accidentally on that occasion, had let a chip fall from the table, had stooped for it as he did now and had been impressed by the tale told by Vargas's feet. The heel of the right boot rested on the toe of the left and was pressed down hard. That was all. But it told eloquently of tense nerves. All that Vargas displayed of himself above the table was under the most rigid control; like most men he had his safety valve and Steve had found it.

So now, with a mere forty dollars at stake, Vargas had gone rigid inside! That could be only because he, too, had made the discovery at this moment; rather, that he just glimpsed it and was immensely eager to be certain.

Thereafter, by imperceptible degrees, the game became a duel between Steve Cody and Vargas. The others played on to be sure, but even they began to sense that the two other men were out for blood. Tad Harper plunged, won wildly a time or two, but fell heavily to an innocent-seeming but deadly hand held by Vargas. That was the beginning of the end for the young fellow and soon, hot-faced and with a jaw that quivered despite his effort at control, he shoved back his chair. Within half an hour Slim Brilliant and Connie Miner had paid their prices for a new lesson and were eliminated.

"Want to quit, Steve," yawned Vargas. "You an' me ——"

"It's early," said Steve. "Let's make or break."

So they stripped the deck and went on. The stakes were higher now, the play swifter, and in twenty minutes the game was over. Steve Cody gathered up into what looked like a hopeless jumble all the bills on the table. Yet he knew that when he could have time to sort, he would be able to tell from whose pocket nearly every bill had come. His apparent nervousness had not been without result and faint creases down the middles of bank notes, and across corners identified them for him.

"You got a regular bundle of hay there, Steve," laughed Vargas. "Better get a truck to haul it home or stop at the bar and get it in bigger bills."

"Going my way, Tad?" asked Steve.

"Yes.—How about a game tomorrow night? I'd like a chance to get some of that hay back."

Slim Brilliant cocked his head to the side, drawling:

"Say, kid, where's your bank? You spilled quite a wad jus' now, an' want a comeback tomorrow! Been robbin' the Firs' National somewhere?"

Tad swung about on him angrily.

"Mind your own business, Slim," he snapped.

"Oho!" cried Slim, and laughed.

There was a general scraping of chairs. Vargas sat where he was and lifted his feet to the table top.

"Tomorrow night?" he inquired idly. "Suits me. All right, Steve?"

Steve, first at the door, went out. Tad followed him. The others remained with Vargas.

CHAPTER VII

ON a gray, sodden morning with lowering skies and dripping eaves, Corinna awoke dancingly happy. She burst out of her room treating the wintry morning to as pretty a vision as a little brand-new butterfly still slightly crumpled from the drab cocoon. She pirouetted into the bustling presence of Aunt Mary in the kitchen, blew that motherly old soul a kiss from the doorway, somewhat in the fashion of the preliminary bombardment of a fairy attack, then bore down upon her objective and made a captive of her in a pair of strong and eager and, this morning, joyous young arms, and administered the second kiss at close range and upon a beaming cheek.

Aunt Mary provided breakfast and did her own surmising behind the barrage of good-natured morning chatter. Corinna was made for sparkling happiness, but here of late there had been many and many a time when shadows chased her smiles all away; when even, as the housekeeper knew full well, behind those shadows was a dreary little world of misery.

" She heard yest'day that her daddy's a mite better," mused Aunt Mary, turning the brownest and most delectable of hot-cakes. " An' what's more, that good-f'r-nothin' scamp of a brother of hers has come in at an almos' respectable hour five nights runnin'. That's why."

No doubt the astute Aunt Mary was, as usual with her, right in her findings. Corinna, for her part, had done no analyzing; who wants to dissect spontaneous joyousness anyhow? She did know that those things were true. She had heard Tad come in last night; she had listened to his quiet footfalls, fearfully at first, then with a sigh of content when they were obviously steady; she had struck a match and looked at the little clock by her bed: not yet midnight. Then she had slept—and she had dreamed. Her dreams, at which of course Aunt Mary could not arrive with all her acumen, had colored her waking as golden-shot mists trail their gay wisps across a morning sky.

" It's been a funny winter," Aunt Mary remarked from her place over the stove—Corinna was eating at the kitchen table under a window. " You're lucky, child, to find your firs' winter here so mild an' wide-open, rainin' mos'ly, when it do rain, at night, with lots of nice shiny days."

" It's not shiny today," said Corinna. " I wanted to ride up to the other end this morning, too."

" Mos' likely, knowin' how you feel about it, it'll clear off right away! "

" I'm afraid the weather man isn't as obliging as you, Aunt Mary."

" If it was a *man* that run the weather," sniffed Aunt Mary, " you'd be gettin' moonlight every night, sunny days all winter an' nice big fat stars to order, an' it wouldn't matter to him if it never did rain an' cricks dried up an' grass died an' stock went hungry. Thank gracious no man's runnin' the weather, Miss Corinna; leastways no man that comes under them two eyes of yours."

Corinna laughed at her, named her a hummy-humbug and strove to dispose of the matter of men with a wave of a spoon.

"Wavin' spoons don't make things any diff'rent, as far as I c'n see," maintained Aunt Mary. "Since you come to this here ranch they's been more young fellers with their hair slicked an' red neckties on, lookin' for a strayed critter or comin' pretendin' to borry a monkey wrench or somethin', than a body'd likely see in any ordinary seven years. An' I notice how mos' of 'em manages to stay to dinner or supper, long's they're here. I dunno, but it looks to me like they's goin' to be a good many ranches go to rack-an'-ruin if you don't make up your mind one way or t'other real soon. An', long as you brung the subjec' up, they's one young feller that used to have a mite of sense, at least f'r a man, an' that's David Laribee; an' seems to me ——"

Aunt Mary, sensing something amiss in that she had been allowed to run on at such length, turned about sharply and just in time to catch a glimpse of Corinna at the far end of the hall, tiptoeing out on the porch.

"I caught you, you rascal!" came a lusty assurance to the vanishing Corinna. "An' I don't blame you, creepin' out on me rather'n hear the truth spoke short, snappy an' fearless. When I was a girl ——"

"When you were a girl, you were simply scandalous!" Corinna called back to her. "Oh, I know every bit as well as if I had been there.—By the way, Aunt Mary, how old were you when you were married the first time?"

Aunt Mary, her broad smile not to be seen by the girl

now on the porch, sniffed a second time and lifted her voice to maintain:

" You been talkin' to the Jedge. Of all the unhung liars, ol' Jedge Bull is the one that ought to be hung first."

Corinna stood a while looking out across the wet fields, up into the gray sky from which now a mere drizzle was falling; the rain had started in a couple of hours before dawn and now began to thin and allow quick hopes of blue skies to spring up again. Regarding that picturesque small section of the world spread out before her eyes, she found herself humming softly certain lines which, though as yet she did not consciously recall their connection, had been singing themselves in some remote corner of her brain since a very particular dream had visited her and had done its part to tinge the new day. While pondering now whether she dared make the six-mile ride, twelve miles there and back, or whether she'd be sure of a drenching, she was humming to her own gay tune:

> " In dayes of olde,
>   When Knightes were bolde,
>   And Ladyes verie faire . ."

" Who's afraid of a wetting? " asked Corinna, and returned to the kitchen. " I'm going to put on a slicker and a pair of horribles and go riding, Aunt Mary. Will you tell Tad when he comes down? I'll be gone a couple of hours."

" All right; I'll tell Tad an' any of the young men that happen by lookin' for lost cattle."

" Is the Judge an old liar, Aunt Mary? "

She drew a sharp, very shrewd look upon her.

"No," said Aunt Mary. "He ain't. Get right down to it, he ain't. If the Jedge says anything, an' ain't jes' jokin' at the time, then it's true. I've heard tell afore now of men that their word was as good's their bond. Well, in mos' cases I've met up with, it was because their bonds weren't no earthly good. But the ol' Jedge is that-away; what he says is gospel; what he says he'll do, he'll do, no matter which-away the wind blows.—Why?"

"Oh, nothing," said Corinna, smiling mysteriously, and ran silently up the stairs. Coming down again in big hat, slicker, riding breeches and boots, she again confronted Aunt Mary, and this time with such a look in her shining gray eyes that the housekeeper marked it and responded to it by exclaiming in mock-gravity:

"Laws sakes! You're jus' wastin' ammunition, child!"

"What on earth are you talkin about?"

"Makin' them big eyes at an ol' woman like me. Unless you're jus' practisin'! If one of them young fellers was here now —— Or even if the ol' Jedge was! He'd up an' say, soundin' legal, 'Young woman, there's places where you'd be shut up in jail, lookin' like that, disturbin' the peace ——'"

"You're a dear and I'm going to call you Hummy, for short," laughed Corinna. "But I was just thinking about something. You're always so wise about everything from weaning calves to making hot rolls,—do you know all about dreams?"

"I do, that! If you'd had time, now, to have had a nap after you et them eleven hot-cakes ——"

" Aunt Mary!—Tell me, then; what does it mean to have the same queer dream three times in succession? "

Aunt Mary appeared to be sunk deep in profound meditation. At length she put her lips close to a cluster of bronze curls under an old hat brim and whispered dramatically:

" It means—a feller! "

" It's such an odd dream," said Corinna, " that I'm going to tell you." She sat on a corner of the kitchen table, one boot swinging. " There *is* a man in it, but ——"

" That ain't the queer part that's so odd-like, is it? " was the sarcastic comment.

" I've dreamed of him three times," said Corinna, and now her hearer was not altogether sure whether she was laughing inwardly or was half serious. " And I don't know who he is! I dreamed —— Let's see. He came riding; out of a black forest, every time. On a great big beautiful horse. And he was all dolled up in—you'd never guess, Aunt Mary!—in shining armor! Like one of King Arthur's Knights, you know! "

" Uhuh! I know. Knights! Lordy, my firs' one was a sheepherder! "

" They do say, though," insisted Corinna, " that dreams are bits of—of symbolism. They mean something, don't they? "

" They sure do," conceded Aunt Mary drily.

" Well, if there ever was any such thing as symbolism in anybody's dream, there must be in mine. For out comes the Knight, just the same each time; and would you believe it, Aunt Mary, I've never got a glimpse of his face! "

" All covered up in armor, huh? Might even be a South Sea islander or an Eskimo!—But look here, if you never see his face, how do you know it's the same feller all the time? Might be three of 'em, takin' turns."

" No; he's the same each time. He's quite distinctive. His armor is all nice and shiny; he has a plume and though his helmet is always closed, I can tell him by the big silver star he wears in his casque. I call him from that the Knight of the Silver Star."

Aunt Mary began to laugh.

" You're fibbin' to your Aunt Mary about as fas' as you can sling words together, so now get out, you an' your Knight of the Silver Star; I got a big batch o' bread to bake, an' I mean to start early. How can I tell it's a fib? This way, child: Girls have been dreamin' dreams since a long time afore I was one of 'em, an' young fellers has come an' went pretty free through them dreams, an' never one yet with his face hid!—You jus' scat now, an' don't waste any more ammunition; it might come in handy yet before the day's out."

Corinna departed gaily, but once out on the porch she stood again, very still, looking across the fields, across the black ridges beyond in their thin mysterious veilings of thin shower and cloud wraiths. It *was* odd, how the dream came and came again, it was baffling and it was vaguely troublesome. Why should she herself, since in all final analysis she must be responsible for her own dreams, hide from herself that face behind the helmet?

" I'll have to look over my old Malory," she decided. " Maybe there is a Knight of the Silver Star in it, but I can't remember any."

As beautiful even as that richly caparisoned horse of her dreams was the one which she saw now all of a sudden coming at a swift gallop from the spot where the trail led from the pine-timbered ravine. So gallant a figure did the rider appear, a neck scarf floating back from his shoulders, and so apt was his arrival amidst the girl's musings, that for an instant she grew rigid, startled. The mists behind this new, eager arrival were like gauzy curtains breaking apart for a vision to ride through.

"I wonder who —— Oh! It's you, Dave Laribee! "

She greeted him with a queer little laugh, just a trifle shivery, and Laribee, as he swung to the steps below her, looked up at her curiously.

"You thought I was someone else," he said when he stood level with her and so looked down from his superior height into her face which was rosy in its welcome. "Don't you know me yet, Corinna? "

"I didn't expect you so early—it was the horse! " exclaimed Corinna. She ran down the steps and strove to make the acquaintance of the high-headed, restive golden sorrel. "Is it a new one, Dave? "

"Yes. I've had an eye on it for a year. One of Steve Cody's horses. I talked him into selling it last week." He followed her down the steps and held the horse still to be patted and admired; such, at least, was the obvious excuse, though all that David Laribee wanted was to be close to her. He looked very handsome this morning in his rough riding outfit as Corinna found time and opportunity to observe while seeming to be concerned exclusively with the high-spirited horse. "Yes," Laribee ran on, "I admit I am early. I am on my way into town, and just took a long shot at catching a glimpse of you.— What is it, Corinna? " he demanded sharply, looking at her wonderingly.

" What is what? " laughed Corinna innocently, though her eyes sparkled.

" The way you're looking at me. As if —— Oh, I don't know; we'll say as if I were a pane of glass and you were seeing visions through it."

" Visions? " repeated Corinna, her head tipped provocatively to one side after a quaint birdlike fashion quite her own. " Maybe I was just thinking. You see, when you appeared all of a sudden, dashing along out of the black forest, your scarf floating out, you were just like a knight, all plumed and ready to—to charge dragons and things."

Though Laribee smiled back at her there was a yearning behind his smile which was as sober as tears. And though he spoke as lightly as she, Corinna understood well enough how under his light words he yearned toward her.

" Those knight-chaps were the lucky birds," said Laribee. " They strutted their stuff in gay old style and they had all the breaks. It was the simplest thing on earth: Your knight got himself into his shell, forked his horse and before the dew was off the grass he was sure to find the Damsel in Distress. She was the one right Damsel; all he had to do was go out and break a few heads in her honor and she was waiting when he came back. He clasped her in his arms ——"

" I wonder he didn't mash her up terribly, in that iron shell you're talking about! "

"There were drawbacks," grinned Laribee, his hand inching along the bridle reins toward Corinna's. "That embrace must have lacked intimacy and warmth! But the idea is that his Damsel in Distress was annoyed only by the sorts of things, caitiffs and so forth that he could knock over with a stick. Whereas nowadays——" His hand slipped down over hers. "Oh, Corinna, my dear, if it were only so easy to make the sun shine all the time for the dearest damsel, whether in distress or not! "

Very gently Corinna slipped her hand out of his and stepped back. For after all she was not sure. If she could see behind the closed visor of her dreams, would it be David Laribee's eager, handsome young face, David Laribee's adoring eyes which would be disclosed?

"My troubles," said Corinna gaily, "speaking for the nearest if not the dearest damsel, are quite blown all away, I think, so no knights need apply."

"Your father is better; I'd heard that," said Laribee. "And Tad? "

"I think Tad is coming to himself again. He's been the old Tad of late; he has been coming in early; he has been behaving himself. I think it's just that he has thrown off certain influences which for a while, in their newness, had him hypnotized."

"You were going to ride? " he observed abruptly. "Not into town, by any chance? "

"No, the other way, if the rain holds off." She returned to her place on the steps above him. "And since you ride so early, of course your errand is urgent and I must not keep you."

He swung back up into the saddle.

" Not terribly urgent. I'm off for a word with the Judge. There's a man he has been looking for for a long time —— Hello! " He had noted a swift change of expression in her eyes and turning to look back over his shoulder in the direction her glance had taken, observed that not he alone rode early this morning. " Who is —— Why, it's Steve Cody! "

Steve Cody it was, recognized by Laribee while Corinna was still wondering who this second horseman could be to ride out of the pines, Laribee leaping to the quicker recognition through knowing the horse. It was a tall rangy black, one of Cody's finest and one that Laribee would have bought along with the golden sorrel had Steve been of a mind to sell.

From the rapidly approaching horseman, Laribee turned back to Corinna, his eyes quick to ask what his lips left unsaid. But she could only shake her head.

" I can't imagine what would bring Mr. Cody here at any hour," she said thoughtfully. " He has never been here before."

So, faintly curious, they watched in silence as the tall black horse bore its rider swiftly on to them. A twitch at the reins brought the animal to a standstill close to Laribee's, as Steve Cody touched his hat brim and said briefly:

" Hello, Laribee. Miss Lee, may I have a word with your father? "

" But he is not here," said Corinna. Recalling all too vividly her one encounter with him, conscious of a former resentment surging up within her, she was as stiff as it resided within Corinna Lee to be when occasion warranted. Seeing how he looked piercingly at her as though he found it hard to believe that Charlie Lee could be away so early in the day, she added crisply: " My father is in the hospital in San Francisco, where he went two weeks ago."

He pondered the information a moment, a frown of uncertainty making his eyes look blacker than mere black.

" Is he expected home soon? "

" No," answered Corinna.

" Are you and Laribee going somewhere? "

Laribee answered for her.

" No; I'm on my way into town. Miss Lee is riding in some other direction."

" I wonder if I might have a word with both of you? "

" Fire ahead," laughed Laribee. " We're both here and listening, Steve."

Steve reined his horse about.

" I'll ride half a mile with you, Laribee," he said, and turned to ask of Corinna: " Will you wait for me a few minutes? "

Corinna wanted to say a cool and emphatic, " No! " She wanted to say " No " to anything and everything he might ask. And yet she hesitated and in the end asked, making the words sound aloof and very far from invitational:

" Is it very important, Mr. Cody? "

" Otherwise I'd not trouble you," he returned in her own impersonal manner.

" All right. I'll wait."

Again he touched his hat with the slightest hint of a

grave inclination of his head and he and Laribee rode off together.

" Well, Steve? " asked Laribee, staring hard at his companion's face. " What's the excitement all about? "

" Let's pull up here a shake; I don't want to keep Miss Lee waiting." He stopped his horse in the meadow, eased himself sideways in the saddle and began rolling a cigarette. " You know of course what my one job is, Laribee."

Laribee's eyes flashed. Never to be forgotten were the days when he and Steve were boys together, when the Cody home was home to both, when to both of them Steve's father had been little less than a demigod.

" Of course," he said curtly. " You want to get the devil who killed him."

Steve did not look up from his meticulous cigarette-making.

" I'm up against a pretty stiff proposition, Laribee. Do you want to come in on it? "

" How? What can I do? "

" As a deputy sheriff? Wait a minute until I explain. I know how you feel; you are pretty nearly as keen for a squaring of the account as far as it can ever be squared, as I am. I am starting the job and may get away with it. On the other hand it's altogether possible that I'll stub my toe and fade out of the picture. In that case I'd like you to carry on. Will you? "

" You think that whoever it was that got him is going to try to bump you off? "

" It was tried last night," and having lighted his cigarette, he looked Laribee straight in the eyes at last. " It will be tried again, never fear. And if I should get

wiped out, well, Laribee, you're the only man I know
to go ahead with it."

"Tell me about it," said the frowning Laribee. And
when he had been informed of the shot fired in the dark
on the rocky trail, he asked swiftly: "Who did it? Got
any idea?"

"I spent the rest of the evening with them," Cody
said, so casually that Laribee stared at him harder than
ever. Then with a little, weary-seeming gesture, the
gambler added: "Just a couple of kids, Laribee, working
for hire. They made it so simple, how they had just
arrived straight from Halcyon, how they had expected
to get some money off a man and had failed. But my job
isn't with such as those two."

"But with the man who hired them?" Laribee said
quickly.

"Vargas? Well, Vargas comes into it. But we'll go into
all this later, if you're with me, Laribee."

Impulsively Laribee shot out his hand.

"I'm with you, Steve. It—it would have gone sort of
hard on me, to be left out——"

"I know. I'll look you up later and we'll go into things.
Maybe this afternoon? You're not long in town?"

"Just in and out. I wanted to tell the Judge that a man
he has been looking for——"

"Not Spike Freedom?" demanded Steve sharply.

"The same." Laribee's eyes asked questions but after
a second his lips busied themselves with the words: "One
of my men saw him back in the mountains yesterday. For
some reason which the Judge has never told me, he is
mighty anxious to have a powwow with that hombre."

" So long, Laribee." Steve whirled his horse and turned back to the ranch house.

Corinna watched him in the frankest of curiosity. She had seen how the two men talked together down in the field and had marked that impulsively proffered hand of Laribee's, grasped with what from a distance seemed as much like impulsiveness on the gambler's part as she could imagine in him. She had scarcely noted how Laribee at the end had turned and waved his hat in good-by to her.

" Since I can't talk with your father," said Steve, when again he had ridden to the porch, " I'd better talk with you. Is Tad around yet? "

" No."

" You were going riding. Will you get your horse and ride a little way from the house with me? "

" So that Tad won't see or hear? " she demanded, and grew apprehensive at her own words.

He nodded gravely.

" Shall I saddle for you? "

" I—I haven't said that I would come! "

" No. You haven't said. I hope, though, that you will come."

" Why should I? " she demanded hotly.

" For Tad's sake."

" You told me once that you would not help. That you were no friend of Tad's."

For a little while he sat very still in the saddle, eyeing her as though he meant now, once and for all, to make up his mind concerning a certain girl named Corinna Lee. He could not have missed the lovely picture she constituted on this morning which had been so spontaneously gay for her, yet it was not with a girl's beauty and piquant charm that he was at the moment concerned, but rather with the girl herself, the real Corinna who could be thinking her own thoughts while the outward Corinna smiled or frowned.

" Tad," said Steve at last, and only when he had taken his time about appraising her, " is mixed in a pretty bad mess. Maybe he can be pulled out, but it will take the two of us to do it."

Then and then only did she forget everything but Tad, and her eyes filled with alarm. She had been so happy, too, thinking that Tad was her old, dear Tad come back home!

" I will come," she said, her voice hushed now. Desperately afraid that Tad might wake and hear, she even tiptoed down the steps. " I'll get my own horse; you ride around to the far side of the barn. I'll be right out."

She ran in haste across the yard, vanishing through the wide stable door. Cody rode around the corral and waited for her just out of sight of the house.

CHAPTER VIII

A QUEER sense of unreality, baffling and faintly oppressive, briefly clouded Corinna's consciousness. Here were she and Steve Cody riding together, passing furtively from the open space behind the barn, striking into the dripping pines beyond. She and Steve Cody! It seemed incredible, though a fact; impossible, even. And yet all the while there was upon her that other odd sensation of familiarity. It was as though they had ridden thus before, and by this same trail, with the rain stopping, with the sky overhead ominously dark with swollen black clouds, with an almost uncanny light spread everywhere so that wet trees and grass were of an unearthly vivid green; such a light as sometimes lies athwart the world when somewhere a rainbow is arching.

They rode in silence for a little while, tacitly agreed on putting some small distance between themselves and the ranch house before speaking, and as they rode Corinna sent many a quick, searching glance at his face which, seen in profile, impressed her with its cameo-likeness. He looked straight ahead and seemed merely very thoughtful.

" We need not go far," he said without withdrawing his eyes from the aisles among the pines wavering before them. " Just beyond this timber we can stop in the little clearing where it won't be so dripping wet."

To herself Corinna said, " He shuts himself off from all the rest of the world. . . . He said that he has no friends. . . . It is as though he built up a wall about him or withdrew into a shell. . . . I am not afraid of him! "

The final thought came almost explosively. For she had been desperately afraid of Steve Cody, the gambler, afraid while she was with him at that terrible road house, afraid when she saw his mirrored face as he shot a man down at her side; most of all afraid in the depths of many black nights thereafter when she lay sleepless in her room and a fevered memory like a nightmare re-called his every look and word and gesture. Why now had her fear departed so suddenly? Because she thought of him as a sheriff and not as a gambler, as an official and not as a man? Or perhaps just because she had seen him and dear old Dave Laribee shake hands? Or, most of all, because he had started up new fears not on her own account, but for her wayward half brother?

" Tell me! What is it about Tad? "

They were in the little clearing which Steve had mentioned, a grassy slope with the willows and alders and red madrones of Willow Creek upon one side, with a straggling forest of conifers on the other. They stopped their horses with one accord and looked at each other, her eyes frank with concern, his very keen and bright, and very watchful for any faint fluttering signs to tell him what kind of an aide he might find in Corinna Lee.

He began with feeling her out, thus:

" Will you promise me at the outset that nothing which I tell you will be repeated? "

" No! " said Corinna promptly. " How can I? It is too early to promise anything, blind like that, when I haven't the least idea what it is all about."

He liked that, though no reflection of his approval showed itself in the steady gaze he bent on her; had she promised too lightly he would have been disappointed in her. He continued gravely:

" Will you trust me, Miss Lee? "

Though she flushed then, she managed to answer quite as steadily as she had responded to the first question.

" No.—I'm sorry, but how can I? How can one trust anyone who is, after all, an utter stranger? "

" Right." Again he approved, but she could not know that. " We'll get at it another way. I take it that you are very anxious to keep Tad out of serious trouble. Maybe it's too late for that; I don't know. I am going to tell you what I do know, telling you because Mr. Lee is not here and I think you can help. If you run off immediately to Tad with all I tell you ——" He broke off with a shrug. " In that case," he amended, " I think between the two of us we will put the boy behind the bars for a good long stretch."

He saw how intently she listened to his every word, how she strove to gauge his inflection, to read his soul through his eyes, and he marked how, though a slow pallor followed her recent flush, her eyes were steady and courageous. She was not going to fly into hysteria.

" At least," she said in a faint, far-away voice, " I will promise not to say or do anything in a hurry of excitement."

" I played cards with Tad last night," he said casually.

" He lost a good bit of money for a kid, and I made it my especial affair to win every cent of it."

She winced; she had let her belief follow her eager hope that Tad had given up gambling. But to Steve she said quickly:

" It is Tad's hope—oh, he is so foolish, I know!—to make a big winning. He wants to help us with the ranch. We are heavily mortgaged, you know ———"

" The money which Tad played with and which I won," Steve told her with no more ado, " was marked money. It was some of the money taken from the stage in the holdup last fall."

If he had wondered how she would take the news, he was not kept waiting for the knowledge. The blood flooded back into her cheeks in flaming anger, and her eyes flashed at him as she cried:

" It's a lie! Tad isn't like that. It's a lie, I tell you! "

" No, it's not a lie; it's just the truth. I have the marked bills in my pocket ———"

" I don't care. Anyone could have marked them; you could have marked them yourself."

" I warned you that if we are to help the kid ———"

" I don't want your help, Steve Cody! " she told him passionately. " I don't know why I came out here with you. I was a fool ———"

" You are being a fool now! " he told her sharply. " If you refuse to look squarely at things simply because they are disagreeable ———"

She laughed in his face, making a brave attempt to fill her laughter with ringing scorn, yet being hard put to keep a tremor of doubt and fear out of it.

" I am at least glad that Tad is going to learn what sort of a friend you are! When I tell him ———"

" You are forgetting, aren't you? You were not to rush off to tell him anything, without first taking time to think." For his own part Steve was taking time; he was very deliberate, pausing a moment, then adding gravely: " If you did lose your head and blurt this out to him, you'd be forcing my hand. I'd follow you and put the kid under arrest, charged with highway robbery. I'd have to do it, to keep tab on him, and that way I doubt if we'd ever find out who did rob the stage."

When she caught the drift of what he was saying she was confused by a swirling medley of emotions. She spoke with less assurance now, yet with new hope.

" But you said that Tad—that he had the stolen money! "

" Which does not mean necessarily, does it, that he robbed the stage? Couldn't he have come by it since? In some other way? "

" Why, of course! " she cried excitedly. " If," she amended, recalling how in hot haste she had given him the lie on this very point, " if you are sure it is that money which Tad had? Then he must have got it from someone else! "

" From whom," he asked bluntly, " would Tad be getting three hundred dollars? "

" Three hundred! "

It was at the moment a lot of money. What with the purchase of the ranch, the necessary expenditures to get started, the family exchequer had run very low, so low indeed that there had been trouble keeping up the interest payments on the mortgage.

" You'll begin to see why I came to you ———"

" But I don't see! You should have gone to Tad first of all."

But he shook his head emphatically.

" Last of all, rather. That would put him on his guard; he would not tell; we'd perhaps never find out."

" Tad, when he understood what it was all about, would tell you. He wouldn't lie to you ———"

" Then he'd simply keep his mouth shut."

" And you want me, Tad's sister, to connive with you? What you are asking me to do is act like a spy on Tad! "

" Exactly." He was very cool about it, accepting the word which Corinna had flung at him as an end of all discussion. " If you are to help me and therefore help Tad, I think you'll have to spy on him. If you can't bring yourself to that, well then, I guess you can't help."

" If you require the services of a sneak, you have come to the wrong person, Mr. Cody! " she flared out at him, and gathered up her reins to go.

" If you don't care enough for the kid to play the part I am asking, I certainly have come to the wrong person," he retorted, and added sharply, " Remember it will be your balking at a word, even more than at the actual deed, that will be as responsible as much as anything I do in putting the damned young fool behind the bars."

She bit her lip, fighting back the angry words which clamored for expression.

" You don't believe Tad robbed the stage? "

" I do not."

" Then what danger is he in? How can you speak of putting him in prison? "

He shrugged.

" He is caught with the goods on him. He will refuse to talk. What's the answer? "

" You mean he will shield someone else, the guilty man? "

Again he shrugged.

" I mean that if you would help me, always with Tad's interests in mind, I believe we could save him from his folly. It's just a hunch at that."

It was his attitude rather than all that he had said which made her more fearful than ever for Tad.

" Maybe," she said hesitantly, faltering among her words, hating compromise with a form of deceit which he had seemed to suggest and which smacked to her of betrayal of a loved one, " maybe I had better hear what you were going to suggest. What do you want me to do? About Tad? "

" I want you to spy on him." He emphasized the detested word; there was to be no quibbling over it. " I want to find out where the rest of that money is; there were three thousand dollars. He said he would come back tonight for another game; I want him watched. If he has the whole amount or half of it or a third, I want to know. I want now to know whether you think he has a considerable sum of money in his possession. If, during the day he goes anywhere to get money, I want to know where he goes and, most of all, whom he sees."

His perfect calmness forced itself upon her and in the end served to aid her in quieting her own racing mind.

All of a sudden she was sure of one thing: He had not lied when he told her that Tad had had the marked money and had lost it at cards. It was a terrible concession to make, yet she made it. Tad in possession of the fruits of highway robbery! But Tad himself was not the highwayman! She clung to that belief with all the might of her love and faith. Then what? Tad had received it from a friend, and that friend was the robber and thief. And Tad, though accused himself, would refuse to betray his friend. That must be what Steve Cody believed.

" And you won't arrest Tad—if I do what you ask? "

" Not if I can help it. It is not Tad that I want.—Look here, Miss Lee, I'll tell you something even though you won't promise me to keep it to yourself. I am taking chances on you, and that is because I think you have sense enough to realize that you will only make trouble for yourself if you talk to anyone about things which for the present are best left alone. I know who two of the men are who held up the stage. And I'll tell you their names: Whitey Robbins and Boney Marks. What I do not know——"

But she interrupted him, saying swiftly:

" Whitey Robbins! He is the man whom you shot! "

" Yes. I tell you of him because I want to ask this question: Did you ever see him and Tad together before the holdup? That was toward the end of last October, you will remember."

" Why, I saw Whitey Robbins—the very day it happened! "

Her admission came with a rush; only after it was out did she catch her lower lip between her teeth, fearful of admitting too much. She bent her head and put her hands over her eyes as though to shut out a blinding flash of light.

" Here, at the ranch? " he asked quietly. And then, when she did not answer and did not look up: " And you saw Tad with him? "

" No! I was alone and I saw him and another man." She dropped her hands; they caught at the horn of her saddle, gripping hard. " I did not know who it was then; but a few nights later I saw him when—when you shot him down at my side. So I know it was Whitey Robbins."

" And it was here? What was he doing on your ranch? And who was the other man? And what about Tad? "

It seemed to her that, however unwillingly, step by step she was coming to his side, allowing herself to be drawn into some sort of a conspiracy centering about Tad, and whether that conspiracy were for Tad's salvation or un-doing, how could she tell? Most of all was it clear to her that if she did not draw back now, if instead she answered these last rapier-swift questions, she committed herself to all that Steve Cody asked of her. So she lifted her eyes to his and looked at him long and fixedly, yearning for some true knowledge of him. He returned her look, un-derstanding, waiting, adding nothing to shape the issue. And, oddly enough, since his expression did not change and no flicker to guide her came into his eyes, suddenly her fear of him rushed back upon her. It was a queer sort of fear, since it did not enter her mind that he would raise a hand against her and she did not dwell upon the fact that the two of them were beyond call; it was not that sort of dread at all, but a vague, nameless thing not based in any way on physical danger.

"I won't answer. I cannot tell you anything else, Mr. Cody. At least not until I have talked with Tad."

"You are making a mistake. From what you have already told me I think that you could help me make everything clear. If you talk with your brother, he'll bind you to silence. And if you would only trust me ——"

Trust? He had used the wrong word.

"Why should I trust you? How can I trust you?" she cried hotly. "What do I know of you that would make anyone put confidence in you? I know that you are a gambler; I know that when I came to you, begging you in simple humanity to help me, you sneered at me. And I saw you shoot a man, and it was not your fault that you did not kill him. And you are not sorry for what you did, not ashamed; you are proud of it, I think! Even the office you are now allowed to fill, how did you get it? I don't know; who rightly does? By trickery, bribery or how? And you ask if I could ever trust you! No! "

Later she might wonder at herself and at her boldness; now the words came unchecked and she was unafraid as she uttered them, knowing that whatever the man might be, she was safe with him.

But she did see that she had quickened him to anger; his eyes hardened and he was very grim about the mouth when, having heard her out, he said coldly:

"Look here, Miss Lee, I haven't made it my business going 'round talking about myself. What I've done, I've done and there it stands. But ——"

Thus far he had been impetuous, yielding to heady

impulse for one of the rare times in his life. But he checked himself, breaking off abruptly, and shrugged as if in indifference and turned away from her to stare straight ahead again. Corinna, her pulses quickened, looked wonderingly into his set face. He had set his will to veil his eyes, but her glance was swift and keen, her intuition great, and in that swift flash of time she saw that they seemed to be looking into vast distances, and that they were no longer stern—no longer agate-hard—but were sad human eyes.

" Tell me," she said softly, impulsive in her turn. " What is it? What were you going to say? "

" Nothing."

" But it was something!—I said things which per-haps —— Oh, the world is becoming terrible! "

From those infinite distances he brought his brooding eyes back to hers.

" You saw me shoot Whitey Robbins; you saw him try to shoot me in the back."

" Yes."

" Something has come over me," he said, and there was a queer new inflection in his voice. " What, I won-der? Maybe it's just the oath I took when I stepped into this office which I took by my own means and in my own way! Maybe it's seeing Tad, a good kid, going to hell? Tad, and other kids that might go square, given a chance! And maybe "—his eyes narrowed and points of light seemed to burn in them—" maybe it's you, Corinna Lee! "

He startled her and she stared at him in amazement.

Then of a sudden he laughed. It was the first time she had ever heard Steve Cody laugh.

"It's all in our stars, isn't it?" he queried in such a tone that she was all at sea as to whether he was in earnest or jesting. He flipped back his coat so that she could see the badge of his office pinned to his shirt. "Something has come over me, and maybe after all it's just this—a star. Is it making me over?"

And now it was his turn for sheer wonderment, so startling a change came over her. She stared with widening eyes; she seemed shocked and grew pale, then all at once her face flamed scarlet. She blundered among words.

"It is a star. A silver star! I did not know—that is, I did not realize—not consciously ——"

"I don't understand," he said, frankly puzzled.

Then Corinna laughed. Laughed from a saving sense of relief, realizing that of course he could not understand. In her first moment of confusion it was as though it had been to Steve Cody, not to Aunt Mary, that she had recounted her dream.

"I am going back to the house now," she said hurriedly. "I will think of all you have said. I will not say anything to Tad. I will even see if I can find a way to help. There is something I can tell you, if when I have had time to think, it seems right that I should."

"About Whitey and the other man?"

"Yes."

"But I will have to know now."

"No. Not now. I want a little while. I will ride back here right after lunch; will that do?"

He nodded and Corinna, scarcely waiting for the nod, flashed away, racing in headlong haste back to the house. She wanted to be alone, most of all to be away from him; she welcomed the wet cold air in her flaming cheeks. And, herself puzzled no less than Steve Cody, as she rode she repeated his words, making them her own:

" I don't understand! "

CHAPTER IX

" ME, I'm a great hand for readin' the newspapers," said the Judge. "Ads, scan'le, editorials an' even the news if there is any. An' in such int'lectual pastimes I've run acrost a certain word recent that sticks in the mind like a cuckle burr in a sheep dog's hair. It's a fine, upstandin' word, an' I'm for it. Inhibition, she is. There bein' no ladies present, boys, I'd like to use that there word. Speakin' of Spike Freedom, me, I've sure got Inhibition."

The Judge, David Laribee and Steve Cody sat at an early lunch in Steve's cabin, served by the dreamy-eyed young Indian buck who was the general factotum of a ranch requiring little. The three had arrived at that stage of the meal where a man's gestures grow leisurely, and when, as witness the Judge, he may find time to rest the fist-gripped butt-ends of both knife and fork on the oil-cloth, blade and tines pointing straight up, to be peered over while he grows vocal ad lib.

Laribee, who always enjoyed the Judge, grinned encouragement for him to sail ahead and make all clear. Steve, seeming to have newly fallen into the pernicious habit of looking at his watch every minute or two, regarded his conversational guest rather absently.

" This here word, Inhibition," said the Judge, knife and fork steadily erect, " popped up recent in my experience, along of Prohibition, I seem to remember. I looked

115

it up once in my ol' dictionary, an' it means anything you'd give your right eye to do an' can't somehow get it done. Which brings me to Spike Freedom an' how I'm inhibitionated. What I'd like to do would be come up with that gent, all alone on a serene Sabbath mornin', when all the rest of the world was sleepin' off its night-before, an' for choice I'd pick a spot where Nature is at her sweetes' an' lovelies', which is to say far from the mad-dog human crowd." His two fists tightened about knife and fork. " I'd sure like to paint that ornery hombre with stripes like a zebra; I got an ol' varmint-skinnin' knife, nice an' dull an' full o' nicks, with which I yearn to take his hide off in strips. Them strips of his own green hide I'd like mighty well to bind about his neck, so's when the sun shone out on 'em, they'd shrink an' choke him to death."

" That would be just by way of getting started to work on him, wouldn't it, Judge? " chuckled Laribee.

The Judge nodded soberly.

" That would be jus' the start, m' son," he conceded, and the mild blue eyes raised to Laribee's face looked wistful.

" What did Spike Freedom ever do to you? " asked Steve, pocketing his watch once more.

" Who said he ever did anything to me? " queried old Judge Bull innocently. " Shucks, Steve, I'm jus' public-spirited."

He and Laribee had devoted several of the fresh morning hours to riding mountain trails, seeking the man who, Laribee had heard, had been in the neighborhood no longer ago than late yesterday afternoon. But it began to appear that Spike Freedom was resolved on maintaining a degree of privacy which the Judge began to find maddening. You heard of him infrequently at this, that or the other place; you looked him up and he was nowhere in evidence. The Judge had even advertised for him in the local paper: " If Spike Freedom will show up at my office he will learn something to his advantage. Also I'll pay money to any man that can lead me to him. Wm. Henry Bull."

About eleven o'clock the disgruntled Judge and Laribee had drifted by Steve's cabin, and to men who had breakfasted early and ridden hard an early lunch was welcome. Steve himself informed them that he was expected elsewhere shortly, and offered no more detailed information.

" Me," said the Judge, talking pointedly to Laribee, " it wouldn't surprise me over much if it was a lady Steve's goin' visitin'. Look at that thing, there, will you? " He pointed. "A lookin' glass hung on the wall an' big enough for an elephant to look himse'f over in. That spells vanity, Dave, m' son, an' it sort o' suggests a female-girl in the woodpile, huh? "

Steve took the trouble to explain; about the glass, that is. Were it not for that and certain practice shots fired before it, it was altogether possible that instead of Whitey Robbins now inhabiting a hospital cot it might have been Steve Cody.

" Only how the blazes," demanded the Judge, " did you know he was goin' to pull his work where a mirror'd be hangin'? "

" A hunch, that's all," returned Steve carelessly. " It was a cinch he'd shoot from behind; Vargas's Place was as good as any; and that big mirror of Vargas's had only been put up a couple of weeks before. A man couldn't help thinking of it."

"A gambler an' his hunches!" scoffed the Judge. "Well, at that, I dunno. A hunch is a hunch, an' I guess it's worth while givin' 'em a whirl.—Ridin' toward town, Steve?"

"Riding alone this time, Judge," returned Steve noncommittally, and looked at his watch. Laribee laughed and rose, saying he'd go get the horses.

"Dave's another man that's got the lookin' glass habit," observed the Judge, looking as guileless as a lamb while watching his host for signs. "Keeps his whiskers under control, hair cut an' combed, an' wears neckties every day same as if it was Sunday, mos' generally red ones, too, I notice. Well, him an' Corinna Lee would make quite a team at that, huh? You've seen her, ain't you, Steve?"

"Didn't Laribee tell you we both saw her this morning?"

"Why, I believe he did! She's a cute little trick, ain't she? She's got as curly a pair of eyes as ever made every jasper that looks into 'em sort of feel he was cut out to be a poet, an' a smile that ought to be against the law unless the girl that owns it is game to keep all the nice promises it makes. Notice, Steve?"

But for all his sagacity and curiosity the Judge drew only a blank and finally mounted his mule and rode away with Laribee in meditative mood.

From the cabin door Steve watched the two out of sight; then he went to the barn, saddled his blue roan and struck off into the wooded slopes at the northern end of his ranch. Once in the forest he altered his course, swinging off to the east, striking into an old trail, beginning to turn south. Thus, in a roundabout way, he would return to the Lee ranch. It was only twelve o'clock now; he would be early at his meeting with Corinna.

The trails which he followed led him through a bit of the wildest of all this mountain country, a region of dusky forest lands where noble old spruces and yellow pines stood like sturdy pillars supporting the arch of the lowering sky, where the atmosphere was like that of a hushed cathedral; through miles of this uncut wilderness, when at last a sharper sound made itself heard above the murmur of the tree tops, and down in a steep, narrow gorge Wild River raced along, thundering over its many falls, waving its white banners, roaring out with its clash of many voices. And now Steve turned south, keeping the river just out of sight on his left, following a timbered ridge, headed toward the Lee ranch and particularly toward the one convenient ford, which, at this time of year, a horse and rider could negotiate. This was not the crossing that the Judge and Laribee would use, where the county road ran on toward High Town, but one which today served Steve's purpose better since he desired to come unseen to the spot where Corinna was to meet him. Where the river ran out into a bit of rich meadow land that had once been a lake, the coursing waters spreading out to flow less turbulently and less deep, he spurred Blue Boy down to the hissing edge, achieving the farther side some fifty yards farther down stream. From here he struck into a gallop, speeding up and down the long slopes, weaving in and out among the pines, arriving shortly before one o'clock at the little clearing. A few big fat drops of rain spattered upon him and he looked anxiously up at the leaden sky.

"She'll come, even if it does rain," he decided.

And in time Corinna came hurrying, though only after his certainty grew veiled in doubt and in the end was on the verge of vanishing utterly. The moment he saw her face he knew that it was no mere girl's trick and whim that had kept him waiting; her cheeks were flushed and her eyes looked frightened.

"I am sorry I came so late," she exclaimed eagerly. "I—something happened——"

And there she let it stand for the moment. Just how could she explain? For certainly she could not tell him the amazing thing that had happened! She would have to tell him part of it, or swiftly make an end of the implied conspiracy in which he and she were about to join against Tad and for Tad's sake; she would have to tell him something of Vargas's unexpected and astounding visit. But that Vargas, reeking with conceit, as sure of himself as any matinée idol among his fair idolaters, had bluntly advised her of his hopes, of his expectations of one day making her Mrs. Vargas, there would be no telling! And yet Vargas's presumption, absurd as it was and therefore not quite so hideous as it would have been otherwise, was the thing which put the hot color in her face and a look half of fear, half of abhorrence in her eyes. What had occurred was like the memory of a nightmare now. Vargas, whom in all her life she had seen but once, Vargas, who had seen her that once only and who had stared and gone on, wanted her. Not only that but he meant to have her. He saw no reason on earth why she should not be overjoyed because he had come to her, offering to buy her.

"Is that terrible man—Vargas—a madman?" was what she blurted out as Steve Cody, silent and puzzled, looked at her.

His brows shot up in that queer quizzical way they had, one slightly higher than the other; he demanded sharply:

"Vargas was at the house? That is why you are late? Is he in the habit of coming out here?"

"It is the first time. He—he acted strangely——"

"Yes," he answered her first question soberly. "Vargas is touched with madness. Most men are, aren't they? He has a fixed idea. He thinks he has it in him to be a Napoleon, an Alexander the Great, a Cæsar. A touch of madness or just an overswollen vanity? He has his own way generally. Those who flock about him are drawn by a will stronger than their own. He is a shepherd over a flock of sheep. He wants to change his sheep into wolves, himself to be the pack leader. That's Vargas."

"He came to see Tad. To warn him. He told Tad and then he told me about the marked money. He says that you have it and that you mean to make trouble for Tad."

Steve listened thoughtfully. In those hurrying words there was no explanation of the confusion and fear he had sensed in her. Had Vargas's errand been only as she described it, he had but shown a friendly interest, a desire to help her brother. So, of course, there was something which she held back. Something to make her ask, "Is he mad?"

Steve suddenly repeated her own words, "Vargas acted

strangely? " and added to them, " Was he making threats? "

" No, no. He seemed to want to help." Her distress in speaking of him was obvious; she hastened to turn the talk back to Tad and his dilemma. " I have thought things over as I promised; I am going to trust you, after all. I am afraid for Tad."

" Fine. First of all, do you think he has the rest of the money about him? He'd hardly be carrying it in his pocket, would he? "

" It isn't anywhere at the house; it isn't in his room," she told him steadily. " I looked. I don't know whether or not I am doing a vile thing, but I am ready to spy on him." Like Steve, she had determined that there should be no quibbling over words; the deed was the thing and must stand by itself. " No; I don't think he has it about him."

" And you have no idea from whom he got it? "

" All I know is that I saw those two men the day of the stage robbery—and I told Tad—and he seemed excited over it. Shall I tell you all that? "

" If you please, Miss Lee." He spoke crisply and his eyes were narrowed as they were bent piercingly upon her. He added more gently: " Once and for all, I pledge you my word that I am hoping and trying to save the kid from his own folly."

She nodded hurriedly.

" If I didn't feel that, I wouldn't be here now."

" So you'll tell me about seeing Whitey and the other man? And how you happen to be so sure that it was the day of the holdup? "

"I like to ride alone back in the mountains," said Corinna. "When you came this morning I was just about to start. That day I had taken my lunch and had ridden to one of my favorite spots; it is at the far end of the ranch, so it must be four miles from here. I tied my horse in a little meadow and nooned in a grove of aspens by a spring. It was a lovely Indian summer day, I remember; I found a sunny, secret place all ringed about with big ferns and read the book I had brought along. When I heard voices I was startled. Through the ferns I saw the two men on horseback. One of them was Whitey Robbins; I had never seen him before and never saw him again until—at Vargas's Place, you know."

"The other man?" he asked.

"I don't know who he was. A tall, thin man, very dark, almost like an Indian. He had a sharp, high-pitched voice and his head looked like a Plymouth Rock's egg, so bald and brown; he had his hat off, mopping his face."

"Boney Marks," said Steve.

"They came up out of a steep ravine where there's a fork of the river. At first I was frightened, thinking that they were coming straight to the spring, but they didn't see me and rode off into the woods. I didn't catch any words that I remember. As soon as I was sure that they had gone I ran to my horse and hurried home. It was late afternoon then; at the corral I met Tad coming in from High Town. And I remember that before I told him anything about the two men he told me of the stage robbery; he had just heard of it in town."

"And you say that he was excited over what you told him?"

She hesitated, looking troubled and uncertain. But suddenly she lifted her head with a little gesture of decision and spoke quietly and with no further hesitation.

" He was very much interested. Late as it was he insisted on my riding with him to the place where I had seen the two men. And I know he has gone back up there many times since. Almost every day, I think."

" But he didn't tell you what he was looking for? "

" He told me," said Corinna, and looked at Steve anxiously, " that with so many fresh mining claims having been discovered during the last couple of years in our mountains, he saw no reason why there mightn't be gold on our ranch. He had been out every day prospecting. That is what he has told me," she added rather faintly.

" You left him just now with Vargas at the house? "

" Yes.—Vargas was asking him to go back to town with him; Tad, I think, didn't want to go until later in the day. He said that he had some things to do before he could get away."

" I'm glad you've told me all this. Now I wonder if you would ride with me as you did with Tad that day, showing me where you saw Whitey and Boney Marks? "

She nodded and asked no questions, though she could not see what possible end was to be served by going now to a spot visited by the stage robbers more than two months before. In silence she turned her horse toward the mountains and Steve, reining in beside her, warned her that no doubt they were in for a wetting; in the far northern distance thunder rumbled and now and then gusts of storm-breath shook scattering drops from the low cloud banks.

" It doesn't matter, I'm dressed for it," said Corinna, and pricked her horse into a gallop. " And there's a good trail; it will take us only half an hour to get there."

At times Steve Cody rode behind her and she fancied that she could feel those keen eyes of his on her back; at times, where there was trail room, he rode at her side and she could not keep her eyes from stealing flashing glances at his face. As hoofs hammered and her pulses strummed with them, her thoughts seemed to become part of a universal throb. She had said that she did not and could not trust him; after all, she did trust him. In riding with him now, deeper and deeper into the solitudes where many a day passed without anyone riding this way, she was entrusting herself to him. More than that, she was giving him Tad's confidences. Why this sudden change in her? Now and then, as his flapping coat was blown back by a gust of wind, she glimpsed the shining badge pinned to his shirt. Was that the answer? A silver star and a dream? Out of them had she builded her a knight?

The wind rushed screaming at them across a darkened glade; down came slanting sheets of rain as though the saturated clouds above had been slashed open, spilling their water not in mere drops but in torrents. Head down they rushed across the open space and into what shelter was provided by a grove of pines.

" Cloud-burst," said Steve. " It will be over in a minute."

But for fifteen minutes, waiting, they sat their horses

under the pines. The rain did not cease altogether, but the heavy downpour passed them by and they rode on, still toward the mountains, which were a purplish black in the grip of the storm.

" It's not far," called Corinna against the wind. " Just over a low ridge ———"

" And I begin to think I could lead the way now! " he amazed her by answering. He pointed ahead and off to the left. " Yonder, wasn't it? And they rode up out of a cañon so steep that you did wonder for a moment how their horses could have climbed down and up again? They came up from the river, didn't they? "

She nodded and her eyes asked him how he knew. He reined in close to her and their horses slowed down.

" You needn't go any further; I can find my way on from here," he told her. " It's going to storm again."

" How do you know where I saw them? " she asked curiously. " And what do you think you are going to find there? There is something ———"

" Come ahead, then," he returned. " I'll show you. You never went down the steep bank into the cañon there, did you? "

She shook her head and now followed him; they rode up to the crest of the low ridge and where a tiny meadow was cradled between two smooth humps of earth she showed him her secret place among the ferns and pointed out the spot where she had seen the two riders come up out on the gorge. Here they dismounted and Steve led the two horses away into the shelter of thick timber at one side of the trail.

" It's simpler, also safer, to make the rest of our trip

on foot," he advised her. "If Whitey and Marks rode out from here, it's a cinch I know where they came from. If you'll follow me we'll be there in five minutes."

There was no sign of trail now, so they zigzagged down a precipitous slope which pitched almost sheer into a woodsy tangle of alder and willow and aspen whence rose the roar of rushing water. There were times when they dug in their heels and slid. Once Corinna lost her balance and careened full tilt into him, to be steadied by his arms about her. She flinched back and away; for a wild second with her heart beating furiously all her old fears of him swept over her. But he appeared unmoved, and certainly, after that involuntary tensing as he caught her, did not hold her captive as he might have done, but freed her the instant she stood securely. They went on and down in silence; Corinna inching along with care too great to permit of another slip.

When he stopped and pointed again and called out something, she could not hear what he said, so great a roar came up from the river where spray among boulders flashed to the tree tops and with such a steady thresh and hiss did the rain lash among the leaves. She looked where he pointed and could see nothing save the line of brushy trees, the dark race of water and the white lacings of foam. She came closer and peering through the whipping branches saw something white gleaming faintly through the bare branches; it looked like an old dead log fallen across the stream.

"It's an old bridge," he told her. "It's been here ever since I can remember, but not many know of it or what's on the other side. Whitey would know! I'm going across; will you wait here? "

She nodded and watched him go. He parted the branches, seemed to be walking freely and easily, and vanished among the trees on the other side. A moment she remained where she was; then she followed to the nearer end of the bridge. It consisted of two logs, dropped parallel and close together, with bits of plank nailed crosswise, making a runway a yard wide. The swollen stream hissed close under it, spray flying over the top. She looked across; the whole distance was not over twenty-five feet and, drawn on by curiosity, she followed where he had led. The first few steps she took timidly, hesitantly, and at each step she was on the verge of going back. Yet she went on and when at last she had gone fully half-way she scurried across the remaining distance, her heart in her mouth. She felt as though the logs were slipping, as though the rush of water so close underneath were about to swirl them from their ancient anchorage.

Before her, among boulders which had rolled from the mountainside and thick growths of fern, she saw a track left by Steve's boot; he had penetrated the thicket straight ahead, which now shut him from view. She called to him, all of a sudden conscious of the oppressive loneliness of the place in its heavy wintry mood. That single track indicated a direction; she found a second beyond a clump of ferns and followed on. Then she saw the stone house not a score of steps away and stood staring at it incredulously. A stone house—perhaps hut was the better word—here in the wilderness of their own ranch, and she had never dreamed of its existence.

CHAPTER X

It was as cold and gloomy and altogether as forbidding a place brooding in the dark ravine as was conceivable, yet Corinna hurried eagerly forward to it. She stopped at the narrow doorway; the door itself leaned crookedly against the wall, insecurely anchored by one rusty hinge. The shadowy interior yielded up no details to a first glance but seemed sullenly set upon guarding its secrets; then Steve's voice saying, " Hello! So you came along, did you? " reached her sounding hollow in that rock-walled emptiness, and she saw him standing in the middle of the room.

" Spooky old shop, isn't it? " he said lightly, as he joined her at the door. " It's always been a sort of den of thieves; couldn't you guess it? Maybe old houses, like old men, have memories!—Ready to go? I'll go with you as far as the horses, then come back here to look around."

" Maybe that's what ghosts are—the things which old houses remember? " Her tone did not match his for lightness; it was more natural to shudder here than to laugh. Yet there may be a thrill even in a shudder, and certainly Corinna was of no mind to budge so soon from what appeared to be the very threshold of all the gloomy mysteries in the world. As her eyes grew accustomed to the shadows which hung like black veils over everything, she darted quick inquisitive glances into all the corners.

129

" You think that those two men had been here? That they hid the money here and that Tad found it? "

He nodded thoughtfully, as he too stared curiously about.

" Why not? Whitey, an old-timer hereabouts, would know of this place; he'd know how lonely and little visited it is. If he and Marks had the money on them they'd hardly take it straight on into High Town. Where is a likelier spot to hide anything? The robbery took place on the grade near Oak Flats; that's a good twenty miles from here. They circled off to the north, struck south again and came this way.—Anyhow, since we're here, I'm going to have a look around."

" They wouldn't have left it here all this time! "

" The next day Marks was killed, you remember. And the next night Whitey went to a hospital. Yes; if they left it here at all, as far as they are concerned it would be here yet."

" And if —— "

" If Tad found it here? " He shrugged. " He might have moved it all. On the other hand, he may have figured it out that it was safe here until Whitey could be up and about again. In which case, Miss Lee, he may have ' borrowed ' the three hundred only; and he may be planning yet today to drop in for some more. It's all guesswork, of course."

" Tad wouldn't —— " she began, but rather sternly he cut in, reminding her that Tad had gotten the money somehow, and it was rather to be hoped that he had found it here than come by it in any other way.

She shivered; this place was cold and damp and dreary,

the rain beat thunderously on the old shake roof, pouring through at a dozen major leaks, and despite her raincoat she was uncomfortably conscious of an all-pervading chill dampness. She wondered rather vaguely how such a place ever came into being, lost in so lonely a hollow. Steve could have told her something of it, the old Judge a very great deal, for it linked the present with those other days when Buck Bull and Curly Cody were young, when there was lawlessness akin to the new lawlessness of today, when stolen stock had been hazed through the mountains on the way to the state border line, and when Joe Vargas had been swung high for many misdeeds in general and another man's crime in particular.

Corinna felt that the ranch would never be altogether clean and wholesome again until men came here with dynamite and blew the old house to pieces. When she shivered a second time it was not alone because of damp and chill; to her this place was shuddersome and seemed to exude evil like some poisonous fungus. From the cross-beams above, blackened with time and smoke, to the wet walls and rotting floor, everything her eyes chanced on repelled her. There was a black fireplace in which rain-water gathered, a bunk filled with mouldy straw, a bench and a crooked homemade table. A narrow door was across the room from the one at which she had entered; she tiptoed gingerly across the disintegrating floor and peered through. At the rear was the second and final room, a small cubby-hole with one small inadequate window high up.

While she took all this in, Steve Cody was busying

himself with trying to hit upon a likely hiding place for the loot which he suspected of having found its way here. He sought a loose stone in the wall, in the hearth; a recess in the crossbeams; a cubby-hole in a corner. He examined the bunk, probing the straw, looking beneath. Then, with Corinna withdrawn to the front doorway, he went into the smaller room and searched there.

"It's a long shot, of course," he said, coming to rejoin her and standing at her side, head down while he rolled a cigarette. "It may never have been here; it may have been removed. In fact, the reasonable thing to suppose, since it was discovered, is that the man who found it lost no time in changing its hiding place. Just the same ——"

"You have known Tad only a few months," she said thoughtfully, staring off through the driving rain, "but you must know him pretty well. He isn't hard to understand, is he? Did he ever strike you as—as a thief, Mr. Cody?"

"No," he returned promptly. "Not a thief. But ——"

"But," said Corinna, "he might do what so many men, really meaning no harm, have done when they used money which did not belong to them? If Tad found that money he might do just what you said a while ago; 'borrow' from it. He would mean to play cards; he would be sure he was going to win; then he'd return what he had taken. Don't you think Tad is like that?"

His head inclined to bring the end of his cigarette to the match in his cupped hands, and no less to give her his silent "Yes."

"So," she concluded with a little weary sigh, "if he

did find the money here he would not have moved it. He would have taken some, maybe, meaning to bring it back. When he lost that, he might ' borrow ' again."

She was looking at Steve now and, with still more to say, checked her words. He was looking past her and did not seem listening; she began wondering if he had heard a single thing she said. That he had heard he made clear enough by saying quietly, his voice hushed:

" He's coming now. I caught a glimpse of him through the willows. It would be best if he did not see you."

She caught her breath and involuntarily started to draw back into the stone hut.

" No. I am going to let him come in, if that's what he wants. Outside, quick. Behind the house. Out of sight."

She darted out, panicky lest Tad should find her here, and ran hurriedly around the corner of the building, breaking her way through ferns and buck brush. Steve Cody followed at her heels. At the rear of the house he pointed toward the depths of the thicket.

" In there," he whispered. " I'll stick close here. I have to see what he does."

Corinna, excited, torn this way and that, ashamed to be a party to any espionage of Tad's actions, terribly anxious for him, vanished in the clump of saplings, leaving a trail of broken bracken behind her. Steve stood very still by the high rear window, through which he could see into the smaller room and through its open door into the larger.

Tad, at once furtive and yet in haste, stopped only a second at the front door, looking about him, then hurried into the hut. Evidently he had no fear of anyone being here before him; after that one instinctive survey which missed all trampled signs which must have been obvious to a really suspicious eye, he went straight about his business. Steve saw him stand on the rickety table, which threatened to give way under him, reach high into the hut's gable end and thrust his fingers into a crevice between two stones in the rough masonry.

Steve waited to see no more from that vantage; the winter afternoon was drawing on to an early close, the dark day was already half-night in the house, and details might easily escape him. He moved swiftly yet quietly from his place, going back to the front of the house. And as Tad, putting something into his coat pocket, stepped back to the door, Steve confronted him.

"Steve! " cried the boy, and gave back a pace or two. "What do you want here? "

"Let's have it, Kid," said Steve, and put out his hand. "You know what I mean."

"I don't know what you're talking about—you've been —— Damn you, Cody! Spy on me, would you? "

Steve shrugged.

"Put it any way you please, Tad, old man," he said gently. "What you've got to keep in mind is that I'm sheriff now. And what I say in a case like this, goes. Fork over."

"What are you driving at? " Tad snapped back at him. "'In a case like this! ' Like what? "

"The loot of highway robbery, then. Three thousand dollars, left here by Whitey Robbins and Boney Marks. Let's have it."

"You're crazy! "

"Better go slow, hadn't you, Tad?" Steve's voice, without being raised, took on an edge. "You dropped three hundred bucks to me last night. They were marked bills; didn't know that, did you?"

Tad, head down, feet shuffling, was for a space of time a picture of moroseness and indecision. Suddenly he jerked his head up, his eyes glaring into Steve's.

"How'd you know so damn' much about it all?" he demanded sneeringly. "Unless you were—the third man!"

Steve did not pretend to misunderstand. It was at this moment that Corinna, hearing their voices, crept from the bushes and to the little window at the rear. She raised herself on tiptoes and peeped in. Tad, having been about to quit the room, had his back turned to her; Steve, being just outside and facing her, catching what pale light still pervaded the dreary afternoon, did not move his eyes from Tad's face.

Tad, failing to hear the swift denial which he had expected as he made his bitter accusation, cried hotly:

"You, Cody, are an infernal yellow dog! Vargas has told me a lot about you today. You're trying to double-cross him; you'd double-cross me. You turned on your own father while he was alive, and by God, I wouldn't be surprised if you were the man that shot him! To grab what property he had; to grab the sheriff's office, using it to hide behind while you pull dirty deals like this!"

Corinna, in consternation, gasped; then, fearful of having been heard, ducked down, her hand clasped to her mouth. She heard Steve saying, with cold repression: "Yes? All of that? Hand it over, Harper."

" I'll see you in hell first! You've no more right to it than I have. If you robbed the stage, it's not yours. If you didn't, still it's not yours. Stand aside, Cody! "

" Better get this straight, hadn't you? It's not Cody you're talking to right now; it happens that I represent the law ——"

Tad's jeering laughter barked at him.

" You! You representing the law! Say, that's rich.— And now I'll tell you something, Mr. Sheriff; I'm fed up with you."

" Been talking with Vargas, haven't you? "

" Well, what of it? "

" Nothing. Anything else you've got on your mind? "

Tad, tense and nervous and rapidly growing distraught, broke into full-mouthed, violent cursing.

" Damn you, yes. Because I've kept my thoughts to myself doesn't mean that I'm a fool."

" That's right enough. Blabbing is the fool's part."

" Well, I'll blab now if I like. It's about my sister; I want you to keep away from her. Get that? "

" We needn't discuss Miss Lee, need we? " came Steve's voice very deliberately. " I've asked you a couple of times ——"

" Never mind that. That part of it can wait," Tad blazed out at him. " I know that Corinna was fool enough to go to Vargas's Place once to see you. Yes, Vargas did tell me. He's a friend of mine; Vargas is all right. He goes roughshod and he plays 'em high, but by high heaven and deep hell he's square with a pal ——"

" You've been reading melodrama," Steve told him coolly. " Can it."

Tad flung up his head, his face hot with color, looking very boyish and defiant and reckless.

" There's more than that," he ran on, a tremor in his voice. " Before I was out of bed this morning I heard voices; one sounded like yours. I put it up to Laribee a while ago when he rode by with the Judge. Laribee said, Yes, you had come to see Corinna. Now lie out of that if you can! "

" I don't intend to lie out of it. Was that any crime? Did I need to ask you? "

" Yes, it was a crime; for a man like you to open your head to a girl like her. After this you keep away from her, hear me? "

" Oh, I hear you." To Corinna, crouching under the window, his voice of a sudden sounded weary. But instantly all weariness departed from it as he said more sternly than he had yet spoken: " I'll take that money now. Now, Harper."

Tad, the fair brows puckering over his blue eyes, strove to carry himself as he thought that a man should.

" I haven't got a gun on me and I know that you're always heeled," he said, with an assumption of a nonchalant swagger. " Take the money, Mr. Gunman Sheriff. I'm on my way and "—the rest of his words poured out wildly—" when I'm through telling my sister what I know about you, you won't want to show up where she is as long as you live! If you've been meeting her on the sly, taking advantage of her father's being away, knowing he'd shoot you down like a dog——"

" Better be going, Tad," said Steve curtly. " Also, you'd

better do a bit of straight thinking for yourself, and get all of Vargas's nonsense out of your head."

"I've given you your warning, Steve Cody," cried Tad, and left, walking briskly, going back through the thicket to the bridge. Corinna, from the corner of the house, watched him cross the stream and climb the steep bank beyond, vanishing among the pines. She hastened to rejoin Steve.

"He really did have it!" she said breathlessly. "He gave you the money."

Steve opened his hand and showed her the bank notes; from his pocket he added to it that smaller wad of bills which represented his last night's winnings from Tad.

"In all, pretty close to three thousand dollars," he told her when he had counted. "Yes, it's the loot from the stage robbery. See these hair-line pencil marks?" He indicated them on several bills. "Well, I've got it now, even if I don't understand the whole deal; and at that, I can guess pretty close. There were three men who did the thing; two closed in from in front, another guarded the rear. The two front Johnnies got the swag and dusted. The third man cut back and around a hill. I'd guess that the two were Whitey Robbins and Boney Marks, and that they stopped here on their way back to High Town, riding in a sort of semicircle to keep in the clear. Anyway, the money was cached here. Then somebody extinguished Boney Marks—perhaps thinking that he had it on him?" He shrugged. "You've heard it rumored that I killed him? Well, I didn't."

"But Whitey Robbins thought it was you!"

"He would," said Steve disgustedly. "He has no more

imagination than a Dutch cow; I'd happened to have had a lively word or two with him and his side-kick. What more natural than Mr. Nit-wit Whitey should remember just that far back and come shooting? "

He stood with his head down, idly smoothing out some three thousand dollars in bank notes which he was but remotely conscious of holding, so deep was he in his own preoccupation. She flashed a glance at what of his face was to be seen under the dripping hat brim.

" Why, I'm not the least bit afraid of him! " she thought swiftly. " He is just fine—and he doesn't go around shooting people! People misunderstand him and lie ——"

" Eh? " said Steve with a little start, and jerked his head up. " Pardon; I didn't catch what you said."

" Why, I didn't say anything! " gasped Corinna, in her own turn so startled that the blood rushed into her face, a brief tingling fear upon her that she had actually spoken aloud. " I—I was just going to say that I must hurry. Tad will be looking for me. I want to get home as soon as I can after he does."

In silence they went to the bridge and across, and in silence climbed the steep slope beyond and went to their horses. Steve, speaking abruptly just as they were about to mount, gave her a fresh start, saying all without preface:

" I dreamed about you last night."

" About me? " she exclaimed swiftly, and her own dream that had visited her so insistently flashed through her mind. Then she laughed lightly with a suspicion of scorn in her uncertain laughter, and it was quite as though she had said mockingly: " I am supposed to believe that, am I? "

He shoved the toe of his boot into the stirrup and looked at her over his horse's back.

" Perhaps I didn't have any business taking the liberty, but I didn't do it on purpose, so you can't have me shot at dawn for it. And it was a curious sort of dream at that." He rose to the saddle and all the while there was the same odd look in his eyes. " I thought that you were what the old story books used to call a Damsel in Distress and ——"

A shivery sensation went rippling through her. She said, as indifferently as she could manage:

" You've been reading Malory, I expect."

She was glad to be up in the saddle, on the same level with him, not forced to look up at him, not feeling him above her, looking down into her eyes.

" Malory? " he said. " Oh, the *Morte d'Arthur?* Not for a good many years. It's funny, though, that you should mention Malory; that used to be my one book when I was a kid. All that knight-business is great stuff for a youngling, isn't it? I remember—at school I had just learned how to draw a five-pointed star—how I got me an old baking powder can and cut a star out of the top of it. You ought to have seen how it blazed in the sun when I nailed it to the headgear I'd made out of some other tins! Ha! I was the Knight of the Silver Star, no less."

Corinna could feel her eyes getting round. Hastily she averted them, pulling her hat down, tucking in a stray, wind-blown curl or two.

" And now," she said at last, a sort of hush in her voice as she glanced at him and then away to a long lane through the trees, " wearing the silver star of your office ——"

" Say, that *is* funny! " he exclaimed, and stared at her wonderingly. " A star—I had a hunch ——" Inseparable from that quality which makes gamblers is something which quickens to superstition—or that wings with inspiration? He said soberly, a frown of sheer concentration darkening his eyes: " There are some things beyond human understanding! "

Under her breath Corinna repeated: " Beyond human understanding! " Aloud, shaking out her horse's reins and starting suddenly ahead, she said only that she must hurry home.

CHAPTER XI

LATE that same afternoon, the Judge, riding a hammer-headed, vicious looking brute of a mule fondly christened Heart's-ease, rode dispiritedly into High Town. There was a deep pucker on the Judge's brow and for once the childlike blue eyes were moody. This business of running Spike Freedom to earth had grown into a weary, waiting game and the Judge had been tricked by high hope into another disappointment.

He ambled down a narrow side alley which brought him to the rear of his snug little brick office building and to the flimsy shed which on occasion served as a stable. He dismounted and led Heart's-ease inside.

The Judge at any normal moment was too sagacious a man to yield to abstraction while caring for his mount. But today his thoughts were very far afield as he began unsaddling, and his mule sensed and made the most of an advantage. What Heart's-ease did, fulfilling a long and patiently cherished desire, was to swing the hammer head about on the long stringy neck and bite the Judge.

The Judge made his nimble leap, twisting and spinning like a top to get his shoulder out of the way, but Heart's-ease won the odd trick. True, the big yellow, bared teeth secured only a nibble of coat, yet the skin was neatly pinched underneath and the Judge's " Ouch! ", preliminary to a burst of volcanic eloquence, made Heart's-ease flap a pair of long ears in ecstasy.

But that was only the beginning of an intriguing episode. The Judge, while spinning out of the way, laid his hand upon a sizable club, which was suspiciously convenient near at hand. And once he had it in his hands he needed no one to tell him what to do with it. He wielded it as joyously and as efficaciously as any primal ancestor of his ever swung a war club, and as a sort of obligato to the hearty thwacks across Heart's-ease's rump the Judge relieved himself verbally of the most insulting remarks that had ever been made or will ever come to be made of the genus mule. No mule-skinner who has cursed and flailed his beasts for a half lifetime ever made clearer just what a mule was by nature and habit than did the Judge now. Which, of course, is by way of saying that when it came to swearing at a mule the Judge took second place to none.

Heart's-ease laid back the big ears which a moment before had flapped so jauntily, and lashed out with both hind legs. The Judge skipped, shrilled a fresh string of anathema and brought his club down with both hands. Heart's-ease took the blow standing and out shot the two small hoofs again. Barely did the Judge escape them this time, but he did have the rare satisfaction of seeing them crash through the shed wall.

" And there you c'n stay, you this-that-an'-the-other Such-an'-Such! " said the Judge, and dusting his hands went off, leaving Heart's-ease as in a pillory.

In his office he found his sec'etary, Tim, winding up a rather listless day, preparing to go. The Judge was panting a little and took a moment or two to mop his face before trusting his voice.

" Evenin', Judge," said Tim. " I seen the men you told me to. The ground's leased and High Town'll have a new hardware store in no time."

That hardware store was only one of many side issues with the Judge, and just now he was concerned with other matters.

" Tell you what, Tim," he observed, getting his wind, " you jes' step out an' get a wire off to the Gov'nor of Abyssinia, sayin' as how you an' me is startin' for Timbuctoo ——"

" G' night," said Tim.

The Judge sat down in his swivel chair, put his boots on the table, gave them scarcely more than a passing glance and fell to watching the shadows thicken out in the street. He sighed a little from time to time, plucked at his lip and rumpled his thinning hair; as darkness gathered he sat in the thick of it watching figures go up and down on the street, splotchily lighted from windows and open doors. The rain had ceased and the high winds had whipped the clouds out of a great section of the starry sky.

The Judge started at the sound of a step turning in at his door, and a quiet knock. He leaped to his feet, hastily seeking matches. Laribee's voice called softly, asking if he were here.

" Come on in, Dave," said the Judge genially. " I was jes' squarin' around to get a lamp lit."

It was Laribee who lighted the lamp after all, since the Judge busied himself first drawing his shade and fastening his door.

" Well? " queried the Judge.

Laribee eased his long form down into a chair and sat twirling his hat on his knee.

"I just had a talk with the superintendent of the Glory Girl," he said gravely.

"And what's Grady say?" The Judge's impatience would not brook Laribee's slow speech, which appeared to be more marked than usual, as though he had no great liking for his errand.

"Between the two of us we've got our list completed." Laribee made his announcement without any noticeable enthusiasm; he produced a folded paper from his pocket and sat tapping the edge of it against his hat brim. "We've gone slow, as you know ——"

"I'll say you have!" muttered the Judge, and began to stir uneasily. He yanked open a table drawer, got out a box of thin, evil looking black cheroots, indicated their nearness to Laribee with a jerk of the head, bit a generous end off one for himself and explosively discharged the cutting against the far wall.

"And," went on Laribee in the same grave monotone, "Grady and I have checked all along; and we've made no mistake anywhere. The names we have set down we can vouch for; we've got the whole forty that voted for Mr. Cody and ——"

When he stopped there the old Judge said waspishly:

"Dave Laribee, if I had a good ol'-fashioned bowie knife handy I'd rip you from gullet to gizzard. Spill it. You mean that Steve Cody's name ——"

Laribee tossed the paper to the table.

"Look it over. No. We've got forty names without

Steve's. And there were just forty votes cast for Mr. Cody in High Town. If Steve voted at all ——"

"He voted all right," growled the Judge. "I know 'cause I saw him."

All Laribee could do was shrug. It became obvious that Steve had cast his vote for Vargas.

"Never asked him, did you, Dave?" queried the Judge.

"No. One wouldn't ask Steve a thing like that."

"No? Well, I did! Long ago; when you first got this idea of roundin' up our pizzlin' han'ful of lawful men an' true."

Up shot Laribee's bent brows.

"What did he say?" he demanded eagerly.

"We-ll, he was slow about sayin' anything."

"He would be," Laribee nodded.

"An' then, with one eyebrow up an' one down, the way he has when he looks at a place that's on the wall right square behind you, he says sorta of sober-like, 'Looks kinda like rain, don't it?' !"

"Yes. He would say that."

They sat and stared soberly at each other a long while. Presently the Judge, his mouth screwed up and twisted to one side, grappling mightily with a cheroot about to be annihilated, opened the paper and held it to the lamp, going slowly down the list of names.

"Steve Cody," conceded the Judge, "is a kind of a funny bird." The shadow of David Laribee's rather fine eyes merely deepened; he didn't say anything. The old Judge sighed. "I always had a hunch that blood was thicker'n the sort o' corn whisky they make now-days.

I'd 'a' bet a man Steve would have voted for his ol' man even if they'd jus' had a Cody family scrimmage two shakes afore the ballot dropped."

"Well, we know now. I'd hoped too." He shrugged and tried to give the impression that after all it did not greatly matter. "Anyhow, the mere fact that he didn't vote our way needn't mean anything now. There wouldn't be anything left in him of the old Steve Cody I used to know if he wasn't as hard set as you and I are to find the man who killed his father."

"Why, sure!" cried the Judge, perking up. "Me, I'm for Steve. He's a good boy. We'll line this Forty Crowd up for him, get 'em at his back so's he'll know he ain't playin' a lone hand——"

"No, Judge," cut in Laribee, reluctant and yet grim in his reluctance. "We're to play out our own string. This thing was my idea and Grady's. If we've been slow about it, that was because we had to be; it's no kid's job to get the right names in a case like this and make sure that no single man who is not one of us gets an inkling of the thing. We've been sure. We're going to be sure from now on, too. We have a small committee, only three men——"

"Who are they?" snapped the Judge.

Laribee's set face relaxed into a tired smile.

"You're one, old-timer——"

"I guess I better be!" He sank back loosely in his chair, enormously relieved. "Any time there's any arrangements bein' made lookin' to the happy event of tying a rope aroun' the neck o' the skunk that did my ol' side-kick in, I better be one of the arrangement committee! "

" You and me and Grady. We speak for the Forty."

" An' you an' Grady already've stuck your heads together, fixin' things without me? Huh? That it, D. Laribee? "

He bristled and Laribee laughed at him.

" I swear you've got that trick of showing your teeth from chumming up with a mule! Hanged if you don't begin to look like one, too! "

" Ne' mind, m' son. A mule's the nobles' animal, short of a dog mebbe, that Goddlemighty ever created to be a man's true friend. A mule's faithful an' true an' kind an' gentle longside the sort o' horseflesh you straddle when you're goin' anywheres, an' I say so. But we wasn't talkin' about that nobles' order of created quadrupeds. We was talkin' about a inside ring of the Forty. You say it's me an' you an' Grady. How come then you've got all the plans cooked up before I get wind of it? "

" We've made no plans, Judge, and none will be made without you. Only Grady and I, knowing your fondness for Steve, are set on one thing: No plan of any sort which has to do with the activities of the Forty is to be discussed with any man outside of the Forty."

The Judge chewed away at his cigar and at last his eyes came to rest upon his neat, tight boots cocked up on the desk. He looked them over critically, made as though to brush some mud-flecks from them with a horny forefinger, found the task of doubling sufficiently no small one and gave it up with a sigh.

" What's that you said, Dave? Oh, yeah. Well, that's

fair enough, I'd say offhand. I've lived quite a spell, I reckon; when I set in lookin' backward I c'n see across a consid'able mess of happenin's. They used to call it a vig'lance committee. That word means an open eye an' a shut mouth." Yet he sighed. Again he looked at Laribee's list and in a heavy silence ran down the column, thumbing at every name. In the end he flipped the paper back to its owner. " All right, Dave. I'll draw cards with you. You an' me an' Grady gets together in a day or so, huh? "

Laribee rose.

" Yes. Not here, though. Suppose I talk it over with Grady? We'll arrange a place and a time where the whole world won't be looking in on us. All right, Judge? " The Judge nodded; Laribee went to the door, hesitated a moment, then said only a quiet " Good night," and went on his way.

The Judge, too, rose. He put out his light, raised his window shade and reëstablished himself in his old swivel chair, boots up, hands clasped behind his head, eyes sombrely on the street. Figures passed, going about their nocturnal activities. As usual most of them appeared to have business at Vargas's Place. The Judge's eyes went back and forth, back and forth, ceaselessly back and forth, like a cat's. And his busy brain kept clicking away like the delicate bit of machinery it was.

So Steve hadn't voted for his own father? Well, it was hard to believe and it was a bitter disappointment. Yet, what of it? That didn't have to mean anything, as Laribee himself had pointed out.

"It ain't what he did; it's what he's doin' an' goin' to do, that counts," muttered the lone figure, brooding.

But that concession failed to smooth out any of the puckers in a frowning face or troubled mind. Steve's first day in office had been yesterday; Steve had wound it up after his old fashion with a poker game, playing with Vargas and Vargas's crowd. Tonight, what? The Judge perhaps had learned patience from such as Bucephalus and Heart's-ease; he sat on and on, musing and watching and muttering. Many men had gone in at the double swinging doors before he dragged his boots down from the table and got wearily to his feet. But in the end he had seen Steve enter.

"Folks'll be sayin' of him he's one hell of a sheriff," grunted the Judge. He knuckled his skull viciously and relapsed into a gentle, murmurous swearing.

CHAPTER XII

WHEN Steve Cody put in an appearance at that aloof room which Vargas reserved for himself and, on occasion, for his intimates, that same company which had gathered there the night before was in waiting for him and was beginning to wonder whether he meant to come. Vargas himself sat clouded in the smoke of his cigar, silent, apt to snap when spoken to, seeming to be working out puzzles in the thick smoke. The four young hellions, Bird Galloway, Chink Johnson, Slim Brilliant and Connie Miner, turned quick, expectant eyes upon Steve's entrance.

In a corner, still and hot-eyed and sullen, was Tad Harper. He alone offered no sort of greeting as Steve came in. Obviously he held himself in leash; his eyes merely grew hotter and a stain of red crept into his cheeks.

Vargas, instantly snapping out of his heavier mood, was all noisy welcome. He sprang to his feet, clapped a heavy hand on Steve's shoulder and cried out with specious cordiality:

" Bully boy, Steve! We were beginnin' to wonder about you; wasn't sure but what the duties of the new job might be keepin' you away from the ol' pleasant pastimes! " He said it with a laugh, as though the conception of Steve having a duty that could keep him away from a poker game were deliciously funny.

151

Steve merely lifted an eyebrow at him.

" I didn't want to come," he said bluntly. " But, quitting top-dog last night, I guess it's up to me. Let's get going."

" Didn't want to come? " repeated Vargas, and all the while, and during the whole of the subsequent game, he seemed chiefly concerned with a futile attempt to read the gambler's mind. " Haven't turned sour on poker, have you, Steve? "

" Deal 'em up," said Steve.

Those who meant to play began taking places at the table. Slim Brilliant and Connie Miner, it appeared, were only looking on. It was Slim who offered sneeringly:

" Maybe it's the crowd Steve ain't in love with."

" How about it, Steve? " demanded Vargas.

" Right enough," he got for imperturbable rejoinder. " You've got a flock of kids here, Vargas, and poker used to be a man's game. What's more, this outfit shoots nickels, and I'm not keen for a night's work that ends up with a fellow making or losing enough to drop in the blind man's hat.—Let's get it over with. And, win or lose, this is the last time with this crowd for me."

Tad muttered something but his mutterings lacked coherence and scarcely rose above a growl in his throat. Vargas said hasily:

" Come ahead, let's get goin'.—Playin', Tad? "

" You know I can't," said the boy sharply. His eyes sped to Steve's expressionless face. " You know I'm flat. Steve knows it too. And knows why! "

Steve ignored him. Vargas meditated briefly, then

pulled out a roll of bills, ran through them and tossed several to young Harper.

" Count 'em, Tad. That's another hundred you owe me. Sit in; maybe your luck's changed."

" It's due for a change! " Tad cried hotly, and snatched up the bank notes. " Thanks, Vargas; you're one friend a man can tie to."

Steve put his own stake before him; Vargas looked at it keenly, his eyes narrowed, as though bent on registering the smallest details; Tad, looking as intently, gnawed at his lip and his eyes continued to say the things which his lips as yet hesitated to frame.

Tad and Chink Johnson and Bird Galloway played with an almost feverish intensity; they were at an age when remarks such as Steve had just made rankled. They'd show him! As for Vargas, he played close to the table and never lost a chance for those piercing furtive glances at Steve Cody; and, as for Steve himself, he seemed to take scant interest. He made his bets carelessly; he won and lost indifferently; he appeared to be playing against the clock rather than against the other players, with time and not money the stake. A return game was expected of him, therefore he gave it. That was all.

A bit of byplay arose which may have interested him but which he watched as though it were no more than the sparring of sparrows. It was between Vargas and Bird Galloway. The youth's round, bright eyes were unusually cold and vicious; they were the eyes of a degenerate, a soulless and conscienceless machine, a potential killer, and they kept flicking at Vargas like knives. Too obvious for any to miss, it was not all smooth water between Bird and Vargas. And in a poker game there are too many chances for a general battle to drop off into a duel for the evening to pass without the two engaging exclusively over more than one hand. When Bird Galloway won from Vargas there was a devilish glee transcending mere triumph in his look and twisted grin; when he lost to Vargas, Bird's anger flashed high and venomous.

" Vargas has handled the kid wrong somewhere along the line," mused Steve, and watched for a flare-up to burst out into explosion.

He had always regarded Bird Galloway as less an independent ˙individual than a sort of shadow of Chink Johnson, one to think as Chink thought, to follow where Chink led, to hate only where Chink hated. Yet tonight Bird Galloway appeared for the first time to be altogether himself with his own private grievance, and Chink was merely curiously interested and perhaps a trifle puzzled.

But when at last an explosion did come, Bird Galloway had nothing to do with it, nor had Vargas. It was Tad Harper who at last broke under the strain under which he had labored so long. His luck had not changed, and the chief reason was that Tad Harper was no poker player but of a temperament which should have kept him away from gaming. He played with his heart rather than with his head, and he encountered old man Disaster at almost every turn. And curiously enough his larger losses were to Steve; perhaps that was because Tad was so ardently set on making his winnings in that particular quarter. He measured his young velvet-horns against a seasoned pair of antlers and got himself gored for his pains. He fidgeted and twisted in his chair as though on a seat of thorns; losing, he plunged to recoup and lost again. Time and time again, having a wish to father his thought, he misjudged his opponent. The greater portion of his borrowed hundred dollars went to swell the stack of currency in front of Cody; and in the end, when Tad staked all that was left him on three queens, Steve covered him and laid down a full hand.

 . . . And Steve had dealt. That gave the boy the loophole his tempestuous brain clamored for. He surged to his feet, his face red, his eyes blazing, crying out angrily:

"Cheat! Crook! You damn' card sharp, you!"

Steve watched him narrowly, but did not rise and did not speak. Slowly he gathered in his winnings. Tad's raging voice swept on until Vargas jumped up and caught him by the shoulder, naming him a fool and commanding silence.

"Take your lickin' like a man, can't you!" he snapped contemptuously. "He cleaned you fair enough."

But Tad was not readily to be coerced. Bitterness seethed within him, its vapors were in his brain; he shook with passion.

"I called him a cheat and he sits there swallowing what I said of him," he shouted, and tried to shake Vargas off. "He's all that and more, and we all know it. He's a dirty double-crossing dog that's buckled on a sheriff's badge to hide behind. He robbed me ——"

"Close your trap!" thundered Vargas. "I'm goin' to have no trouble here. I tell you he won from you fair enough."

" I'm not talking about just tonight. You know what I mean. So does he."

Steve continued to watch him but was utterly dispassionate about it.

" And what's more," shrilled young Harper, " he's a cur and a coward! Hear me, Steve Cody? "

Steve cocked an eyebrow at him, and that was as much of an answer as Tad got.

" Afraid to stand up for himself ——"

Vargas caught him by the shoulder and propelled him, expostulating wildly, to the door. At time of need Vargas could be his own bouncer as well as any. Out went Tad and the door slammed.

So the game ended. Vargas, coming back, said briefly to the others:

" On your way, you kids. I want a word with Steve here."

They shrugged and departed, only Bird Galloway making any rejoinder. From the door he flung back sourly:

" Don't you go kiddin' yourself like Cody does that we're all jus' kids, Vargas."

" Beat it! " said Vargas, and slammed the door a second time, seeming utterly unconcerned with Galloway's evil sneer.

" Getting out of your hand, isn't he, Vargas? " asked Steve casually. He pocketed his winnings and stood up.

" Hell with him," grunted Vargas. " Something's turned sour on his stomach." He shrugged heavily. " I'll take care of Bird Galloway when I haven't got anything else on."

" Don't let me keep you. I'm on my way."

" Hold on a minute, Steve. Let's get in the clear. Young Harper told me quite a tale. He says he found some money; three thousan' bucks an' that you lifted it off'n him."

Steve rolled himself a cigarette, lighted it and turned to the door.

" Hold on, I say," said Vargas insistently. " You know what money that was, don't you, Steve? "

" Well? "

" It's the money that somebody robbed the stage for. You know that as well's I do.—You're sheriff now. But you're Steve Cody, too. Kind of funny that, ain't it? "

" Laugh then."

" That's no kind of answer. You've got the money; you don't deny it. You spotted the marked bills here las' night; you went after Tad an' got the rest. The whole three grand. Now what? "

" Now? Well, Vargas, if you want me to get really confidential with you for the one and only time, I'll tell you this. I've got a room at the rooming house down the road and it's getting close to sleepy time."

Vargas's red-brown eyes hardened. He made a move as though to step between Steve and the door, thought better of it and said sharply:

" It's come to the place where you got to show your hand, Steve. You're either keepin' that money, figurin' it's yours as much as any man's, or you're returnin' it to them that owned it when the stage was robbed. Which is it? "

The faintest of smiles touched the gambler's lips.

" I used to think that I was my own man and could do pretty much as I damn' pleased," he said pleasantly. " Nothing to date has happened to change my mind. See you later, Vargas."

He went out, slipping swiftly through the door, standing a moment in the darkness at the side of the small building, then going on his way. That way led him deviously through the darkest of convenient shadowy places at the rear of buildings and at last into the road near the stable where he always housed his horse. But he had no affair at the stable; he circled it in turn and finally approached the small, isolated cabin where Grady, the mine superintendent, lived. Steve took up a place under one of the pines, his body having the effect in the gloom of having merged with the tree trunk.

He had tossed away his dead cigarette and did not light another. Time passed and he did not stir, but seemed possessed of a more than human patience. There was a light in the house; it made yellow lines about the drawn shade.

In time his patience had its reward. He saw a man hurrying up the gentle slope from the street. Steve guessed who it was the moment his ears caught the sound of footsteps and his eyes made out the vague blur of a figure. It was only when the door opened, however, and his man stood in the light that he knew he was right. The door closed immediately on Vargas's entrance.

Steve moved away, this time going to his room.

" That's a part of what I wanted to know," he said to himself, not without satisfaction.

CHAPTER XIII

DURING this time and the days that followed, every up-stage brought a letter to Corinna Lee from her father in the hospital in San Francisco and every down-stage carried a letter from her to him. It was those letters but what was not said in them that sent Corinna traveling and, to quote Judge Bull's later words, " helped mix the whole damn' hasty puddin'."

Lee, down in San Francisco, wrote nothing but cheer and optimism; he was "laid up there for a spell, but everything was rolling high and in no time at all he'd be forking the friskiest horse on the ranch and riding it clean off its legs." And just because of that cheery tone in all his letters Corinna, whether logically or illogically, began worrying. If there was any logic in her feminine determination, made in a flash and carried out at the first opportunity, it was based on a fact known to Corinna alone. That fact was that day after day she herself sat down and wrote her father a cheery letter without a shadow in it, conveying the impression that life was all undiluted joy with her, and all the time she was holding back from him her mounting concern over Tad. Said Corinna to Corinna: " He wouldn't tell me if anything did go wrong."

So she prepared for the journey down out of the mountains, to the railroad and to San Francisco. Her preparations consisted in packing a bag, in giving Aunt

Mary a vacation with injunctions to visit her brother's family over at Halcyon, and in begging Tad to stick close to the ranch and run things during her absence.

Corinna had missed her father far more acutely at this particular time than she would have done during ordinary circumstances. He had been both mother and father to her; she had always run to him with her problems of the hour; to him alone had gone her little confidences. And now she longed for his clear yet sympathetic understanding and his hand, if not to lead, at least to point the way. Since her experience with Steve Cody at the stone hut she had felt herself a very small and futile being trying to cope with a fate which masked its true face from her in terrifying uncertainties.

What had dreams to do with the hard facts of life? What had an ancient book of impossible romance to do with a girl's trying to shape her own acts correctly and at the same time striving for a proper influence on a wayward brother? Yet it remained that she could not dissociate Steve Cody, gambler and sheriff, from a splendid young knight whose emblem was the silver star. He held a fascination for her which penetrated to the roots of her being; while she was with him, hearing the clear tone of his voice, seeing his dark clear and untroubled eyes, she believed in him and something within her swayed toward him. But their short hour together had passed and she did not see him again. Tad she did see daily, and Tad was all bitterness toward the man whom for a spell he had heroized. Since he did not know and Corinna did not tell him that she had any knowledge of the three thousand dollars in marked bank notes, he did not refer openly to them. Yet he did convey to her his certainty that Steve Cody was in possession of stolen money, and that the gambler meant to keep it. Further, Tad more than hinted that Steve himself had been one of the three men who robbed the stage.

Corinna would not believe this. Yet she longed for her father and his fine human understanding, that she might shift something of her new burden of responsibility to his shoulders. She wanted to believe in Steve Cody and in her heart, wherein one arrives at faith without the cumbersome processes of reason, she did believe. But a feverishly active mind, grasping on this and that and the other fact and pondering those countless rumors which might be either fact or fiction, gave her no rest. It was not alone her own life and her own happiness which concerned her, but her half brother's as well.

So, with no one else to turn to at this juncture, yet desperately bent on doing the sane thing, she deafened her ears to romantic whisperings and carried her troubles to the one quarter which suggested itself in her need. She would be away several days; she could not unburden herself to her father before he was well and at home again; but what she could do was go early into High Town, where she was to take the stage, and at least share her responsibility with the old Judge. That he had always spoken kindly of Steve Cody was in reality the determining factor in her decision.

Carrying her little hand bag, she went to the Judge's office. She found him and his secretary mildly quarreling over some small point of routine which did not seem greatly to matter one way or the other; hesitantly, as the

Judge bounded to his feet and Tim regarded her as he always did, as though he was not to be put upon and did not and would not believe all that his eyes told him of her, Corinna began a sort of apologetic request for a few words in private. But the Judge, seemingly electrified by her mere appearance in his untidy office, heard never a word of it. Gallantly he bore down upon her, catching her free hand, relieving her of her bag, beaming and expanding.

"After this there'll be no livin' with me, I'm that set up over your droppin' in," he chuckled at her. "My, my, you do look sweeter'n any picter this mornin'. Where'd you get all them dimples? You know you got to be careful; you're apt to go an' start a riot with a couple of eyes like that! "

"You know you're just looking at my new dress," Corinna smiled at him. And Tim, caught off guard, nodded his head vigorously; yes, that was it. It was just a dress. No girl could be as pretty as she made out!

"Goin' somewhere? " queried the Judge.

She explained and again intimated that she did hope that she might have a few words with him. She was going down on the stage and it would be leaving in a few minutes.

The Judge whirled on Tim, who was already reaching for his hat.

"Tell you, Tim," he said gravely, "you jes' step out an' see if you c'n get a clear wire through to Constantinople; there's that cargo of platinum, you rec'lec' ——"
Tim departed. "Now! " said the Judge, closing the door and returning to her.

Then all of a sudden his face changed and his eyes grew very sober. For he saw Corinna sitting with her hands tight-clasped and her head down and realized that something must be pretty much out o' gear somewhere. She had come to share some confidence with him, and it was goin' to be hard sleddin' for her. She wanted to say something, yet she didn't want to say it—— He put a hand very lightly on her shoulder.

" Now," said the Judge again, but gently this time, encouragingly.

She lifted her head and looked rather searchingly into his eyes.

" I don't know what to do," said Corinna. " I came to tell you something, for you are so much wiser than I. And now—I don't quite want to go on with it—and I don't quite dare keep silent."

" Yep; things get like that sometimes." He nodded sagely. " I know how it is. The works gets all gummed up with a lot of things all cross-cuttin' one another." He sat down facing her, put his two plump hands behind his head and smiled encouragement. " I've noted, Miss Corinna, in a long an' wicked career, how things when once you get 'em nailed down in words ain't quite as bad as when they're jes' floatin' aroun' sort of vague-like in your head. Let 'er fly; I guess you know you c'n take a chance on me."

" I do know," she said warmly. " You have been such a good, dear friend to us."

" Don't go makin' me out any angel," he admonished her genially. " I'm the villain of the play, you know, that hol's the mor'gage on the ol' homestead!—Now,

what's worryin' your pretty head? Tad been up to something he'd better left alone? "

She nodded, tightened the grip of her two hands on
each other, lifted her chin and made an end of hesitancy.

" Yes. And more than that. It's about Tad and—and
about Steve Cody. You're his friend, aren't you? "

" Tad's?—Oh, Steve's? Sure I am. Let's have it."

"I am betraying a confidence, I suppose." She shrugged
rather wretchedly. " I don't care if I am."

So she told him her whole story; that is, the whole
facts of the case, since what did romantic dream-stuff
have to do with a tale one could tell? The Judge's little
facial puckers tightened as he heard her out, and he kept
nodding away at every point she made quite as though
he knew it all before and was therefore not in the least
surprised or concerned. But she did read concern in his
eyes.

" That happened a week ago? And you saw the money
yourse'f? " Corinna nodded. " An' you say Tad says
Steve's never handed it over where it belongs? " She
gave him another nod and, for full measure, a sigh.

" How's Tad know that? " he snapped. " How's he
sure Steve ain't forked the money over? "

" He says that if it had been returned everyone would
know about it now. He says Steve is gambling a great
deal; he is sure that he is using the money himself."

" Tad better keep his mouth shet," muttered the Judge,
and got up and went to stand at his window staring out.
When he turned and came back to her Corinna was
amazed at the expression on his face. He was smiling once
more and seemed serene, untroubled.

" Tell you, Miss Corinna," he said cheerily, " you jes'
hop along an' grab your stage; it'll be smokin' down the
mountains in no time. I'm glad you tol' me all this; jes'
you travel down for a good visit with your daddy, an'
leave all this on my fat ol' shoulders. They won't sag
none under it." He chuckled again and Corinna, watching him suspiciously, was sure that all this seeming
light-heartedness was summoned up for her benefit, and
that deep down he was no less perplexed and ill at ease
than she herself.

" I'm glad, too, that I told you." She rose and took up
her bag. " Yes, I'd better go now.—Of course, what I've
told you is just between the two of us? " For despite her
better judgment she did still feel guilty and ashamed; in
her heart, she kept saying over and over, she did believe
in Steve Cody!

The old Judge watched her go and made no offer to
accompany her to the stage. The puckers gathered again.
He slumped down in his chair and brooded. Now and
then little ominous muttering noises disturbed the silence
of his office. The stage rocked and clattered by; a handkerchief waved; he did not note or see.

The Judge sat very still for a long time, but when he
did move it was with emphatic and almost galvanic
abruptness. His open palm smote his table top and he
exclaimed:

" Why, she loves him an' don't know it! Lord—Lordy!
What a thing that would be for Steve, if he only had the
sense to see an' was man enough for it! The poor little
scared kid is thinkin' twice of him to every once of Tad—
an' the thing ain't dawned on her yet! "

After that one violent outburst he relapsed into still brooding and for a very long time had no eyes for anything that passed before his window. He slumped lower and lower in his chair; he pulled at his lower lip as though his only affair of the moment lay in wrenching it loose from its moorings. In the end he rose ponderously, shook himself, jammed his hat down over his brows and went about seeing what he could see.

First of all, Grady, the mine superintendent. If the money had been returned, Grady would know. It should be simplicity itself to go to the superintendent's office and get the desired information. Yet there was truth in Tim's dictum that " the Judge couldn't get close to anything without circling all around it and sneaking up on it from behind." He had no slightest intention of telling anyone what Corinna had told him. And he wasn't going to ask any leading questions; and he wasn't going to tip his hand in the least by appearing to seek Grady out. He'd meet him accidental-like. And he'd come at what he wanted to know obliquely.

So he went considerably out of his way to find David Laribee. To Laribee he gave the impression that he had thought of nothing since their recent interview but the Forty and what it might achieve. The thing to do was for their Inside Ring, as the Judge liked to term the smaller committee within the greater, to meet without delay and get started functioning.

The meeting took place that night and, despite Laribee's first objection, in the Judge's office. He had thought the matter out and had the pat answer to any objection.

" If the Forty is to be any 'count on earth, it's got to

run smooth, without any hitches, an' it's got to be able to act as quick as chain lightnin' at any time. Which means that our Inside Ring can't run under a lot of handicaps; we got to be ready to get together on a minute's notice an' not to have to go slinkin' off to a hole in the mountains to do it. Let folks see us together; let 'em get used to it, an' that-away they won't think any more of it than when they see two dogs nosin' in the road."

"They'll wonder what we're up to ——"

"Not long, they won't. I'm gettin' a new hardware store started, ain't I? An' I've got some irons in a few other fires, ain't I? All right; that takes money, don't it? Me, I've give' you an' Grady a chance to horn in with me. We're pardners; see? "

Laribee saw the advantages of the Judge's suggestion. But he failed entirely to see what it was that caused the old fellow to demand this first session. For, during an hour's talk behind their drawn shade, the Judge appeared to deal in generalities which had been discussed by pretty nearly every man in the county for months. That somewhere during their conference a reference was made to last winter's stage robbery was natural enough and had no particular importance to either Laribee or Grady; the Judge's dreamy remark, "Well, I guess you've seen the las' of that three thousan' bucks, eh, Grady? " drew only an affirmative nod from Grady, and talk led elsewhere. Yet the Judge, quite in his own fashion, knew what he had set out to learn. The money had not been returned to Grady.

And Grady was bound to know, if anyone did, mused the Judge. Just the same he did not stop with this one investigation. Early the next morning he was on his way to Madrone, forty miles away, and the courthouse. He appeared to have business with the county clerk, looking up titles of lands in which it seemed that he was interested; he chatted with all his old friends, going from one office to another. In due course, and actually without invading the district attorney's lair at all, he managed to encounter John Bingham in one of the corridors.

" Well, well, well, look who's here! " cried the Judge. The old fellow was a power in local politics; further, he had been a Bingham man and a friend. The district attorney was glad to see him, and in spite of the fact that the Judge claimed to be in a hurry, dragged him into his office for a twenty-minute chat. The Judge went away, beaming good cheer, like a man who did not know that anywhere in the world there was a shadow as big as your old hat; yet once alone all the puckers came back into his face, and in his eyes dawned a look that was akin to suffering. The district attorney knew no more than did Grady of any recovery of the lost three thousand.

The Judge returned to High Town, as perplexed and uncertain as to the next move as Corinna had been. The direct step, of course, would have been to go straight to Steve Cody, but direct steps were not the old fellow's habit, and in this particular case he deemed that he could not possibly serve any useful purpose by startin' shootin' when he couldn't even see the target. The hot haste of youth lay safely behind him; he philosophized that a man was more apt to stub his toe an' break his fool neck by runnin' headlong in the dark than by watchin' his step; he went about very much as usual, which is to say with his innocent-looking blue eyes taking in everything in the landscape.

But he wasn't ubiquitous, and he couldn't see through walls, and so he missed a certain happening which, without doubt, would have forced his hand and drawn his swift interference. Grady sent for Steve.

As once before, Steve found the mine superintendent alone in his cabin; it was early evening and Grady led the way to the same lamp-lighted room in which they had had their other brief talk. They sat down; Grady lighted his pipe, leaned back and looked long and searchingly at the man for whom he had sent. Steve stared back at him as keenly, waiting for the heavy-jawed young man to speak his piece. After this initial skirmish of glances, Grady delivered himself of one of his thick-shouldered shrugs by way of preliminary information that his was not the responsibility for what he was about to say.

"Last time you were here, Cody," he said abruptly, "we talked about the money which at various times is sent up for the Glory Girl's pay roll. You'll remember? " Steve nodded. Grady expelled a cloud of smoke and added crisply: " Well, at that time I told you it wasn't up to me to arrange ways and means of getting funds in here safely. That's up to the Old Man at the other end. Also, it's up to him to ask help from you or to kill his own rats alone."

"Help from me? " said Steve with the faintest hint of lifting brows.

"Help from the sheriff's office, if you like that better," said Grady. " I got word this morning that I was to advise with you. We are getting some currency in on next

Thursday's stage. It's a bigger wad this time, and the Old Man seems nervous about it. Seven thousand dollars, instead of a mere three or four as usual."

"And I'm asked to help see it comes through? That's because you or your Big Chief thinks that there's a play going to be made to nab it on the way?"

Grady frowned and shrugged.

"Personally, it's nothing to me who nabs it. My responsibility doesn't begin until the money is delivered at this end; even then it's only partly my responsibility, our cashier of course being the man to handle it officially. No; I'm not in the least worried over it myself; I'd say it's safe enough. But my orders are from headquarters, and they are to put it up to you that that money is coming in on next Thursday's stage."

"There's a lot about my job that I don't know," Steve told him coolly. "If I'm to chase all over the country watching private shipments of cash or ore ——"

"I told you it wasn't up to me. I'm carrying out my orders." He consulted a pencilled memorandum on the pad in front of him. "I am to tell you that seven thousand dollars are coming up on the Thursday stage; that the money will not be in the bag; that it's in a pack in a battered old hand bag carried by a passenger who's a stranger hereabouts, a city man, who'll ride on the driver's seat. And when I've told you that I've told you all I know."

"No one then knows but you, the shipper and now myself?"

"That's the way I thought it would be," said Grady, "and of course that's the way it ought to be. No; the

Old Man's private secretary knows; the man who is bringing it knows; the stage driver knows ——"

" Why not publish it in the papers? " queried Steve lightly. He rose and for a moment stood looking down thoughtfully at Grady's upturned massive face. " Well, so long."

" So long, Steve," said Grady, and seemed glad to have the interview over with. " Anyway, I didn't wish this on you. It's the Old Man's doing."

This meeting took place on a Monday evening, three days before the money was to arrive. Three days also, as it chanced, before Corinna was to return. During this interim the Judge, keeping his eyes open, told himself that he might as well have kept 'em tight shut. Steve, whatever might have been his occupation, did not once appear in High Town. The Judge, building up an elaborate excuse to take him by Steve's mountain cabin, found him away from home; the Indian boy did not know where he was. So back to High Town rode the Judge and found among his scanty mail a little note from Corinna. Her father really was doing splendidly; all his worries were over; yet he'd remain in the city for a while yet. She herself was coming home Thursday. There was a bit of a post-script which made the old Judge smile crookedly:

" I'm almost sorry that I said anything to you. Somehow I *know* that everything is all right. Please don't say a word to anybody."

It was simple enough and should have required no great effort to get written. Yet it was a rather messy-looking postscript. The Judge read the letter, holding it at arm's length, his head cocked backward the better to see; then he put on his glasses and studied the concluding lines, concerning himself with words which Corinna had scratched out. Originally she had written, " Somehow I *know* that he ——" That " he " was deleted.

When Thursday afternoon came with drizzling rain and an early dark already spreading throughout the mountains, the Judge cocked his hat at a jaunty angle and rose from his desk to meet the stage. As he opened his door Tim, who had already quit for the day, came hurrying back, advising him excitedly:

" Another holdup, Judge! Somebody stuck up the stage down at the Double-S curve on Red Dirt grade."

" What's that? " snapped the Judge, and glared at Tim as though blaming the news-bringer for anything that might have happened. " Who says so? The stage ain't even in yet! "

" A man just rode in ahead on horseback; one of the Cutter boys, I think. The stage'll be here in a minute."

" Corinna Lee's on it," muttered the Judge, and shoved Tim out of his way.

With long whip snapping and his six lathered horses at the run, the stage driver brought his passengers, his mail bags and his rage into High Town. A crowd gathered as crowds will; his red face was lost in the throng; a little, dapper man on the seat at his side leaped down and vanished, calling on every man into whom he bumped to show him the way to Mr. Grady of the Glory Girl; voices shouted asking details and other voices, no less excited, began making much of their story.

Through all this milling, ever tighter-packed throng,

the Judge made his way with elbows and grunts, until at last it was his plump hand which helped Corinna Lee down. He saw at a glance that she was highly nervous and looked frightened; she caught his arm and clung tight to him.

"Way there!" bellowed the Judge, again attacking the crowd, beating a path through it. "Make room, you jaspers.—Come ahead, Miss Corinna; you jes' stick tight to me an' we'll get out o' this mess. They get as het-up over a dinky little stick-up as if the sky was fallin' down."

In a faint, shaking voice, Corinna said: "It is!" The Judge wasn't sure that he had heard aright; he took a good look at her face. It was pale; her lips were trembling; he could not understand the expression of her eyes. They were anguished as if something truly terrible had happened.

"Nobody killed, was there?" he demanded.

"No, no! Oh, thank God, no! But —— How can I tell you?"

"Never mind in a hurry; you're jes' nacherly all shook up. Let's get off the street; come into my office an' get your secon' wind. A thing like this ain't anything, once you get used to it."

In his office Corinna subsided into the chair which he shoved forward for her; for a moment she sat with her white face buried in her hands. Then with an effort she lifted her head; her anxious eyes looked straight into his.

"It was Steve Cody!" she whispered.

The Judge started as though she had slapped him. Then he frowned and bent toward her, coming close, saying curtly:

" What was Steve Cody? "

" He was masked. He had a big handkerchief over his face. He did not speak a word. He just gestured. He made the man get down; the one sitting with the driver. Made him open his bag and hand over a little package. All the while he had a gun in his hand, and nobody dared move or speak. Then he—he just rode away."

" His face was covered? He didn't say a word? And you say it was—was Steve? "

That look in her eyes was one of agony as she sat there nodding.

" How in hell do you know? " blazed out the Judge. " If you couldn't see his face an' couldn't hear his voice— how the hell do you know? "

" I just know," said Corinna wearily.

" Does anyone else know? "

This time she shook her head in negation.

" No one seemed to know."

The Judge said, " Hmp, hmp, hmp! " and went trotting up and down the small room. An uncontrollable urge to laughter seized Corinna; he looked like some little cherub or elf man they had caught and put in a cage. But suddenly her laughter trailed away miserably and she hid her face in her hands, fighting hard against breaking down and crying.

" Hey, there! " commanded the Judge querulously. " You're all high-strung like a fiddle string that's ready to go pop." He scrubbed his head vigorously with the knuckles of both hands and then jerked up, erect and purposeful, like a soldier at attention. " Look here, you are tired and you are imaginin' things." He had himself in hand nicely now; he even achieved one of his low, mirthful chuckles as he came to her and put his hand very gently on her bowed head. " Look up at me." She did so, her eyes swimming with tears. " Answer me this: Could you go into a court room an' swear that it was Steve that robbed the stage? "

" No! " she exclaimed eagerly. " How could I? I tell you I didn't see his face; I didn't even hear his voice. How could I *swear* to it? "

" Exac'ly. Now, that's fine. Because, since you couldn't swear to it, it's because you ain't sure!—You made a mistake, that's all. It was some guy that was built like Steve ——"

" I *know*," said Corinna, and would not have it otherwise. She did not know how she knew; she just knew.

The Judge swore softly under his breath.

" Anyhow, you'll leave it all to me? You won't say a word to anyone else? " Corinna shook her head emphatically; he could not guess how grateful she was that she need do nothing further now that she had told him.

" Well," he said steadily, " you better skip along home. An' you can take this from me: You made a mistake. It wasn't Steve. I ain't always guessed Steve Cody jes' right, but I'm dead sure now. It wasn't Steve."

They went back for her bag, which she had forgotten in the stage; the Judge accompanied her to the stable where Tad had left her horse. Tad himself, it was learned from the stable boy, was expected but had not returned. The Judge saw her started on her way in the dusk, and turned back along the road, looking for Steve.

CHAPTER XIV

Not the anxious Judge alone, but the superintendent of the Glory Girl also sought Steve Cody, and no less urgently. And Steve, advised of the impatient interest of both men, elected to see Grady first.

Both, knowing his habit of leaving his horse at the stable, had left word there for him. When he rode in at an early hour that night the stableman, swinging up his lantern to make sure of him, greeted him with:

" Where you been, Cody? Hear about the holdup? "

" What holdup? " said Steve.

The man told him with all that eagerness which so naturally goes into a recital of any stirring happening which the teller prides himself on being first to make known. Steve appeared only mildly interested, certainly far less concerned than the man who gave him the news.

" By the way, Cody, they been askin' for you. Ol' Jedge Bull wants to see you. So's Grady."

" Give my a horse a good rubdown, will you, Jake? " asked Steve. " I've had to ride him hard today." Coins chinked, going from hand to hand and Steve left the stable.

Yes, he'd see Grady first. Though, had he been actuated exclusively by curiosity, he would have gone first to the Judge. For he had no doubt that Grady's business had to do with the stage robbery, and he wondered what the Judge's could be. If it too were concerned with the holdup, it would be interesting to learn just what the Judge knew or thought that he knew—and just what he thought he could do about it all.

Grady came hurrying to the door before Steve had had time to knock.

" That you, Cody? Fine! Come ahead in."

Steve entered silently and when the door had been locked followed the mine superintendent into the room where their former interview had taken place. A cloud of smoke hung in the air; Steve sniffed it, glanced at the pipe in Grady's fingers and said carelessly:

" What kind of stuff do you smoke in that trash-burner anyhow? Smells more like a cigar than a pipe."

" Squat! " invited Grady crisply. " The big thing in the world tonight isn't brands of tobacco."

Steve sat, first moving the chair meant for him, placing it so that his back was to a corner of the room whence he could, if so disposed, have doors, window and Grady before his eyes. Grady settled himself in his own chair with something of an air; the way he nested down in it might suggest, depending on his observer's flight of fancy, either a setting fowl or a man establishing himself firmly in a place from which he meant to issue ultimatums. Then, to create further confusion in the impressions which he gave, that face of his, with the heavy underslung jaw, became oddly reminiscent of a bulldog's. Even his eyes, none too large, seemed to have become smaller and keener and brighter with some sort of bulldog grimness.

" Now! " said Grady.

Steve had not removed his hat; he pushed it far back on his head so that his face, the face of a gambler who had no need to shadow it since it gave away no secrets, caught the full lamplight. His thumbs he hooked in his belt. His eyes were busy, while his tongue was still, and Grady would have been surprised could he have known how much of his thought Steve had already caught.

" Now! " said Grady, the second time. He gripped the arms of his chair; his strong square teeth bit into his pipestem. " About this new robbery, Cody."

It would have helped him to get started had Steve spoken; had he explained how he had just arrived, and had first word from the stableman; had he evinced even a hint of curiosity; had he in any way whatever " tipped his hand." Steve's attitude merely remained that of one who was willing to listen.

" Damn it, Cody," snapped the other. " This thing is open and shut."

There was no doubt that Steve heard. You could tell by looking at him that he heard. And that was all you could tell.

" All right," said Grady. He took a deep breath as though he were going to dive. After all, Grady was only a Number Two man and perhaps he began to feel like the little boy who went rabbit hunting and scared up a man-eater. " If you want it in words a child can understand, here it is: The stage was robbed and—and you did it."

He tensed in his chair before the final words were ejected; he was ready to spring to his feet. But his caller remained unmoved. Further, he remained maddeningly silent. His rôle was still that of a listener.

" Well? " demanded Grady.

"Well?" said Steve coolly.

"You heard what I said?" Steve nodded. "Well, what about it? What have you got to say for yourself?"

"Nothing, Grady."

"You don't deny it?"

"Do you want me to?"

"You know it wouldn't make any difference if you did! I've got you dead to rights this time."

"Ye-ah?" said Steve.

Grady frowned; he was not sure, but he fancied there was the hint of an irritating smile on Cody's lips.

"Yes. Dead to rights. Want me to tell you how I know?"

"This is your party, Grady."

Grady's thick hands remained very tightly gripped on the arms of his chair; under his coatsleeves no doubt the muscles of his arms were corded, ready to do their part in jerking him forward and getting him to his feet. For all that Steve looked merely idly interested and not in the least dangerous, one could never tell.

"How many men, do you suppose, knew that the money was coming in on today's stage?"

"You told me that several knew. Lying, were you?"

"You're damn' whistling I lied! No one knew, outside the Old Man and myself—but you! Not the stage driver; not even the poor rabbit that brought it in his satchel. He thought it was some papers, important but not irreplaceable. Just the Old Man, myself—and you!"

When Steve stirred then, Grady did leap to his feet. But all that Steve did was stretch both arms high over his head and yawn.

" I've had a day, no mistake," he said carelessly, and Grady could not be sure whether it was what one might call a steely glint or a purely mirthful twinkle in his eyes. " Guess I'd better trundle off to bed early."

" You're a cool party," cried Grady. His voice was sharp with truculence; he was like a man who had tried to push over a rock wall and in the end grew wrathful with the insensate thing. " If you think you can get away with this sort of thing —— Look here, Cody! You are in for a nasty spill unless you mind your step. That three thousand from last fall's holdup; you got that. You've had it over a week; you're figuring you can get away with that? Today, another seven! A haul of an even ten thousand! "

" Good night, Grady." Steve stood up and for a moment looked down gravely into Grady's flushed face.

" No you don't, Cody! I haven't started yet. I set a trap for you and you fell into it. I told you about the money on today's stage, being sure you'd go after it; and you did. I accuse you now of being in possession of ten thousand dollars that belongs to the Glory Girl."

Steve shrugged and moved toward the door. Grady called angrily after him:

" Hold on there! Nobody knows this thing but you and me. I could wipe you out—like that! " Figuratively he wiped something out with a snap of finger and thumb. " I'm willing to stand your friend ——"

From under an up-tilted line of black brows Steve regarded him somewhat critically, somewhat humorously and somehow altogether insultingly.

" Friend? No thanks."

"A word from me will yank your damned sheriff's star off you! It'll put you behind the bars, Cody. I warn you."

Yet even despite the open threat it appeared that Steve was going and had nothing to say, nothing to ask. Just then an inner door opened and Vargas stepped quietly into the room.

"Hello, Steve," he said casually.

"Hello, Vargas," was returned to him in the same tone.

"I'm in on this, Steve," said Vargas, mouthing at his cigar. "Suppose the three of us talk it over sensible."

For once Steve appeared to hesitate. Then he shrugged and returned to his chair in the corner.

"Grady's got something on his mind," he said indifferently. "Maybe, if you're trailing your luck with him, you can help him to speak his piece."

Vargas grinned broadly and the hot red-brown eyes flickered from face to face. He perched on Grady's table, swinging his leg and fell to examining his stump of a cigar. Then his eyes again flashed up to Steve's.

"It was a plant, of course, like Grady tol' you. Me an' him framed it together. You see, Steve, ol' horse, we sort of itched to know jus' where you lined up."

Steve nodded and made himself a cigarette.

"Now we know," said Vargas.

"You're damn' right we know!" cried Grady, and strove for emphasis and an expression of power by slapping his knee; he must have made his own flesh tingle but got from Vargas only a twitching frown and from Steve not even a glance.

"The point," said Vargas, "is this: We know where

you line up. That's one thing; the big thing, after all. But there's another, the little thing, an' it ain't so terrible little at that. It's a matter of ten thousan' bones, Steve, ol'-timer. We done our part, Grady an' me; an' we're in line for our share. Split it three ways, an' we're with you."

For the first time Steve laughed. It was a soft, chuckling laugh, and made Grady's flushed face go redder while Vargas's eyes narrowed swiftly. The two waited for him to speak; Vargas, for one, should have known better. Steve did not trouble to add anything to the laugh.

"Let's call it a night," said Vargas suddenly, and shot a warning glance across to Grady. "Steve here knows where we stand. So far as I know there's no hurry. It's a split three ways, Steve; since you took the main chances an' did the dirty work, say three thousand for me, three for Grady an' four for you."

Again, and because he knew Steve Cody of old, Vargas was wise enough not to press matters. He slipped down from the table and led the way to the door.

" Goin' my way, Steve? " he invited in friendly fashion.

" Only part way, Vargas." Steve, ignoring Grady, went with him, adding, " I'm all set for a run-in with the old Judge. He's sent for me too." He chuckled as he and Vargas went out. " He's a wise old coot! Maybe a little bird's been telling him things. What if he wants a split, too? "

Grady, who after all was perhaps only a Number Three man, called after them, trying to follow Vargas's cue, to be affable. His " Good night, boys," went unanswered, and a slamming door ended the interview.

CHAPTER XV

STEVE tossed his hat in at the Judge's door, stood a moment as though awaiting results, then entered with what, for him, was next door to a broad, good-humored grin.

" Well, what's on your mind, Judge? " he asked as he swept up his hat again and put it on. He conveyed the impression of being extremely easy in his own mind, as carefree as a colt.

But the Judge only glared at him sourly. Before saying a word he went to the door and locked it; he took another look at his shade to make sure it was drawn all the way down over the window; then as stiff as a ramrod, he demanded bluntly:

" Steve Cody, what for a man have you turned out to be? "

" Care if I sit down? " asked Steve equably. " I'm saddle-weary." He glanced about the room before selecting the chair which suited him, one drawn up to the Judge's desk. " Mind if I make myself a sort of roost to hang a leg on? " He pulled a drawer half-way out and cocked one boot up on it. " Now for your puzzle-quiz: What for a man am I anyhow? Say, you know I hadn't taken time off to think that over! And a man ought, now and then, huh? " He began ticking points off, finger and thumb of his right hand making captive of finger after

183

finger of his left. " I can ride first rate; been breaking a
new saddle horse this week, and sticking on him for five
consecutive minutes passes a man as a bronco buster.
Tally. I can play a satisfactory hand at poker; I'm clean
to the good over two months' play now. Check. What
comes next? Nowadays the measure of a man is in his
gentlemanly accomplishments, isn't it? I'd say handling
a gun comes next ——"

" Are you shootin' 'em straight, Steve? "

Steve, yielding to his mood, pretended misunderstand-
ing.

" Stand a thin dime on edge across the room, and get
out of line ——"

" Are you shootin' 'em straight, Steve? "

Steve sighed but an afterglow of his broad smile remained.

" Here I stepped in, feeling all pepped up like it was a
new deal all around and the deck full of high cards, and
you're laying for me. To give me a roasting, I'll bet a
hat! Well, hop to it, Judge; I'm wide open and defence-
less. I made myself liable when I asked what you had
on your mind. Drill away."

" You're actin' kind o' funny, strikes me," said the
Judge suspiciously, squinting up his blue eyes.

" And I'm feeling kind of funny," chuckled Steve.

" I never heard you runnin' over with words this-
away ——"

" I'm running over with ideas, that's all. It's a great
world, Judge Bull! Ever notice? "

" God, He made it a great world," grunted the Judge.
He attacked a chair, yanked it viciously to him,

preëmpted it and cocked his own heels up. " If you damn' fools would only leave it the way He intended t——"

" You've got your start now, old-timer. Blaze away and see what you can hit."

In his turn the old Judge sighed. The hardness dissolved in his eyes and they grew frankly wistful. He remembered suddenly how he had had his last talk here with his old friend, Steve's father. He recalled vividly how the other man had looked, how he had spoken; how he had put a handkerchief up to his face to wipe away an expression which betrayed his yearning. They had spoken of Steve on that occasion; it had been the Judge who asked the elder Cody which way Steve was voting.

" Steve," said the Judge, now somewhat sombrely, " I asked you once straight out how you'd voted las' fall. Maybe it wasn't any of my business an' maybe it was. Well, I know now. You voted for Vargas."

Steve took all the time he required in answering. He leaned far forward, for a moment in danger of toppling his chair over, and captured a pencil and pad from the Judge's desk; he sat, head down a little while, busy with making the sort of designs a man's fingers are so often responsible for when his mind is far afield, circles and crosses, linked into chains, pierced with arrows; all that sort of thing. At last he tore off the outer leaf of the pad, crumpled it and fired it accurately into a waste-paper basket.

" Fire ahead, Judge," he said crisply.

" You don't deny that then? " And the Judge's tone was eloquent of his faint hope that Steve would deny.

"Let's have the rest of it," Steve said. "You didn't send for me just for that."

"No.—You're runnin' with Vargas an' his crowd right along, Steve."

It wasn't a question; just a well-known fact. So Steve made no remark upon it. Suddenly the Judge's manner changed and sharpened.

"Me, I've stuck up for you, Steve Cody, whenever there was wild talk about you; that's because I figgered you to come clean, man-style, by the time you'd climbed plumb to the top o' Fools' Hill an' had a good look 'round. This sheriff business, I said it would make a man of you; I helped put you in office. I figgered you all the time as your daddy's kid, that's why; an' when they make a fairer, squarer man than my ol' friend Steve Cody, Senior, I'm here to tell 'em it'll be some job. Yes-sir, I've stuck up for you all along the road, an' it was because of him, an' because I couldn't figger you, bein' his kid, without bein' somehow like him.—An' now are you for lettin' me down, Steve?"

"As how?" demanded Steve coolly, his pencil poised over the pad.

"You want it straight?"

"Pick your spot between the eyes and pull the trigger."

"Ten days or so ago you recovered the money stolen from the stage just before election. Three thousan' dollars. You've got it yet. What's the idea?"

"Who told you?" said Steve swiftly.

"*She* tol' me," the Judge informed him sternly. "She as ought to think well o' you, Steve; as, if I'm any jedge which I ought to be, is willin' an' wishful to think well o' you."

Steve's eyes flicked at him, then returned to the pencil slowly twisting in his supple fingers.

" There's worse'n that, Steve; a damn' sight worse. There's what happened today. Guess I don't need to put a name to it, do I? "

" Guess you do, Judge, if you want me to follow you."

The Judge jerked forward; it was only a harsh whisper when he said:

" You stuck up the stage, Steve!—Oh," he cried sharply, forgetful of the caution which had lowered his voice, " are you gone crazy or what? My God, boy, can't you see how you're slippin'? An' where you're slippin'? Slam the brakes on; come clean with me; get your head screwed on right an' get your secon' wind, an' I'm with you. But you got to do a rightabout so awful damn' quick it's dizzy work, or I'm shed of you an' you'll trail your own misery hellwards."

Steve's eyes, with a queer look in them, clung steadily to his.

" You seem to know an all-fired lot, Judge," he retorted. The tip of his tongue touched his lips as though they suddenly had gone dry. He stiffened visibly, like a man preparing for a blow, when he demanded curtly: " Who told you? "

" That you'd held up the stage? "

" Yes."

" Does that matter? "

" Yes."

" It's a fac', then? "

" Who told you? "

" I'd say," came the evasive answer, " that by now more'n one party knows. For it's the truth, ain't it, Steve? "

" She told you." Steve stared at him, then shook his head as though weary and dropped his eyes to his pencil. It began drifting back and forth across the pad.

" The truth, Steve? " queried the Judge, more anxious than ever.

Steve did not look up; his pencil did not stop. " Yes," he snapped. He seemed more occupied with what his fingers were doing than with any talk of the Judge's.

" My God! " The word came explosively and it was something in the nature of an explosion that the Judge came up to his feet. " Up till now I'd hoped —— What 'n hell did you do it for, Steve? "

" What does a man generally pull off a thing like that for? Better sit down a shake, Judge; I've got to do a bit of thinking."

The Judge ignored the command; he began that jerky trotting up and down which was characteristic of him at moments of high nervous tension, sometimes looking at Steve as at some horrible monstrosity, sometimes staring blankly at nothingness. With lightning rapidity he built up plans and they crumbled as swiftly. With everything to be done there was nothing to do! He wouldn't believe this damned thing, and yet he did believe it. Because he knew now that it was the truth.

" Steve Cody," said the Judge very sternly, coming to a dead halt and looking straight into the moody black eyes which at last were lifted to his, " either you square yourse'f in a big fat hurry an' turn over the loot you been liftin', or I'm through with you. Got that? You come clean or I'll turn you in—an' I won't wait until mornin' ! "

" Judge," said Steve evenly, " did you ever hear about the little pastime of a man minding his own business? It's never too late to learn, you know."

" Why, you infernal whippersnapper! You damn' this-an'-that such-an'-such! "

" Steady on, Judge! " Steve seemed to grow icy now that the old Judge began to fume. " I know what I'm doing and I'm not to be interfered with."

" If you think that I'll stan' aside an' let you make a monkey out'n the county, me along with the rest of 'em, playin' that ol' gag of sheriff an' stick-up gent ——"

" How about taking a minute for some thinking? Now figure it out: Just what can you do? "

" I've thrown this thing in your teeth an' you've admitted it ——"

" Hold on; that's a good stopping place! What of it? It's just the two of us, isn't it? Suppose you try to tie this thing to me and say that I admitted it; suppose then I laugh at you and politely inform the world that you're a liar and always were? What then? "

" It can be proved, you fool! "

" Who'll prove it? " Steve shot back at him.

" Corinna Lee, that's who! " the Judge fired back at him, just as hotly.

For the fraction of a second the Judge thought that Steve was taken aback. But it was always hard to be sure of Steve's emotions; hard, at times, to be sure that he experienced any whatever. When he spoke, after that brief hesitation, it was boldly and coldly.

" Making an accusation is one thing, Judge; proving it before twelve men good and true—but not too good nor too true as a rule to be whipped into line!—is quite another. My impression of the thing which has happened is this: A man with his face covered, riding a horse which he had temporarily commandeered and which could in no way identify him, a man who did not betray himself by speaking a single word, held up the stage. Now you know as well as I do that no individual on that stage is going to be able to make a jury believe that he or she could recognize the holdup man! There'll be the rest of the passengers to swear that no glimpse was caught of his face, no sound of his voice heard. And so your proof that you're talking about is all shot full of holes.—Further, you might be interested in knowing that I've got a tip-top, iron-clad alibi."

" You would have," grumbled the Judge. " Vargas, I suppose? Or some of his gang? "

" Vargas is, after all, what in loose parlance you might call a friend of mine. Yes; I think you could count on Vargas and some of the other boys remembering that they were with me, or had seen me, far afield at the moment the stage driver slammed on his brakes and put his hands up."

Consternation scrawled itself all over the Judge's face. For once he felt no call to employ finesse; for once he did not care if his every thought were read. Most of all was he hurt; something within him was tortured. He had made allowances all these years for youth; he believed in Steve Cody and, if you wanted the whole truth, loved him like a son.

"Guess I'm gettin' old," thought the Judge drearily. "Wornout an' milk-an'-water." Then he caught himself up short and bristled. Namby-pamby was the next thing he was about to accuse himself of being, and he would not have it. He turned a pair of hard and implacable eyes on Steve Cody. "I've broke bigger 'n' better men than you, Steve Cody," he said steadily. "An' what I've done once I c'n do again.—Get t' hell out of here!" His voice was swept up into gusty rage. "Scat, you polecat."

Steve rose, sat perched a moment on the edge of the desk with his hands behind him, then shrugged and got up from that seat.

"Better watch your step, Judge," he said curtly. He turned the key and was about to open the door. "I'm on my way."

And then, all without warning, the Judge was treated to the biggest surprise of the evening. Some strange change swept over Steve's face; no longer was it a mask but rather a countenance which before the Judge's eyes grew more expressive than any he had ever looked into. It was eloquent of some strange pleading; it conveyed a command for caution, for silence; it promised revelation to come. Steve's hand shot out, pointing with tremendous nervous eagerness, indicating something on the Judge's desk ——

He whipped the door open, stepped out, slammed it behind him.

The Judge stood rooted to the floor for a paralyzed second; then his first urge was to shout after the departing man. He clapped his hand to his mouth and hurried to the desk. In full sight was the note pad which had engaged Steve. On it was written Steve's message:

" Somebody's listening outside. I'm out on a limb. Go slow, Judge, for God's sake! Look in your drawer. Not a word to anyone. See you later."

The stupefied Judge just stood and stared, all at sea. Then he dived at the drawer which Steve had pulled out for a foot rest. In it was a snug packet, not wider than three fingers, tied with string and sealed with a half dozen stamps. Written upon it in ink were the words:

" Containing $10,000, belonging to the Glory Girl. Entrusted for safe-keeping to Judge Bull, by Sheriff Steve Cody."

The Judge turned it over in his hand. Then he bethought himself of an unlocked door and attended to it in haste. Again he turned the packet over. A bit of string and this flimsy sealing between him and what he wanted to know! A big-bladed jackknife made a short end of obstacles. Sure enough there was the pad of bank notes; ten thousand dollars. Also a letter addressed to John Bingham, District Attorney.

The Judge slumped down in his chair and began to swear. And, queer combination, as the gentle curses rose to his lips a moisture as of tears gathered in the childlike blue eyes.

CHAPTER XVI

AT a much later time the Judge relieved himself of an observation which may be set down here as being not inapropos.

"The Good Lord took a full week o' workin' days," said the Judge, "to get Him a pretty considerable big job done. Yep, it was a real smart job, with suns an' moons an' stars an' planets, some of 'em so far off our big telescopes ain't picked 'em all up yet. An' the key-idea of the whole works was that everything was to go roun' an' roun', the heavenly bodies, so to speak, roun' one another, an' all happenin's in sort o' circles, what they call cycles nowadays, like day an' night an' the seasons o' the year an' such-like. Everything to turn an' spin an' whirl, y' know. An' I guess He dusted His han's off an' stood back and said, 'Let her flicker!' an' then come the firs' shock. It was a fine bit o' machinery, all right; but the whole dumb works jus' stood still as a balky mule. Then what? Quit on the job? Nary. The Good Lord went an' made Adam, an' Adam he jus' sat on a rock an' didn't even take much notice. So then He made Eve—an' lo an' behol', the wheels all started turnin'! Talk about a commotion! Whew!—An' if you ask me, Miss Corinna, what that firs' girl looked like, face an' figger an' cut of the eye ——"

"But I don't ask you," laughed Corinna, very gay.

" And besides, Aunt Mary has one of your especial cakes in the oven and I promised to help her."

But all this was very much later.

Steve Cody, leaving a mystified Judge behind him, announcing " I'm on my way," in a voice sufficiently loud to be heard by any eavesdropper, went straight to the stable, to his horse and out of High Town. The night was fine, cold yet exhilarating, dark yet with stars gleaming here and there through rifts of drifting clouds, and he was acutely in accord with it. The campaign into which he had thrown himself, striking boldly, was such as could have recommended itself only to a man who gambled with his life. He had walked into Grady's trap with his eyes open; Grady had rushed into Steve's net with shut eyes. Since that first night when Steve had called at Grady's office, and Grady had said sharply into the dark, " Is that you? " and then had not taken the trouble to explain who it was that was expected, Steve Cody had drawn his own inferences. As he was ever prepared to stake a big wager on a suspicion that he topped the other fellow's hand, or that the other fellow might be bluffed out, he was ready to play the game with Grady. And now?

He rode slowly into the mountains, headed back to the solitude of his cabin. He was at once zestful and of a mood for quiet thought. He lifted his eyes to the stars and was concerned with their brilliant lights, no less with the invasion of fat black clouds into starry fields; the stars were blotted out but they came again. He was both at peace and ready for the next move in the game. His mind shuttled forward and back, and also knew moments of calm musing.

When after a while he heard hoofbeats, coming on with a rush far off somewhere behind him, he merely drew aside from the trail to let the impetuous one pass by. Tad Harper, perhaps, hurrying home? The thud of hoofs came steadily on; Steve, from his place a score of paces from the traveled way, saw the dark forms sweep on, a horse galloping, a man slouching in the saddle, riding loosely. The night made the two into a blurred centaur, then gathered them into itself. They vanished, for a few moments the receding hoofs hammered through the whispering silence, then they too were gone. Tad Harper, no doubt.

As a matter of fact, it was Vargas. Yet how suspect that? Steve reined back into the trail and rode on, again in tune with the hour. He came in time to that forking of the way from which a wagon track led off to the old Byron Motley ranch, the Lee ranch now. He did not stop or turn aside, but his thoughts did. So Corinna held him both thief and stage robber, did she? Well, why not? What should she know of him in one way or another save through such rumors as flew her way? And rumors always made the worst of things; evil was what gave them wings. And it was sheer unreason to want her to think other than she did; had he not taken his stand, willfully misleading the countryside, determined on making the whole county misjudge him? Yes; that way he would slip under the guard of such as Vargas and Grady; that way, in time, he would learn a very great deal and, in the end, the one thing he was set on knowing.

But Corinna! Why couldn't she know? In his place, he would know about her, no matter what she chose to seem.

Was man's intuition then, or at least a gambler's, so much higher than woman's, vaunted as it was? He had read her to the heart that first time he saw her at Vargas's Place, looking " like she had dew on her! " He had gone to her, ostensibly to help Tad, truly to help her, since she would suffer where Tad suffered. And he had thought that she and he understood each other. Not as two ordinary persons ordinarily do. In some other, richer way. When they spoke of dreams—when he harked back to his boyhood and his Malory, and their eyes met and both he and she seemed snared in some spell cast by that naïve old singer of knightly ways——

" I'm going to get hold of Tad one of these days and make a man of him. The kid has a lot of good stuff in his make-up. Let's see, S. Cody; we're going to clean house a bit—when the big job's done. At first there'll be a lot to do right at home; getting the old place back in shape, like it was when—when I first got it. Want the job, Tad, as general foreman over that and the other ranches? "

But Tad passed out of his mind, which centered on Corinna. A queer mood fastened itself on him. Sudden vague and illogical fears for Corinna filled his mind; he started into a gallop, finding himself growing moody and, as it seemed to him, all without rhyme or reason. She was all right; what earthly menace could be threatening her? The only cloud in her sky was Tad, and didn't Steve mean to straighten the boy out before he could get himself into any serious difficulty?

Yet though he pressed on, farther and farther from Corinna at her father's ranch house, he did not shake off that insistent and growing sense of dread. He kept telling

himself that Corinna was all right, no doubt by now
spending a happy evening with her brother—but while
he was assuring himself his hands pulled his horse from a
gallop down to a trot, to a walk, to a standstill. He turned
in the saddle, looking back, seeing only the black pine-
clad hills and the sky no less black save for its few clear
starry spaces. After a moment he shook his head and
named himself a fool and rode on. She, thinking of him
as she did, would not thank him for obtruding himself
and his formless fears upon her.

Had he known that it was Vargas, not Tad, who passed
him in the dark he would not have delayed as he did in
"playing a hunch." But he had no inkling of Vargas's
secondary obsession which had sprouted out, green and
vigorous, from the major one. Vargas read his Cæsar,
his Alexander, his Napoleon, and said within himself,
"Me, I am like that." He was a supreme egotist. He said,
"What those guys did, me, I can do." He made money;
he made himself a power of a sort; he looked always to
new heights; being very vain, he was very cocksure of
himself. And so the sprout upon the main obsession was
inevitable: He looked at Corinna, who was so very different from women that he knew, and wanted her; and
he did not for an instant entertain a doubt that she or
any other girl would say no to him.

What Tad knew, Vargas knew. So, for example, he
knew that tonight Aunt Mary was with her brother's
family at Halcyon, for Corinna, not wishing to curtail
the housekeeper's vacation, had not written that she was
returning; he was aware that Tad himself had ridden
yesterday with a hectic crowd that had raced off half-

cocked to Red Dirt, where some wild rumor had it that another gold strike had been made; he knew that if Corinna had written her half brother of her home-coming, Tad had not gotten the letter. And so tonight Vargas chose to make his call, confident of finding Corinna alone.

And alone she was, and distraught and weary and very, very unhappy. It was not only that this had been a trying day of train and stage; the heavy weight upon her spirit was the realization that Steve Cody had robbed the stage. Since her afternoon alone with him in the woods she had thought more and more kindly of him; though she had gone to the Judge with her suspicions, subsequently she had regretted her act and had built up all sorts of extenuating explanations. Now she could only despair for him and strive futilely to persuade herself that he and his misdeeds were nothing to her. But she could not shake off her sadness nor fail to sigh over a dying glamor.

She moved restlessly through the quiet house; her steps, though she went softly, echoed eerily and formless little fears started up like ghosts. Overwrought, she started at every slight sound.

She wondered anxiously about Tad, hoping at every instant to hear him coming. And so when quick footsteps sounded on the porch she ran to the door all eagerness, crying in an access of glad relief, " Hello, Tad! It's time ——"

Vargas stood there looking in at her. Her words broke off with a gasp and she drew back hastily, as a fresh horde of fears came rushing upon her. His hat was on and the upper part of his face was in shadow from the broad brim, but the lamplight revealed his massive jaw, freshly shaven, and his mouth set in a firm straight line. While she could only stare speechlessly, he came in and softly closed the door; his spurs rattled and clanked, their chains dragging the floor. He remembered his hat and removed it; now in the fuller light she saw his eyes, those strange hot-brown eyes in which was so much of mastery and cunning and vain arrogance. In them, before he spoke the first word, she read his errand.

" I wanted to see you," said Vargas.

Corinna's almost overpowering impulse was toward flight; she had never been so afraid of anything in her life as she was now of Vargas. But she remained motionless, facing him as one might confront a beast of the jungle come upon all unexpectedly and at close quarters, lest the first hint of panic precipitate attack. She tried to tell herself that it was absurd to be so frightened, that he came only to make her a call, that he could not possibly know she was alone.

" If you'll excuse me a moment to go and call Tad —"

" Tad ain't here," said Vargas.

She had even taken the first step but grew rigidly still when he spoke. She had seen herself in eager expectation going deliberately to the hall door, calling, " Tad! Mr. Vargas is here;" going on into the hall, then breaking into a run to the bunk house where a little while ago she had heard the men's voices. Now, confused, she said quickly:

" Aunt Mary ——"

" She ain't here either," said Vargas. " She's over to

Halcyon. That's why I picked tonight. I wanted to talk to you."

The blunt words served to increase her misgivings; since he did know that she was alone he must read her purpose in the transparent excuses she had made. But Vargas gave no sign of having sensed her self-betrayal. He stood twirling his hat with both hands and for a brief moment those two hands held her fascinated gaze, they were so brutally strong. When she looked swiftly at his face his eyes were unwinking, steadily appraising her, bold in their admiration. She flushed hotly and said as calmly as she could, her voice cool but a little hurried:

" I hope you will excuse me tonight, Mr. Vargas. I have just come home and am tired. Some other time ——"

" No," said Vargas, shaking his head. " Now." He seemed to hesitate, and for an instant dropped his eyes to his hat. Looking up swiftly, he added: " You see, I think a heap of your brother."

So after all he was not finding it as smooth sailing as he had anticipated. Face to face with her, despite his bold look, he failed to be direct and outspoken. He had come to talk not of Tad but of himself, then of her. He held himself no man to whip the devil around a stump, yet with this moment at hand, with himself and her alone together, he approached from an angle, seeking her blind side.

" You see," he said slowly, that still bright gaze bent unwaveringly upon her flushed face, " Tad owes me money. Seven hundred dollars, now. He gambles; he can't win. Steve Cody picks 'em clean when they're sof', like Tad is. Now seven hundred dollars ain't much to a man like me, but there's a plenty of folks that figgers it's a lot of money."

Corinna, with perception keyed up to the point where it missed nothing, saw at the outset what direction the man was taking. He wanted her, he meant to possess her, he was clumsily approaching the matter of the purchase price. Here was the sort of man to look at a girl, to estimate her value to him and to pay the price. How otherwise should a Vargas woo?

She realized with a start that his voice had been rumbling on and that she had not heard all that he said. It was something about " bein' a friend of Tad's, of tryin' to give the kid a show, of bein' willin' to snap his fingers at what a lot of folks would call a pile of money ——"

He went on, beginning to speak more swiftly, sure of himself now; he was telling her about Vargas, the man he was, most of all the man he was going to be. She caught her first true glimpse of Vargas's dream. Had he not missed election as sheriff he swore that already that dream would be realized. Never mind; things were all right anyhow; he was in a position to dictate; he had Steve Cody by the back of the neck and could shove his face in the mud. . . . This country, remote from the outside world, aloof and self-sufficient behind the ramparts of the mountains, rich in agricultural possibilities and in gold, was Vargas's in prospect, as good as his now. " It's goin' to be like a kingdom like there used to be in the ol' days. Me, I'm king of it! Every man in office will be my man; if a man gets in trouble it will be me who says, ' Put him in the pen; ' me who will say, ' Hell, he's a friend of mine; turn him loose! ' Me, I'll own lands an' mines; I'll have a thousan', maybe ten thousan' men on my pay roll."

He had not yet spoken the words, "And you can be the queen! ", but Corinna heard them singing through every note of his rhapsodizings. She knew, whether he had actually told her or she had gleaned it among the things left unsaid, how in his fancies he builded himself a palace of the sort that would rear its fantastic walls in a bartender's dream; how he made laws and dispensed justice both high and low. She realized that the only limitations to the man's grotesque ambitions were the limits of his own imagination. And she realized too, marking a new sudden flash in his eyes, in which there was an intimacy which enfolded her like an embrace, what his next words would be. He took a swift step forward, coming so close to her that he towered over her.

" Corinna——"

The tenuous thread by which all the while she had held herself from flight snapped then; in his voice as in his eyes, in his hands coming up from his sides now, she read the same horrible message, his unclean coveting. She whipped back, her heart beating wildly; the hall door stood open——

But quick as she was, Vargas was quicker. The hot brown eyes had watched her too narrowly, that quickened brain of his was too alert with suspicion and cunning, to miss her slightest gesture or fail to read its significance. At her first stir his hand shot out and clamped about her wrist.

"No," said Vargas heavily. "No. Don't you go—Corinna."

She writhed out of his clutch; he released her lingeringly when he made sure that her retreat was toward
a corner and that he could come between her and the
door. But as she withdrew he followed her.

" Don't you dare touch me! "

Already he had touched her. And now, because of that
contact of his hard hand against her soft warm wrist,
he abruptly lost all his slow speech and ponderous move-
ment, and flared up like fire. She was in his blood now,
she mounted up to his brain.

" God, girl! You're—you're beautiful." He paused and
she could hear his quick, hard breathing. " Why, I guess
I could have any woman I wanted—an' I want jus'
you!—Listen to me! There's nobody here but you an'
me; you listen to me ——"

" No! " cried Corinna, as he took still another purposeful step toward her. She darted back; she tried to
scream for help.

Vargas was almost upon her and meant to clap a hand
over her mouth when the front door burst open. Both he
and she whirled and saw David Laribee standing in the
door, staring incredulously in on them.

" David! " cried Corinna, and ran to him, clutching
his arm with both hands.

Laribee, at first only puzzled, then amazed, suddenly
realized just what sort of scene he had interrupted. He
put an arm protectingly around Corinna's shoulders.

" I guess you'd better go now, Vargas," he said. And
when fury flamed up in Vargas's red-brown eyes and he
started forward, Laribee said again: " You'd better go
now, hadn't you, Vargas? "

Vargas stopped where he was, for a moment seemed to hesitate, then went quietly to where his hat lay, picked it up and went out. They listened for his steps and heard him go down to the yard and ride away. Laribee went to the porch to look after him, then came back and closed the door.

"I didn't know you were home; I thought I'd drop in for a chat with Tad ——" Laribee looked white around the mouth. He was just saying anything, oddly constrained.

"Oh, David! Oh, thank God you did come."

"My dear, my dear," he said hoarsely, and drew her tenderly into his arms.—That a man like Vargas should even sully her with his eyes! He couldn't get it into words; for a spell he was quite inarticulate. A profound gratitude overfilled his heart that he, David Laribee, had been permitted to arrive when he did.

And in Corinna's heart was a thanksgiving so great that it crowded everything else out. Breathless, she looked up into Laribee's face and saw it transfigured by his emotion, which rose from his great love for her.

"You came just in time," she whispered, "to save me ——"

He muttered something about Vargas.

Yes, of course, it was from Vargas that he had saved her. But from nothing else? From herself also? A surge of emotions made conflict within her.—She had been very, very happy during most of the trip home, for her father was so much better than she had thought to find him— and somehow, during train and stage ride, she had come to a decision which brought her a new high gladness: It was that Steve Cody was fine and true and honorable. Despite ugly rumors and in defiance of what she knew of him and all that Tad maintained, she had chosen to see in him a heroic figure; and if that figure was at times obscure and uncertain that was only because of those mists of mystery which lend fascination.

And then, crashing into her musings, had come the late afternoon episode; with her own eyes she had seen him rob the stage.

Ah, it was not alone from Vargas that David Laribee was saving her. She was on the verge of panic at realizing that she was falling in love with Steve Cody; she was like one who jerks back when another careless step would have been into an abyss. She blamed her romantic fancies, her dreams themselves, and strove desperately to scramble back to sanity. And now she was in David Laribee's arms and read his soul itself in his adoring eyes, and all that warm liking which from the first she had experienced for him, that good comfortable affection, rose up within her to respond to his devotion. With him was security, salvation.

" Corinna dear, I love you so! "

" Dear David," she said softly.

It was while they stood thus, clinging to each other, deeply moved, that Steve Cody came upon them. He arrived in haste, with no thought of stopping for doors or conventions.

" Corinna! " he burst out.

Both Laribee and Corinna had the quick suspicion that he was drunk. Neither of them had ever seen such a look on his face, so much unleashed emotion, such wildness in his eyes. He took an impetuous step toward them, then halted abruptly. He looked confused. He began speaking hurriedly, excitedly.

" I was riding home. Something—I don't understand! I was so sure that you were in danger. I tried to ride on, but it came again, that fear for you; stronger than ever. I was sure. So I came. Some danger ——"

" It has passed," said Corinna very faintly, and stared back at him in wonder touched with awe.

" It's all right, Steve," Laribee added gravely. " You did have the right hunch. Vargas was here and Corinna was afraid of him. He's gone now."

Even while Laribee spoke Steve did not look at him, but only at Corinna. He seemed puzzled, unable to get his bearings, like a man rudely awakened. She slipped out of Laribee's embrace and made a little involuntary step forward, only to stop irresolutely.

This was the first time in many a long year that Steve Cody's guard had been down as it was now, the first time for his face to reveal his emotion. A skilled fencer may be taken by surprise, shocked into a reckless gesture, but the moment passes swiftly. Almost in an instant Steve was again the Steve the world knew. It was as though he hastily readjusted a mask which had slipped.

" Glad you are all right, Miss Lee," he said indifferently. " I do hope you'll come to overlook my blundering in on you like this. Good night. Good night, Laribee."

He withdrew and closed the door. There was something symbolical in the small, everyday act as he performed it, so gently and quietly, yet with definite firmness. Corinna shivered. It was just in that way that one would close a door if for him the act were rich in significance, and if he meant that it should be closed forever.

But just now Laribee was not in the least concerned with Steve Cody and his manner of departing. The light in his eyes was like a light someone has set in the window, welcoming a beloved one home. He again took Corinna's hands, inert now, into his own and without noting their lifelessness he said in a hushed voice:

" Corinna—mine? " He spoke hesitantly; he was like a man drawn to something which filled him with awe, which he approached reverently. " You know, dear, dear Corinna, how I have loved you since I first saw you. But do you know that, though I have dreamed greatly, I have not really hoped until now? Shall I tell you of the only other love of my life? I have lived much alone; I have sat on my steps through long twilights into evening and dark, looking at the far-off mountain ranges and the stars above it all, and I have loved all that so that it hurt me with just the great beauty of love. I never hoped to make those things mine; just to love them was enough —— "

Then his hand tightened on hers, and his grip and his eyes and his voice all alike were touched with fierceness.

" Mine! " he said.

And Corinna clung to his hands. Just now Steve's unexpected entrance, his wild statement that he had known of her peril, his rush to come to her, had shaken that solid ground on which she had thought to have found footing. A whole host of fantastic uncertainties besieged her. She was very weary; and she was grateful for Laribee's strong arms. Here was haven.

CHAPTER XVII

DEAD ashes. . . . Time itself, but a dreary wind blowing. Well, let it scatter them; thus, in the end, there'd be not even ashes. Only the dreary, empty wind. . . .

When there came a sharp rapping at his cabin door Steve lifted a pair of morose, moody eyes. Otherwise he did not stir. Almost immediately the knocking came again; of course the fellow outside had seen the light shining through a crack, and would not go.

" Well? " called out Steve at last. His voice was like his mood, savage, inhospitable. " Who the devil are you and what the devil do you want? "

" It's me. I'm Whitey Robbins. I got to talk to you."

Steve drummed on the table. Well, it wasn't Laribee. He had feared it might be. He couldn't have talked with Laribee tonight.

He got up and went to the door.

" If you're looking for trouble," he sang out, " you'd better come a-shooting. I don't know a nicer way to wind up a pleasant evening than by drilling you, my friend."

" I ain't even got a gun on me. Hones', Steve. I ——"

The bar came down, the door was swung open and Steve stepped to one side. You couldn't tell, with a man like Whitey. But the albino was in haste to demonstrate that he had no intention of bringing trouble along with him; he stepped quickly into the full lamplight and held his hands for Steve to see, lifted in front of him, empty. He entered; the door was closed and barred behind him.

"You c'n shake me down for a gat, if you think I've got one. I ain't though; I chucked it outside."

Steve considered him sombrely, then went to a chair. He pulled his holster forward so that the grip of the weapon that it housed was most conveniently at hand, and fixed his eyes incuriously but watchfully on Whitey's face. That face, always so colorless, was whiter than ever tonight; plainly the albino was not long out of the hospital and in such physical condition that the ride from High Town had been an ordeal. He in turn went to a chair; he perched on its edge like some evil bird not certain that it meant to tarry.

"I want to talk to you," said Whitey.

Steve did not trouble to return him so much as a nod. Whitey appeared to be seeking a place to begin, then blurted out:

"You said you didn't wipe out my pal, ol' Boney Marks."

Steve realized that something of interest surely was forthcoming, and yet did not greatly care. He felt oddly detached; it was hard to bend his mind to this man's problems even though they doubtless were an intricate part of Steve's own. He kept thinking of Corinna; of Laribee and Corinna.

"You said you didn't kill him," persisted Whitey. "That's what you said. An' you said you had a hunch you knowed who did. An' you said later on you 'n' me'd talk."

It seemed to Steve a long, long while since he had had

that talk with Whitey. Yes; he had had a suspicion concerning the manner of the taking off of Boney Marks.
It didn't seem to matter ——

He pulled himself up sharp. It did matter. It was the
other thing which no longer weighed in the scales.

" All right. Get going. What now? "

Whitey screwed up his face, his pale eyes almost vanishing, as he strove for craft.

" How do I know you wasn't lyin' to me? "

" Lie to you, you damned rat? Why should I? "

" I guess you ain't." Whitey shifted and looked uneasy;
he darted a glance at the door, then wet his lips and
said:

" If you didn't kill him, then who did? You said you'd
tell me."

" I told you that I had a hunch. If you care to come
clean with me and tell me a few things, I think between
the two of us we can get somewhere. If you don't intend
to spill everything you know you better up and dust.
Suit yourself, only make it snappy."

His sincerity impressed itself on his visitor.

" What do you want as I should tell? "

" First of all, this: Who was the third man with you
and Boney when you stuck up the stage last October? "

Whitey bristled and began sputtering, ready denials
pouring from his lips. Steve disgustedly commanded him
to shut up. In a brief silence which followed he rolled
himself a cigarette, did a bit of cool thinking, cleared
his mind as best he could of all but the matter in hand,
and planned his campaign. The first move in that campaign appeared to be the directing of a stream of smoke

across the table into Whitey's face; it was a gesture and eloquent of contempt.

"Listen, you rat," he said coldly, "if I saw any fun in it I could slam you in the hoosegow right now. Count one, for stage robbery. Count two, for trying to bump me off that night at Vargas's Place."

"If you think you c'n frame me——"

"I could. Had I wanted to, I'd have done it before now."

"You mean you ain't goin' to make any trouble for me?"

"Put you in jail?" Steve shrugged. "I'd get just as much kick out of going out and catching a wood tick and putting it in a bottle. So far as I'm concerned I rather think you can go to hell in your own way."

Whitey sighed and was plainly relieved.

"You've just got to figure for yourself," Steve continued indifferently, "whether you'll gamble that I'm telling you the truth or whether I'm lying to you. If you'll be good I'll promise you that I'll not make you any trouble about the holdup.—The first thing you did, wasn't it, when you got out of the hospital and could straddle a horse, was to go to the old stone house in the river fork?"

"Who says so?"

"And you didn't find what you went for, did you? And you'd kind of like to know who got it, huh? Well, I did."

Whitey's jaw dropped.

"I thought——" But he firmed his jaw again and shut his mouth hurriedly.

"Here's one more point for the hesitating," said Steve. "We are alone here; there are no witnesses. If I did want to use anything you might say, you could lie yourself out of it."

"That's so," said Whitey.

Steve had done all the persuading he meant to do. He lazed back in his chair and allowed the other to commune with his soul in silence. Whitey pondered and frowned and smoked half a cigarette before he made up his mind.

"Shoot the works," he said. "I'm with you."

"Good enough. Here's the start: You and Boney Marks and the other guy stuck up the stage and rode hell-for-leather getting out of there. You and Boney got separated from the other fellow right at the jump; I don't know and don't care whether accidentally or on purpose. But you and Boney had the loot, three thousand in bills, and you cached it in that old stone house. Then you showed up in Halcyon and somebody mowed Boney down. You figured me for the job and came hot-foot, and I got you first. You lay in the hospital and figured things out for yourself. You thought anyhow you'd get the three thousand back; now you haven't got even that. But most of all, in spite of the fact that you are the sort of animal you are, you remembered your old pal; and you got it in your head that I hadn't shot him—and you began to think you knew who it must be. That 'third man,' huh?"

"Spike Freedom," nodded Whitey, his mouth twisted evilly awry. "That's my guess."

"He's the man that helped you and Boney?"

Whitey had to glance over his shoulder and all about the room, had to hesitate and finally must lower his voice so that it was hardly raised above a whisper when he said:

" Yes. Spike Freedom."

" Yes? Well, he's slipped the country, hasn't he? "

" I c'n put my finger on the slippery little snake! He's hidin' out, but I c'n nail him."

" Well, why haven't you put a bullet in him before this? "

" I ain't sure." Whitey wriggled on his chair, looking distressed and helpless. " It'd be hell to go drill a innocent guy."

" Would it? " grunted Steve ironically.

" What I thought was that you might know for sure. You said you did."

" I'm not sure. I've got my guess, that's all."

" You think it was Spike? " demanded Whitey, all eagerness.

" I *think* it was Vargas."

" Vargas! " Whitey fairly leaped from his perch. " Vargas? You say Vargas bumped off Boney? "

" I don't say anything of the sort. It's a guess, that's all. You guess Spike, I guess Vargas. Only I know Vargas was in Halcyon that night and hasn't spread the news. And I'm wondering if maybe Vargas didn't know that you three were pulling off the holdup? He might even have put you up to it? Told you what stage to pick? "

" Vargas! " muttered Whitey, and though he agreed with nothing Steve had said, neither did he make any denials.

"Spike Freedom or Vargas, one of them no doubt," Steve told him. "In any case I'll go with you for a talk with Spike. Whatever he knows, and it will be plenty, we'll have out of him before he's a day older. Where's his hide-out?"

"Funny," said Whitey, and began to chuckle. "I'm glad the snake didn't drop wise! Hell, man, he's been hidin' mos' of the time in that same rock shanty where the money was! You see, he was the one tol' me an' Boney about the place; we was to meet up there nex' day. An' me an' Boney, ridin' that way, figgered it a good place to leave it. We hadn't figgered then on ——"

"Never mind," said Steve when Whitey paused. "I don't want all your confidences. But I do want to get my hands on Spike Freedom."

It was not until two days later that they found Spike Freedom. He had been somewhere for provisions and returned to the stone hut in the late afternoon. He approached his hiding place with all due and patient caution; he hid his horse in a thicket half a mile away and completed his stealthy journey on foot. But from a cliffy vantage point across the river he had been sighted, and when at last he knelt before the fireplace his game of hide and seek was played out. Steve, with Whitey peering around him, stood in the doorway and startled Spike with a quiet voice, calling him by name. Scattering firewood in his nervous agitation, the man sprang erect and darted toward his rifle where it leaned against the rock chimney.

"That the way you receive callers?" demanded Steve.

"Who are you? What do you want?" retorted Spike.

He was a little old man whom Whitey termed a snake not altogether without reason; furtive, sly looking, oozing guile. Small watery eyes, red-rimmed, peered out of a face which had been tanned like leather through years of life outdoors and which was fringed with untidy dirty-gray whiskers. He was thin and spry with over-large, knobby hands. He stared and blinked and finally, making out who one of his callers was, muttered:

"So it's you, huh, Whitey? What you up to now?"

"So you're Spike Freedom?" said Steve. "Well, I'll know you next time.—Didn't I see you over at Halcyon——"

"Who're you, Mister?" cut in Spike, fingering his rifle.

"Steve Cody, Sheriff."

Then Spike's bleary eyes, brightening briefly to hard, hot anger trailed away to Whitey. Slowly, lingeringly he set his weapon back against the chimney. He started to say something, then clamped his small mouth so tight shut that his chin beard bristled and thrust forward.

"Light your fire if you want to," Steve told him. "It's cold. We'll have a war talk."

"Sheriff, huh?" muttered Spike and spat on the hearth. He went back to his fireplace, set a match to a handful of dry twigs and soon had a smoky fire burning. His task done, he squatted on his heels and stared into the blaze, a picture of placid patience as he waited to learn what was wanted of him.

"Old Man Patience, is it?" cried Steve. "Well, there's none of it in me right now."

" It gen'rally peters out in young fellers.—Sheriff, huh? " Then his eyes turned again on Whitey; the big knobby hands tightened on a dead stick and it snapped to the sudden tension of his grip. " You're a dirty double-dealin' dog an' ever was an' will be," he said venomously.

Except for Steve's presence and the authority vested no less in him than in his office, the two would have been at each other's throats. Hatred and suspicion glared out of their eyes. But their growls died away in their throats and they listened to him. He leaned against the chimney and looked down on Spike Freedom and made it clear at the outset that he was the one to crack the whip.

" Now then," he went on, while the squatting Spike Freedom began picking at the callouses on his hands, centering his gaze on them. " Here's something that wants explaining: How come that a man like you is always on the dodge, hiding out for months, and yet sticking to the part of the country which you'd think he might want to show a clean pair of heels to? Kind of queer, isn't it? "

" Mebbe it is an' mebbe it ain't. Leastwise, it's my business."

" I think maybe the law wants you."

" Yah! An' what I think, young feller, is that the law's uncommon like folks, wantin' a heap sight more'n it's ever goin' to git."

" Want to talk here, or talk in jail, Spike? "

" Jail! " Spike jeered at him. " You can't come jail on me."

" No? Don't fool yourself. You can just bet your sweet life that I can. What charge would you like to answer to first, stage robbery or murder? "

Spike looked at Whitey and lifted his lip in a snarl of pure animalism, showing his few widely spaced discolored fangs.

"He's got the goods on us, Spike," spoke up Whitey Robbins, taking the attitude which he had been coached into by Steve. "He knows you an' me an' Boney pulled that party. No, I ain't squealed. He knows an' he's got me jugged same as he plans on gettin' you."

"You fool! " cried the old man, quivering with rage.

"Stage robbery is only one point," Steve told him. "The other and bigger thing is murder. What about Boney Marks? "

"I didn't kill him," said Spike stonily.

"Know who did? "

"No."

"All the worse for you. If you did happen to know, I'd be willing to forget all about the stage holdup."

Spike showed his fangs at that. His crooked smile as good as said: "You don't trap me, young feller."

"I'll go back to what I started with," Steve ran on. "It has struck me that a man hides because he's afraid of somebody. And that he sticks close because he's after something. How's that for guessing? "

Spike brooded over the fire, hiding his eyes under heavy lids.

"Who are you scared of, Spike? Vargas, by any chance? "

Spike shifted and spat and began tinkering with his smoky fire.

"And who is it you're trying to get something out of? The same Vargas, huh, Spike? "

" Gum-shoe, ain't you? " jeered Spike.

" No. I just happen to know a few things. I know that you used to trail your luck with Vargas. I know you haven't showed up with him of late. And I know "—here he ran his blazer—" that it was either you or Vargas who shot Boney Marks that night at Halcyon."

There followed a long silence. Obstinacy was in Spike Freedom's every gesture; his bristling attitude reeked with it. But fear was in it too, and after a while a hint of nervous uncertainty. He jerked his head up and turned his watery eyes with a fixed, intent stare on Steve.

" If I'm right and you're thinking you can get something out of Vargas," Steve continued meditatively, " it won't work, Spike. For I'm going to have you behind the bars until I'm sure you're not the man I want; in that case, before you go out Vargas will be in. Think that over."

" I don't know a pesky thing about what you're drivin' at," cried Spike angrily.

" All right. Let's go! "

" To jail? Me? " He whipped back and looked longingly at his rifle; then took stock of the holstered weapon at Steve's side and the ready hands with their thumbs hooked in the belt, and sighed.

" Yes. To my cabin overnight. To jail early tomorrow. You and I and John Bingham will have quite a party. You'll be sorry you were ever born before we wind up. Come ahead, old-timer. Let's travel."

He took up the rifle and stood aside. Spike, muttering under his breath, his voice breaking in rage and chagrin, obeyed an imperative gesture and stepped ahead.

It was only after the trio reached Steve's cabin that Spike made up his mind and told what he knew. And that was only after the matter of the stage robbery and any legal action connected with it was quite cleaned up to his approval. He learned that the money had been recovered; he had Steve's solemn promise not to make trouble for him over that fruitless crime; he had it out with Whitey and got that individual's further assurances that Steve was on the square.

" All right," said Spike, growing sharp and vicious. " Make this skunk of a Whitey Robbins get t'hell out of here; jus' you an' me, Cody, an' I'll spill more beans than you ever thought was in the bag."

" Fair enough. Whitey, vamoose. Here; take this into town for me."

Steve wrote a brief note to the Judge. It said merely: " I've got Spike Freedom. If you want a word with him, come ahead. Steve." Whitey took his departure reluctantly and under protest; it was only when Steve said, " Can't you see he won't say a word while you're here? " that, he withdrew.

Then Spike, suddenly eager to have the thing done with, told what he knew. Here was a case of attempted blackmail; Steve was right in his deduction. Spike claimed that he had the goods on Vargas and that Vargas knew it. Spike had hid because he knew he wouldn't last long if Vargas could find him. From his several hiding places he had issued his repeated ultimatum and so far had got only temporizings.—Who carried word back and forth? Why, of late, Bird Galloway. No, Bird didn't know what it was all about, any more than he could guess, anyhow.

He might know that Spike had something on Vargas; that was all.

" Bird an' Vargas has had some sort of a row; that's why Bird was willin' to chip in on my play; he knew I'd make it up to him if things broke right."

But recently, readily enough admitted by Spike once he got into full swing, he was going about in terror of his life, always changing his hiding places, afraid to go to sleep at night lest he wake to find Vargas standing over him.

" An' now, damn him," he rasped nervously, " since he won't stand in with me he can hang. They're hangin' stock, them Vargases."

Yes, Vargas had killed Boney Marks if Spike was any good at seeing anything as plain as the hand before your eyes. Vargas had intended all along, Spike thought, to kill Marks, hating him like poison. Marks was such a fool. Spike spat disgustedly. It had been Vargas who cooked up the stage robbery for them; then he had made the mistake of thinking that Marks still had the three grand on him, not knowing he and Whitey had been foxy enough to stop on the road and sink it, and had bumped him off. But that wasn't all; not the half of it ——

" You're Steve Cody? Ol' man Cody's son? An' wonderin', I guess, who bumped *him* off? "

" It wasn't Vargas," said Steve coldly. " You can't tie that to him."

" Can't, huh? How do you know so much, young feller? "

What Steve knew or thought was not to be read in a

pair of stern eyes which grew as bleak as winter now, and Spike had to wait until Steve got ready to answer.

"How do I know?" Again there was a brief pause; there were things a man found it hard to talk about. "This is how I know: Whoever it was that shot my father shot him six times. One shot, two at most, would have been enough. Therefore it wasn't Vargas."

"Why not? Since when has he been stingy with lead?"

"I've figured it out. The killer was either a man with some terrible personal hatred of my father—or else a new hand, an amateur at that sort of thing. Vargas fits in neither category."

Spike pursed his lips and finally broke into a dry cackle.

"No? Vargas didn't hate him, huh?"

"No. If Vargas had anything at all to do with it, it would have been only a matter of politics, the removal of an opponent."

"Much you know about it! Listen, kid."

And now, his words galloping, Spike told him an old story, a story which the Judge had recalled to Steve's father that last time the two old friends talked together. It was about a hanging long ago, when Vargas's father dangled from a rope; when Steve's father was one of those who condemned him.

"It was me tol' Vargas about it," confessed Spike, and looked at once fearful and defiant. "Jus' a few days before it happened."

"What are you saying, man? Go on with it; damn you, go on with it! You mean that Vargas killed my father?"

" I seen him do it! " shrilled Spike. " Me an' another
feller followed him an' seen him. The two of us can
hang Vargas an' he knows it an' that's why —— "

Steve caught him by the throat, for a moment glared
at him while the gripping fingers sank into the stringy
neck, then thrust him violently away.

" You knew—you knew and allowed it to happen —— "

" No! " yelled Spike, no longer defiant but weak with
fear. " What I mean is —— Hones' to God, Cody! Yes,
me an' the other feller knew but it was too late. We
went to stop it but we wasn't in time."

" Liar! "

Spike cringed back from him and his shifty eyes were
everywhere at once, seeking some weapon. But Steve
throttled down his anger and got himself in hand and
demanded:

" Who's this other man who knows? "

" No you don't! " muttered Spike, his hand at his
throat about which remained the sensation of fingers.
" You might bump me off, if you didn't need me. Not
another cheep out'n me until you got Vargas dead to
rights; not until he's safe behind bars an' you an' me
an' the distric' attorney gets together. Then I'll come
through. Then I'll hang him, an' hell take him for the
dirty miser he is."

Steve nodded grimly. Ten minutes later, leaving Spike
bound hand and foot and under the watchful guard of
the Indian ranch hand, he started to High Town.

CHAPTER XVIII

WHILE Steve was hastening to High Town, behold the Judge as merry as a grig, or as cheerful as the proverbial cricket, just as you please, turning his back on the town and heading for Steve's cabin. Riding, he jingled his spurs, and jingling his spurs he fell to singing. The favorite refrain of

> " Oh, she's the apple of my eye
> An' me, I'm fond of apple pie,"

assailed the long ears of Heart's-ease, and the ears cocked and flapped and pricked forward and lay back as though the notes were little strings pulling them this way and that. And the Judge, while singing, used his spurs for something else than merely to make a chiming obligato to his vocalizings, and Heart's-ease covered the miles in really creditable time. The old fellow was but newly returned from delivering Steve's letter and the bank notes to John Bingham, where he had tarried long enough to read the letter over the district attorney's shoulder and so come to a rather full understanding of matters heretofore obscure. He had barely dismounted in High Town when Whitey brought him word of Spike laid by the heels. That he and Steve did not meet is only to be explained by the fact that both men, on urgent errands, deserted the main trail for many a shortcut and somehow missed each other in the folds among the hills.

So now the Judge rode to have his long-delayed inter-view with a certain low-life, mangy, egg-suckin', yeller-doggish, shifty-eyed, ornery cuss, otherwise known as Mr. Spike Freedom. Wherefore the rollicking song and bubbling cheer.

"Heart's-ease," said the Judge, and swished his quirt with abandon, "it's a long worm that don't turn sooner or later. Be patient, sweet frien'; at the en' of this ride there's goin' to be something whispered in that off ear o' your'n that'll make your whiskers curl. Whoopee. Hear me, Heart's-ease? What I said was 'Whooopeee! ' Now jus' lay your lean belly down to the earth an' scamper! "

To such effect did Heart's-ease scamper that mule and rider brought up at Steve's mountain cabin while the light of the lowering sun still quivered on the uplands. The Judge got himself out of the saddle much after the fashion a small boy gets a stone out of his sling-shot; he hung the reins over the hitching rack and assaulted the door.

"Hi, there, Steve! " he shouted. "Open up, man, an' let me at him! "

The words came only when he discovered that the door was fastened. There was a silence, then a voice, not Steve's, demanding who was there and what was wanted. A gentle sweat broke out on the Judge's forehead. A delay now, even of an instant, was not to be brooked.

"Open up! I'll poun' your damn' door down; I'll burn you out, you Siwash. It's me, Jedge William Henery Bull come to see a long lost frien'." He meditated swiftly; must be Steve's Indian in there riding herd on the trapped polecat. "Steve sent for me," he added. "Get a move on."

The Indian knew the Judge and was impressed by the authority of his appearance and title. If rather hesitantly, yet with no great delay, he opened the door wide enough for a man to look through. The Judge did the rest. He hurled his weight against the last barrier to stand between him and his quarry and both door and Indian were shoved back.

" Now! " he said. " Now! "

He saw a form lying on a cot and recognized it as it wriggled over and surged up; Spike Freedom trussed up in a fashion to meet with the Judge's heartiest approval. The Judge's eyes fairly sparkled; a deep breath escaped him and he took off his hat and mopped his forehead. Yep; it was Spike all right. Now, let's get everything clear; get rid of anybody else that ain't needed.

" You get out," he said to. Steve's Indian, for once coming to the point without the least circumlocution. " Go up to the barn an' squat. Twirl your thumbs, like this; when I want you, I'll yowl. Scatter."

The Indian did not know exactly what to do. There were his orders from Steve; on the other hand here was the Judge in the flesh, here the Judge's impressiveness and also the fact that the Judge and Steve were old friends. Further than that, Steve had sent for the Judge. With so many considerations to occupy him all at once the aboriginal stood and gawked. But the Judge did neither. Nimbly he caught the Indian by both shoulders, spun him about, shot him out through the door and again said, " Now! " as he dropped the heavy bar into place.

Spike with some difficulty had achieved a sitting posture on the edge of the bunk. With his hands tied at

his back and his feet lashed together, he looked particularly helpless, and as his eyes filled to the vision of
the old Judge confronting him, legs aspraddle, hands on
hips, Spike's eyes fluttered and grew fearful and fell
away.

"You damn' this-that-an'-the-other Such-an'-such! "
said the Judge.

Spike twisted helplessly and tried to rub his nose
against a hunched-up shoulder.

"Lay off'n me, Jedge," he growled. " I'm young Cody's
prisoner; a kind o' prisoner o' the law, mind you, an'
you dasn't lay a han' on me.—I ain't done nothin' to
you."

"You — ain't — done — nothin' — to — me! Say that
again; oh, let me hear them words again! "

"You dasn't," muttered Spike. " You leave me alone."

The Judge hunted himself a chair. He sat down right
in front of Spike and not three feet away from him. For
a long while he just sat and looked at his helpless victim—and gloated. A look of infinite satisfaction dawned
in the mild blue eyes.

"Spike Freedom," he said softly, " I never thought to
see the time when I could jus' set an' look at you an'
find a holy an' sweet'nin' joy creepin' all over me like
a pan o' milk spilt on the kitchen floor. Makes a man
get poetic, don't it? " Deep rumbles became gentle, oily
chuckles. " I don't know's I ever felt so low-down poetic.
Thanks, Spike."

Spike's nervousness increased as he watched the Judge
extract one of his long and vile cigars from his pocket and
set to rolling it in the corner of his mouth.

"Got you, ain't I, Spike?" queried the old fellow amicably. "Got you where the hair's long an' the flesh tender."

"You ain't got me," Spike snarled back at him. "You don't lay a dirty finger on me. Me, I'm workin' with Steve Cody right now, an' he's sheriff an' it's legal."

"Yeah?" The Judge lighted his cigar and, serenely taking his most unfair advantage, blew the acrid smoke in Spike's face. "Looks like you an' Steve was workin' together an' firs' class frien's, at that! Yep; sure does."

Spike's alarm was patent enough; now into his crafty eyes came another look, that of determined if hastily formed purpose.

"You was a frien' of Steve's ol' man, Jedge," he said sharply. "You'd like to know who killed him, wouldn't you?"

The Judge tautened and hitched forward in his chair.

"Well?" he shot back. "Speak your piece."

"I know," said Spike. "Know all about it. That's why Steve has got me here. You lif' your han' to me, an' I'll die with a shut mouth same as a oyster."

"Who killed him, Spike?" said the Judge gently.

"No you don't! You don't get a thing out'n me until he comes back an' says the word."

"That so?" The Judge leaned back comfortably and smoked a moment, directing puff after puff into Spike's face. "Listen to me, kid; I'm goin' to tell you a secret. Nobody knows it but me; now I'll let you in on it. I got Apache Injun blood in me. Bad Apache Injun, at that." He blew the ash clear of his glowing cigar end. "Speak up; tell me who shot Cody ——"

" I'll see you rollin' on the hottes' bed o' coals ——"

" Or I'll jus' nacherally do right now what my Injun gran'dad would 'a' done in like circumstances, with a pale-face tied up in front of him an' a live cigar goin'." He leaned forward with a jerk, and thrust the cigar close to Spike's face. " I'll burn your nose off'n you, you sarpint."

Spike yelled for help. The Judge stoically reminded him that the only man within call was " another Injun." Spike yielded and said that it was Vargas. The Judge resumed smoking. Spike, striving for security, hastened to add that he and he alone could hang Vargas for the crime. The Judge wanted to know the why and the wherefore of that and Spike enlightened him this far and no farther: That he and one other man had actually witnessed the murder and could prove it. No; he'd say not another thing; the Judge could go the limit and do all the things which his Apache blood suggested to him; Spike would say never another word on the subject until Steve returned.

And now it was no longer smooth sailing for the Judge, and Spike, though he did not understand the reasons involved, did mark the change in his tormentor's expression. The blue eyes grew uncertain and troubled; the face so close to his own became an amazing network of puckers.

The Judge jumped suddenly up from his chair and began a nervous pacing up and down. Broken snatches of sentences floated to his interested listener, but since the audible words were chiefly dissociated expletives they conveyed no meaning beyond what was already apparent, that the Judge from being as merry as a grig was now in a very vile temper. What the old fellow was doing was staging one of the grimmest battles of his checkered lifetime, for now he and what stood him as a conscience were locked, so to speak, in a death grapple.

"Looky here, Jedge ——" began Spike, his nervousness growing acute.

The Judge stopped to glower at him.

"You jus' open that mug o' yourn until I give you leave," he growled, " an' I'll jump down your throat with my spurs on an jus' nacherally rake you from tonsil to toe nail."

Spike forthwith subsided into gloomy silence. The Judge resumed his jog-trotting and his inner battle. Just then Heart's-ease outside grew fretful over something and emitted a raucous complaint which concluded with a vicious and clearly audible snap of the big yellow teeth. The Judge started: that little homely sound seemed to have brought him back to the present ——

"Spike," he said, in a voice which trembled a little, "you wished a curse on me them eight year ago. You got to take it off."

"Yah!" jeered Spike. "Like fun, I got to! The way you been treatin' me, you're in a nice fix, I'll tell a man, to come askin' favors of me."

"It ain't no favor, Spike." He spoke with sudden meekness now. "It's only what they call common decency. A joke's a joke, an' let it go at that; but there's such a thing as runnin' one into the groun'."

Now was Spike's turn to sit on the seats of the mighty. His scraggy chin beard bristled; his little eyes grew as evil as a snake's.

"This one ain't goin' to run into the groun' until you do," he announced viciously. "When they dig a hole an' plant your carcase in it, it's a fresh deal. Not until."

"That so?" The Judge hardened again. "You says looky-here; I says the same. Looky here, Spike Freedom: Them eight year ago you an' me made a bet on election. The bet was the man who los' was to ride a mule as long's he lived less'n the other let up on him. Me, I los'. An' I played my string out. I've rode more damn' mules an' more kind o' damn' mules and more ornery damn' mules than any other one man ever see."

Spike giggled.

"You," said the Judge sternly, "tricked me. You got some inside dope ahead o' time an' made a monkey out'n me. Jus' the same, a bet bein' a bet, I've stuck to it. Now I'm through. It's your turn!"

Again Spike jeered, but this time there was a bit of uncertainty registering itself in his eyes. The Judge's tone was meant to carry conviction.

"You're in a bad hole, Spike," went on the Judge, calm now and judicial. "Less'n I get you out, you're in a right bad hole an' you're in it to stay. This here ain't a healthy neck o' the woods for you. You got the goods on Vargas, huh? Well, I reckon he knows it, don't he? That's the big reason you've been so damn' hard to find. Now, you're tied up nice an' proper." On his face dawned an expansive grin. He stepped lightly to the door. "So long, Spike," he said breezily.

"Hey there!" yelled Spike. "Where you goin'? What're you up to now?"

" You mean, you addle-wit, you didn't get my proposition clear? " The Judge stopped, one hand on the bar, and conveyed the impression of being in a hurry, yet willing to give his companion one more moment of his precious time. " I'll say it over, so's a simple mind c'n grasp the main idea: You take the curse off'n me an' wear it yourse'f, an' I'll let you go on indefinite contaminatin' the earth with the breath you breathe.—Now, looky here; bein' outspoken an' straight shootin', I'll tip you my hand: I come out here hell-bent meanin' to turn you loose an' to stick a wad o' money in your jeans an' let you flicker, no matter whether you was wanted for manslaughter, arson or egg-suckin'. Now I can't, seein' as Steve wants to keep you real bad. So for a minute I was stumped; not for long, though. Look in my eye, Spike Freedom! "

" Yah," jeered Spike.

" See blood in it? Well, there's blood on the moon. I can't do what I figgered, but there's a better way. You take the curse off'n me, Spike, or I'll jus' step along hasty an' have a word with Vargas. An' I'll whisper some sweet tidin's in his ear. I'll say to him, ' By the way, Vargas, Spike Freedom's shootin' off his mouth, sayin' he's goin' to pin a certain hangin' matter on you an' right now he's stewin' in his own poison juices, all tied up han' an' foot up at Steve Cody's cabin.' An' then I'll jus' call it a day, an' go an' get me some supper an' let things take their course."

" You dasn't," wailed Spike. He gulped, and strained at his bonds; making his last stand—and to the cold watchful eye bent upon him it was palpably a last stand

—he muttered: " Anyway Steve'll be here firs'; he'll see me clear."

" If I never do another Christian ac' in the worl'," said the Judge sanctimoniously, " I'll sure head Steve off long enough to give Vargas the firs' whack at you. Maybe you think I wouldn't, 'count of wantin' to see Vargas swung for what you say he done? Res' easy, Spike; I'll see he hangs for killin' you, an' so he hangs I'm satisfied. Better start prayin', Spike," and he went briskly to the door and yanked down the bar.

With that gesture he won. Spike, shivering with terror, called him back and swore to do anything on earth to please his old friend.

" Thought so," said the Judge. " Got a horse here? "

" Yes. In the barn, I guess."

" Well, I'll swap saddles. Part of the bargain, mind you, is you trade me your horse, sight unseen, for my mule, which I c'n recommen' very high as havin' one hundred per cent what you might call the pure essence o' mule. You lif' up your right han' —— No, you can't, can you?—All right, you jus' say these words an' say 'em solemn: ' I call the ol' bet off.' "

" I call the ol' bet off," said Spike dismally, and added with greater warmth, " Damn you."

" That's a nice clean curse, an' I don't mind that kind a-tall. Now you go on an' say, ' An' I'll take my turn, givin' you my word of a sneak thief an' a skunk, that the res' of my life I'll walk where I'm goin' unless I c'n get me a mule to ride on.' "

Spike in the course of time made the promise; to be sure, both he and the Judge realized that he had not the vaguest idea of keeping it, yet the mere speaking of the words was hard for him and ineffably sweet to the ears of a man who had dreamed through the years of hearing them.

Then the Judge drew what was perhaps the longest, deepest sigh of his lifetime. He could hardly hold himself still to deliver his peroration, so eager was he to be gone, so did his legs tingle in anticipation of draping them over a real horse's back again. But he held himself in check and spoke ponderously.

" A bargain's a bargain, remember. I kep' mine for eight o' the longes' years that ever drug like a broken-back inch-worm creepin' through mos' of eternity. You think you c'n lie out'n your promise, but you can't. I'll keep as watchful an eye an' as listenin' an ear on your doin's as ever did a fon' mama over her firs' borned. The minute I get an inklin' that you've so far forgot yourse'f as to fork a horse, I'll go look up Vargas an' sick him on you. If in the meantime the grim reaper gets that gent, as I got a hunch mebbe will happen, then I'll take his burdens on my shoulders. I'll go gunnin' for you, Spike Freedom, an' I'll gore you."

And then the self-styled scion of a bad Apache took his departure. He summoned the California Indian, instructed him to guard his prisoner like a pearl of great price, changed his saddle, bestowed a last baleful glare at Heart's-ease and had as baleful a glare in return, and was on his way like a schoolboy out for vacation.

Riding a horse!

CHAPTER XIX

DURING those two days devoted by Steve to running Spike Freedom to earth, and by the Judge to his trip to the county seat, a sequence of circumstances in High Town was acting much after the fashion of a burning fuse; and at about the time that the Judge triumphantly reverted to the equine habit of former days the explosion took place. It was a tragic occurrence which created a brief hubbub and exercised a pronounced influence on subsequent events.

To David Laribee, at a time when his indignation against Vargas flared up hotter than ever before, it seemed that a kind fate had thrust an instrument into his hand. That instrument was Bird Galloway. Exactly what was the trouble between him and Vargas, just where it began and when, was never made altogether clear. Its springs, perhaps, lay in jealousy. Of late, with his own purposes to serve, Vargas had made much of Tad Harper, and young Galloway resented the favoritism. Then came the alliance with Spike Freedom; it is likely, saving for Galloway's mounting jealous anger, he would never have considered Spike's proposition. But consider it he did and so took the first step toward the pitfall of his own digging. Now, when he should have been very cool and wary he allowed himself to grow hot-headed and reckless.

That he had gone to Laribee at all was but an indication of that heady impulsiveness to which he surrendered

234

himself. It was merely that, having come to a decision,
he could not wait. He first of all sought Steve Cody,
meaning to feel him out, sensing that all was not milk
and honey between the gambler and the man who held
himself to be the dictator of High Town. Steve was
nowhere to be found. Galloway then looked for the Judge;
he too seemed to have vanished. At this juncture, growing the more impatient through being baffled, Galloway
sighted Laribee on his way to a talk with Grady.

Thus it was to Laribee that Galloway, overflowing with
animosity, appeared like a sharp-edged tool made for the
task in hand. He told all that he knew of Vargas, which
when boiled down was little more than Laribee already
knew; he poured out all that he suspected and this was
a very great deal.

" He's double-crossed me. For that I'm goin' to pull
down his meat-house for him." The young roisterer's
shambling frame twitched nervously, his sharp-featured
face was sinister and malevolent. His sincerity was
obvious; there was no misdoubting that ancient evil
emotion which shone in his birdlike eyes and rasped
in his voice.

" Why bring all this to me? " asked Laribee curiously.

" I looked for two other guys firs'; the ol' Judge an'
Steve Cody. They was both out o' town."

" Steve Cody? " Laribee lifted his brows. " He and
Vargas are friends, aren't they? "

Bird Galloway laughed mockingly.

" Frien's? Them two? Guys like that frien's to anybody when they got a chance to step on the other guy's
neck to get somewhere? Gimme a rest!—Funny about

them two," he added musingly. " Why, not so long ago
Vargas tried to bribe me an' Chink Johnson to wipe
Steve out. Sure. Five hundred bucks for the job. An'
then nex' thing you know he calls it off. He says it ain't
necessary; figures maybe he can whip Steve into line;
guesses he can use him better alive than pushin' up the
grass." He shrugged and began making himself a fresh
thin cigarette. " Anyhow, one of 'em wouldn't cry if the
other got carried out feet first."

Laribee eyed him narrowly, thinking that here was a
thoroughly unprincipled young scoundrel who, if one
dared trust him, might serve some good purpose no matter with what motives. Yet a clean man dislikes dirty
tools, and he stared frowningly into the quick bright
eyes and was a long time deciding what to say.

" Even yet you haven't told me why you come to me,"
he said at last.

" I know what's goin' on, don't I? " retorted Galloway. " I know you're one o' the gang that wants to clean
up High Town. I know you never drag a spur into Vargas's Place. I know if you could knife him you'd hop
to it."

It was Laribee's time to shrug.

" What can I do to Vargas? Where has he laid himself
open? "

" Leave it to me," said Galloway eagerly. " Ain't I
offerin' to get you the dead-wood on him? " He hesitated, then added guardedly, out of the corner of his
mouth: " There's one man that's got something on Vargas, an' I'll tell you this much: I'll tell you who it is.
It's Spike Freedom, that's who, an' maybe I don't know

the whole of it yet, but I'll find out, an' I do know
Spike's got something on him."

" Do you know where to find Spike? " asked Laribee
sharply.

" Sure I know. Ain't I been carryin' word back an'
forth between him an' Vargas? "

" Where is he? "

Galloway dropped his cigarette and, head down, ground
it into bits under his heel. When he looked up it was
to shake his head.

" That's diff'rent. Spike's got reasons for hidin' out. I
ain't goin' to squeal on him; not unless it works out that
that's the only way I can get Vargas. No, I won't snitch
on Spike."

" Unless it's necessary to get Vargas," Laribee reminded him.

" Yes. That goes. I'll double-cross my own mother to
nail Vargas to the cross."

" Come ahead," said Laribee then. " I'm going to see
Grady. We'll talk this thing out."

Grady was no finished actor, especially when taken by
surprise, but he was a cautious man and not without
foresight. His caution in the past had kept him, so far
as was generally known, far away from Vargas, and now
it held him silent until he had brooded over the new
situation. Since neither of his callers harbored any suspicion of him, his lowered eyes did not concern them
farther than to assure them that Grady was thinking
hard.

The conference was brief; it brought out that there
had been no open break between Galloway and Vargas;

Galloway, so far as Vargas knew, had but taken the first step or so away from his old allegiance and might reasonably be expected to return to it.

"You go back to Vargas," said Grady. " Play your hand carefully and we can use you. We'll pay well for your trouble too, eh, Laribee? You've been close to Vargas, you say, Galloway; well, little by little, worm your way back close to him; closer than ever. You give us strength where we were weak before. The side which has a spy in the other side's headquarters has the bulge on the situation. Hop to it, Bird. We'll nail him, and I guess it will be a satisfaction to you to have a hand in it."

"Watch me," said Galloway.

There was a streak of cleverness in Bird Galloway and a much richer, wider vein of vindictive determination. Therefore, had he been just then the only spy plying his trade in High Town, he might at least have saved his own life in the enterprise to which he committed himself. Only, naturally, Grady gave him no chance.

The whole story was whispered into Vargas's ear that night.

"Yeah? I wondered what had come over the kid. He's been playin' up today an' not overplayin' his hand, at that. You got to admit, Grady, there's stuff in him.— Well, it's his own funeral."

"All you got to do is give him the wrong steer all along the line; make a monkey out of him. You don't have to ——"

Grady let it go at that and Vargas, with one of his heavy shrugs, went about his business. As coldly and methodically as a man might set about any necessary bit of routine business he arranged for Bird Galloway's removal. From the first it must be that he meant to do the thing himself; there were to be no chances taken this time. Further, Laribee and the men he represented would know that Vargas answered their attack thus; it was a gesture; and he himself would play safe.

So Bird Galloway was allowed to live through that first night; Vargas learned the new set-up too late to act. There need be no great haste; likewise, there was no call for any considerable delay. No nervous hurry of an amateur; not tomorrow, during daylight; tomorrow night, rather, and at a late hour.

But these plans went by the board. Whether some shrewd keen sense warned the victim or whether it was mere chance, Galloway on the second afternoon prepared to leave town. He had remarked, and Vargas heard of it, that his pal, Chink Johnson, had sent him word to hit the high spots for Chinese Gully; Chink was in some sort of trouble over there.

Vargas merely shoved the hour forward. In his own saloon he found Slim Brilliant idling at the piano; Slim had a penchant for dreamy music. Vargas got him aside.

"Slim, get hold of Bird Galloway. Tell him Chink Johnson is hidin' in my room out back. Tell him Chink is in dutch; shot a man over at Chinese Gully. Wants to see him quick."

Slim's eyes batted wide open.

"On your way," said Vargas curtly. "An' don't mention my name; I don't want to be mixed in this. Tell him you saw Chink an' he's hurt."

Slim went on his errand; Vargas passed through the

door behind the bar, down the hall and out through the cold sunshine to his private room. When Bird Galloway came in the room seemed unoccupied. He closed the door and stood with his gun in his hand, very tense, at once apprehensive and electrically eager. Vargas had been standing behind the door and shot as Galloway whirled. Galloway clutched at his breast with his left hand and with his right fired wildly. Vargas shot him the second time and he sagged in the middle and dropped to the floor, gurgling incoherently. Vargas, coolly devoting himself to details, ejected his two empty cartridges, replaced them with new ones, gave a dexterous cleaning to the gun barrel with the materials ready in his pocket and shoved his weapon back out of sight.

He had been very swift in every act yet had barely completed his arrangements when the door was flung open and Tad Harper hurried in.

"Vargas!—" He saw the figure on the floor and recoiled. "My God! You've shot him! "

"No! " said Vargas quietly. "I didn't ——"

"I was just coming to tell you—I saw him talking to Dave Laribee —— He tried to kill you? "

"No! Listen, kid; you got to get this straight. You're goin' to be my witness if anything gets stirrin' over this.—Who killed him?—*Steve Cody!* Here; quick." He caught the bewildered, badly shaken Tad by the arm and dragged him to a window; it was closed but the shutter open; a small hole was drilled through it and there was broken glass on the floor. "He shot through there. I saw him as plain as day. Tried to get me, I guess. Shot twice; poor Galloway fired once, wild." Then he jerked his own weapon out and thrust it before Tad's staring eyes. " Not a shot fired, see, kid? See it? "

" Steve Cody! " gasped Tad.

Then the two whirled together as they had their first inkling that Bird Galloway was still alive. The fallen figure twitched and strove feebly to come erect. Galloway was not only still breathing; he had heard and understood; he had caught Cody's name. Most of all did his burning hatred consume him. To go out like this, leaving Vargas victorious ——

He began babbling. They heard his choking words.

" Cody—yes! I tol' him. 'Bout Spike—he'll get you— damn you —— Me, I done it ——"

He sagged again and fell back heavily. Tad, deathly white, nauseated, understanding nothing now, could only stare at Vargas. Vargas however kept his wits about him, knowing he never stood more in need of them.

" If he tol' Steve—if Steve knows where Spike is ——"

Tad in all his confusion thought that he saw one fact clearly: It was that Steve had shot Galloway while trying to shoot Vargas. There was the hole in the window glass; there was Vargas's unfired weapon; there was, most of all, Vargas's story still ringing in his ears. And, an important factor, there was Tad's eager willingness to believe anything evil of Steve Cody.

He saw Vargas frowning, perplexed. What was this about Steve and a man of whom he had heard so many rumors? Tad, with no orderly thoughts, his brain overstimulated, was merely reacting to a mental stimulus when he said dully:

" Steve Cody—I was going to tell you about him,

too.—I don't know what he's up to—I saw him and
Whitey Robbins ——"

Vargas was not consciously listening, his own brain
being crowded with thoughts. But he caught the name of
Whitey Robbins linked to Steve Cody's and jerked his
head up, demanding:

"What? What about those two?"

Tad explained jerkily. From a distance he had caught
sight of the two at the upper end of the Lee ranch. Acting sort of funny, he thought. Remember where the old
stone house ——

In a flash, oddly enough led on toward the truth by
Bird Galloway's vicious lie, Vargas pictured Spike Freedom hiding in the old house in the wilderness, and Steve
Cody finding him. His big square jaw set grimly; he stood
a moment pondering; then he leaped to his decision. He
clapped a familiar hand on Tad Harper's quivering
shoulder; he spoke as man to man, friend to friend.

"Tad, old scout," he said, with a semblance of great
frankness, "I'm in a bad hole. I'll tell you all about it
when there's time. Not now. It's that damn' double-dealin'
Cody. He's the worst crook that ever took a drink in
High Town. You know how he got the three thousan'.
What you don't know, maybe, is that he's the man that
robbed the stage the other day an' cleaned up another
seven thousan'. Now, he's tried to wipe me out an' has
killed Galloway. Nex'?" He simulated gruff laughter.
"He's on the run to kill Spike Freedom, an' Spike's a pal
o' mine ——" Now he set his two big hands on the boy's
shoulders. "I guess you're about the bes' frien' I got,
ol' kid. An' now that I'm in trouble ——"

Tad with an effort steadied himself. Here was one of the big moments in a man's life.

"What can I do, Vargas?" he asked and lifted his hands to Vargas's shoulders so that they held each other at arms' length and looked deep into each other's eyes.

"That's the kid! Frien's? Well, I guess we are.— Look here, Tad ol' man: I've got to stick here a while; I can't leave on the run or they'll be tryin' to pin this thing on me." He shifted his glance hurriedly to the figure on the floor; he couldn't leave until he was sure that Galloway was beyond talking. "But you can. Get me? You can pile on your horse an' be on your way while I'm reportin' this an' getting poor Galloway to the hospital. Beat it for the ol' stone house; get there before Steve Cody can round up Spike. Warn Spike to beat it. Tell him—— Now get this straight, Kid. Listenin'? That's good. You're a cool han', you are.—Tell Spike for me that the deal between him an' me goes; an' it goes the way he says."

Tad squeezed his hand and darted to the door.

"The main thing," Vargas called after him, "is to keep Spike from fallin' into Cody's han's. Don't let that happen, kid, no matter what else does happen. I'm trustin' you; remember that."

Those words quickened the boy's flying steps. Taking the shortest course he ran in at the rear door of Vargas's Place and straight through the house; as he ran he called out: "Steve Cody just shot Bird Galloway. Back at Vargas's room." Leaving commotion behind him he burst out at the front door and to his tethered horse.

He had ridden two or three miles before he realized

that he was unarmed. So he turned in at the ranch house, which he had meant to pass without stopping. He left his horse behind the barn and went hurriedly across the back yard, hoping to enter and leave the house without being seen; he knew Corinna would want to hold him back and there was no time to be squandered in argument. But Aunt Mary saw him through the kitchen window, and Corinna heard the whine on the screen door. She heard, too, the creak of the stairs as Tad went up to his room. As he came down, carrying his rifle, every tread of the old staircase busied itself with that chief joy of all old staircases, the announcement throughout a quiet house that someone was moving with suspicious stealth.

" What is it, Tad? " asked Corinna, waylaying him in the back hall.

" It's all right, Corinna," returned Tad. He was trying to carry himself as he felt a man should in an emergency, but his pallor and a look of high tension in his eyes betrayed him. " I've got to hurry."

" Tad Harper, you tell me! " She caught him by the arm.

" Oh, all right. Only let me go!—I'm hurrying to that old stone house; to head Steve Cody off. He's after Spike Freedom and Vargas wants Spike to get away. Steve would kill him; he's gone crazy, I guess. He's the man that robbed the stage the other day. And that's not the worst of it. He killed Bird Galloway just a little while ago."

" Tad!—He didn't! I know he didn't. He couldn't! You've made a mistake! "

He shook his head sombrely.

" Wasn't I there?—Now let me go."

He jerked free and hurried out. For an instant only Corinna stood and stared after him. Then she ran after him, calling him back. But he did not turn and did not even answer. He hurried on across the yard and about the corner of the barn. When he reappeared he was riding swiftly and soon passed out of sight among the pines beyond the pasture.

CHAPTER XX

VARGAS was all haste and presented a spectacle of the most eager solicitude in hurrying Bird Galloway to the hospital—but that haste did not begin until he was convinced that Galloway was dead. A crowd gathered and eddied excitedly; above its murmur rose Vargas's loud-mouthed protestations. Bird was a friend of his; it would go hard with the man that shot him down like a dog. Who? Why, both Vargas and Tad Harper had heard Bird saying that Steve Cody shot him.

Now not only did Vargas see Galloway carried to the hospital, but he himself brought Dr. Burton hurrying. And thus, playing his hand so craftily to catch public opinion while it was still plastic and shape it to his need, he overreached himself.

" Save him, Doc. A thousan' dollars if you do. He's a friend of mine."

The words were spoken for many to hear; they were to be filed away in memory, to be placed of record against a possible future requirement; words of the sort to chime and echo in a jury's ear. Cool, watchful of every step, Vargas awaited in confidence the expected reply: " He's dead already." But instead Dr. Burton merely pursed his lips and shook his head and set to work. He drove every-one but the nurse out of the room. Vargas mingled with the crowd in the road. He did not dare leave now. He could not go until Dr. Burton came out and made the official announcement that it was all over.

Laribee shouldered through the throng. In High Town, looking for the Judge, he had just learned from Tim that the old fellow had returned only a few minutes before, had had a word with Whitey Robbins, had glanced at a note handed him and had immediately departed for parts unknown. Tim then added what he knew of the shooting of Bird Galloway, and Laribee lost no time in going to the hospital. He and Vargas looked each other coldly in the eye as for a second Laribee hung on his heel, and each was free to reach much of the other's thought. Then he hurried into the building.

"Oh, Mr. Laribee," exclaimed the nurse who happened to be hurrying along the hall, "I'm so glad you've come. He is asking for you."

"Galloway? I'm on my way to him.—Is he badly hurt?"

"He is dying," she told him.

Laribee turned back to the door. Looking over the crowd he singled out a man whom he knew, one of the Forty, and beckoned him.

"On the run to Grady," he commanded urgently. "Tell him what has happened and that I want him here as quick as he can make it."

Bird Galloway was again conscious but almost beyond speech. He gasped, "Whisky," and Burton nodded. As Vargas had said, "there was stuff in him." He made his last tremendous effort and managed a few words to Laribee bending over him. Grady came hastening into the room in time to hear.

"Vargas——" Perhaps he thought that he had said it all, all the words which had been saying themselves over and over in his dulling brain. And his eyes, terrible in their hate and their yearning to return evil for evil, did complete his meaning. He struggled and commingled a few significant words with incoherent mutterings: "Spike Freedom—ol' rock house—quick!—*Spike knows!*"

He babbled something about Steve Cody; he muttered Tad Harper's name and Bird Galloway had finished. Desperately had he clung to his last earthly purpose, one in harmony with all his deeds; he had done what he could toward achieving it. The stubborn spirit had flickered and flared up and now died down, no longer tenanting the limp body huddled on the hospital cot.

"Game kid," said Dr. Burton, and flipped a sheet over the white face.

Laribee spoke swiftly and his eyes, which an instant before had been misty and soft with pity, suddenly flashed angrily.

"There are only four of us who have heard." Beside himself, the doctor and Grady, there was the nurse. "No one but ourselves just now need know that Galloway ever spoke. Get me?"

Grady observed him with troubled eyes. The doctor nodded curtly. Grady then hastened to agree, and a moment later he and Laribee left the room.

"Well?" demanded Grady, and came to a dead halt in the hall.

"Galloway as much as said Vargas killed him. And we'd have known that anyhow."

"He only said the name," Grady demurred.

"In a tone that was charged with accusation! Did you see his eyes?"

" Yes, but ——" He shrugged and dropped his eyes to the toe of his foot, busy with a crack in the floor. " What we surmise isn't evidence, Laribee. More than that Vargas is surrounded by a crowd of his hangers-on. If we lifted a hand there'd be a hell of a mess, and more men killed than Doc Burton could write death certificates for in what's left of the day."

" I know. Well, so long as we keep our mouths shut, Vargas can wait. We'll close in on him when we're ready; later tonight or tomorrow. In the meantime there is Spike Freedom.—Hidden out at the old stone house ——"

" Where's that? " Grady perked up his ears. A comparatively recent comer to the mountains, he naturally knew nothing of it.

" I can lead the way; we can make it in a couple of hours. Let's scare up half a dozen men we can trust and get our hands on Freedom first of all. Come ahead."

Grady could not go on demurring, and so nodded hesitantly.

" I'll go get a gun and my horse," he said, and departed by the rear door as Laribee hurried out the front.

Laribee, on the porch, cast a keen glance over the curious faces lifted toward him; a glance was enough to show him that Vargas was not among them. He hurried on and in his haste it did not suggest itself to him that Vargas might have slipped around to the back of the hospital and there have met Grady when he came out. But then, of course, he had no slightest reason to suspect the mine superintendent.

Sinister rumors flocked about High Town like bats disturbed in some cave populous with their kind. They centered about Bird Galloway and rayed out in many directions to touch Chink Johnson, Vargas, Tad Harper, Spike Freedom and particularly Steve Cody. For the most definite bit of misinformation given out had been Vargas's statement that it was Steve who shot Galloway. This report reached Laribee before he left town, and troubled him. He did not believe it; he held in his own heart that it was Vargas himself who was the killer, and with reason understood by Laribee; yet he was puzzled and concerned. And he was still further perturbed by the frequent mention of Tad Harper's name. While no one seemed to know what Tad had to do with it all, still it remained that many connected him vaguely with the afternoon's tragedy, and it was common report that he had dashed to his horse and ridden out of town in some wild haste of his own.

Thus when Laribee rode out of town accompanied by a hastily gathered handful of the stern Forty, with Grady a sombre companion stirrup to stirrup with him, he was too profoundly meditative to dwell upon any lukewarmness on the mine superintendent's part.

"Vargas is up to something," spoke up Laribee, after a long silence save for the impatient drum of hoofs and creak of saddle leather, the silvery chink of spur and bridle chains. "He slipped away while we were inside."

"Yes?" said Grady, cocking his head about to look shrewdly at his companion.

"Galloway gave us the right tip. It's Spike Freedom we need. Somehow he ties into this whole racket. When we get him we get to the bottom of a dirty mess. If we can't swing Vargas for one thing maybe we can for another. But what if Vargas knows? He'd be trying to beat us to Spike, wouldn't he? "

" Well, we've the head start."

" We'll go by the Lee ranch," said Laribee. " It's on our way, and we'll check up there on young Harper. He seems mixed in somehow. We've got to keep him out of this."

Grady made no answer and they hammered on. Now and then, with Laribee leading and familiar with every foot of the way, they left the main trails for shortcuts; it was Laribee's fear that it would grow dark before they came to their ultimate destination. Already the sun was low and a high wind trailed thickening veils of cloud across the sky. None the less he was determined on a momentary stop at the Lee ranch house, hoping to head off Tad there and so to restrain him from any foolish interference.

At a swinging gallop they swept out of the fringing pines and into the open meadow from which they caught the first glimpse of the old ranch house; at the moment a broad band of sunlight streaked the grassy lands and sent the riders' spindling shadows leaping before them, while the house among the trees stood in a half gloom. Laribee, looking forward eagerly, thought that he saw a figure running out by the corral, but whether Tad or someone else he could not in the least make out. Reluctantly he touched his horse's heaving flanks with his spurs; he had ridden hard into town, where he had meant to rest his horse before starting back to the ranch, and now as he shook out his reins and dashed on decided to change here to one of the Lee horses.

He saw the figure out by the corral stop, pause and then dart back to the house and to a meeting with him and the men accompanying him as they pulled up by the porch. It was Corinna and she, filled with apprehensions, startled at seeing so many men arriving in such haste, groping fearfully for some connection between their arrival and Tad's coming and going, awaited them breathlessly.

" What is it? " she called out before the last horse slid to a quivering standstill. " What has happened? "

" Nothing for you to worry about," Laribee answered her, quick with his lover's eyes to mark the pallor of her cheeks and the alarm in her look. " But tell me first, where's Tad? "

" He's gone! I was just going for a horse to follow him. He was here a minute ago —— Oh, David, it isn't true, is it? "

" What isn't true? What has Tad told you? "

" That—that Steve Cody —— Oh, he didn't do it, did he, David? "

They were all looking at her curiously. She saw only David Laribee and his fine eyes, just now dark with trouble.

" Just what is it, Corinna? " he questioned gently. " What about Steve? "

" He didn't—he didn't kill that man! I know he didn't! "

" Galloway? "

She nodded miserably, her hands twisting, eloquent of an emotion akin to despair.

" Tad said that Steve shot Galloway? " snapped Laribee. And when she could only nod again, not daring to trust her trembling lips, he demanded, sharper than ever: "What does Tad know about it?"

"He says—he says he was there. But —— Oh, I know there is some mistake!"

"My God," groaned Laribee.

Grady, straining forward in the saddle, cried out suddenly:

"That's what they're saying in town. Maybe Cody did do it."

For a moment Laribee was speechless, and the men behind him stirred uneasily and looked at one another questioningly. But the moment passed and Laribee jerked his head up, saying curtly:

"I don't know. We don't know anything yet. But tell me about Tad. What's he up to?"

"I could tell that he was terribly excited. He got his rifle and hurried away. He is going to the old stone house at the river. He says that Spike Freedom is up there and that Steve is after him. And now Tad and Steve—they'll kill each other!" Her eyes, round with agony, were fixed beseechingly on Laribee's. "You must stop them somehow!"

"You mean Tad and Steve are gunning for each other?"

"All I know is that it is something about Spike Freedom, and that Tad says Steve means to shoot him, and Tad will try to hold Steve off—he'll do anything for that terrible Vargas ——"

With the horsemen facing her and the house, she alone faced across the meadow through which they had ridden.

Now she broke off suddenly; Laribee saw her stiffen from head to foot and it seemed to him that her pallid face turned even whiter. She lifted a trembling hand to point.

" There he comes now! "

All turned and looked back. A horse and rider were just emerging from the pines, not yet in the broad swathe of sunlight. It might be anyone arriving, provided it was a man who rode hard.

" Tad? "

" No. It's Steve Cody! "

" At this distance you can't be sure of anything," contended Laribee, with narrowed eyes intent on the oncoming horseman.

" It's Steve," cried Corinna. " I am sure. Oh, don't let them ——"

An instant only did Laribee hesitate. It might be Steve, it might be anyone, even to Vargas himself. It was a moment of groping confusion created by Corinna's reluctant repetition of Tad's accusation. But out from confusion certain facts stood forth: Spike Freedom should be gathered in before he was warned and took to his heels; Tad must be safeguarded from his own headlong folly; Tad and Steve must not meet just now.

" Quick, boys," commanded Laribee. " To the back of the house, out of sight. Whoever it is, he probably hasn't seen us here in the shadows. Snap into it; I'll be with you."

He himself hung back only to say to Corinna, gravely and gently, yet with heavy emphasis:

" You're right; Steve and Tad mustn't meet until we know what it's all about. If this is Steve, will you manage somehow to get him to come into the house, Corinna? If you'll do that—it may save a life, you know ——"

" Yes, yes! Oh, I'll do anything! "

She scarcely knew that Laribee had left her, to join the others behind the house. She did not know when Aunt Mary came out on the porch and called to her. She stood on the steps and watched the rider come sweeping on. How had David Laribee, even at a distance, failed to recognize that rider? No other man in the world carried himself quite as this one did—gallantly—like a knight ——

" I won't believe it! I won't! It's too terrible —— There is some mistake; I know there is ——"

But no mistake in it being Steve coming closer swiftly, borne along by those long rushing strides of Blue Boy's; Steve drawn up now close to where she stood on the steps, his face very stern, those unfathomable black eyes of his fixed on her face, taking in everything, giving out nothing. Steve who had enshrined her in his heart and who now strove to look on her as on one who meant nothing to him.

" They told me in town that your brother had just ridden out this way," he was saying quietly, as though there were no such things in the world as strife and murder and grim retaliation. " Is he here? "

" What do you want with him? " she asked fearfully. Her heart was beating wildly; fragmentary thoughts were flashing through her brain; pictures like nightmares formed and dissolved there. She heard a board creaking somewhere behind her; she turned swiftly. No, it was not Aunt Mary; that mystified and nervously anxious individual stood near by, stock still. Someone in the house ——

"There is something going on," Steve was telling her after the casual fashion in which a man might remark that it was a fine day, "that Tad had best not mix in. If he is here —— But you haven't told me. Is he inside? "

"And you haven't told me what the trouble is? "

"It's about Vargas," he retorted. "I'm after him and I am going to get him ——"

"Vargas isn't here. He hasn't been here."

"No. But I think he's headed for the upper end of your ranch. Tad might throw in with him —— He mustn't! "

"No. He mustn't! I —— Tad was here a minute ago but ——" Oh, she hated to do this thing. It was, after all, no matter how she might name it, betrayal. Judas work. And with Steve Cody the victim. She looked at him piteously, as though begging him to help her. But in his face she read only a stern, bleak determination. She clenched her hands and went on with it. "Will you come into the house a minute? "

He looked at her curiously, but shook his head.

"I'm sorry, Miss Lee, but I've got to hurry. I wouldn't have stopped at all, but I thought I might save Tad a bit of trouble."

"But just a minute! Please! If you will —— Will you, if I tell you you may save a life that way? Tad's life and maybe —— Will you? "

"I'll have to hurry." He dismounted, left Blue Boy standing, and ran up the steps with her. "Hello, Aunt

Mary," he said and at Corinna's heels stepped into the living room.

There were two men at each side of the door, ready for him. With four pairs of hands on his arms he stood rigid, his eyes hard on their eyes, a faint tinge of color running up into his cheeks. Besides the four, there was Laribee confronting him.

"Take it easy, Steve," said Laribee. "I'm sorry, old man; but there was no time for a lot of questions. At least, this way, no one is hurt."

"Suppose you put a name to it, Laribee?" said Steve. He did not look at Corinna, who shrank away from what she had done, but into Laribee's eyes now, and in his gaze was only a high scornful sort of disgust.

"Somebody killed Galloway, Steve."

"So I heard."

"Was it you?"

"No."

"Where are you headed for now?"

"Is it any business of yours?"

"We're making it so."

"Well, then, I'm after Vargas. If you'll mind your own business I'll get him."

"You think he is on his way to the old stone house?"

"You seem to know a lot!—Yes."

All the while Laribee stared back at him, the color hot in his face.

"Steve," he said soberly, "I may be making a mistake. I can't tell. But there's no time to waste talking things over. We've delayed too long already. You will stay here. If Vargas is up there, we'll get him."

He gave a sign to the men holding their captive and without another look turned and went out to rejoin Grady, who had preferred to remain with the horses. A man shook out a coiled rope; Steve was led to a chair and fast bound, his ankles to the chair legs, his hands at his back. They removed his weapons and left him. And only when they were gone did he look at Corinna. She stood grief stricken, the tears rolling down her cheeks.

" A pretty piece of work you've done, Miss Lee," he told her coldly. Then, with a queer, quizzical sort of tight-lipped smile he turned to Aunt Mary. " And you, Aunt Mary? You don't mean to tell me you were in on this deal too, do you? "

" No! No, Steve Cody, I ain't! I've done a many things I'm shamed of; not this, though."

Corinna ran out of the room.

CHAPTER XXI

HAVING achieved what she so desperately wanted, Corinna no longer wanted it. Not that she was more fickle than the other sons and daughters of Adam and Eve; merely that, often enough, success has a bitter taste. Only by bringing down the red apple from the tree does one come to know whether it is as desirable in the hand as on the topmost bough; whether crisp and juicy and edible or wormy.

She had succeeded in keeping Tad and Steve apart; perhaps she had saved both lives? Or one from death and the other from the stigma of murder? But as she watched the little party of horsemen speeding away among the timbered hills, vanishing in the thickening shadows of the pines, Laribee riding gallantly ahead—she noted that he had changed from his jaded horse to Steve's Blue Boy—it was not upon the fine success of her achievement that she brooded. Her thoughts leaped ahead to the moment when they would come riding back.

They would go to Steve where he sat bound, and it was quite as though her fingers had knotted the rope. They would say to him: "You stole three thousand dollars which, more than any other man, you should have returned to its owner; you robbed the stage, and took another seven thousand dollars. You, it is reported, have done many another thing best left undone. Did you kill Boney Marks? We know you shot his friend, Whitey

259

Robbins. Did you today kill Bird Galloway? It is said that you did. Tad Harper says he saw you."

And, bound, they would lead him away.

How much of all this did she herself believe of him? Why, she *knew* him guilty on two counts; her own eyes had served her. And should she doubt Tad's latest accusation? Yet making this concession, for it was a concession, she merely yielded to an imperative cold, logical functioning of reason—and since when has reason dictated to the young, the romantic, the hopeful? Far stronger was something else, the whispering of the spirit within. Call it instinct? Or intuition?

Call it by any name, there remained the Something which had stirred in her dreams, when her golden knight, with visor down, came riding to her succor. There was Steve, perhaps not altogether as he actually was, but as her " maiden meditations, fancy free " made him. Some mystic tie bound him and her. . . . Had he not come racing to her when, though miles away, he had felt the menace of Vargas towering over her?

Head down, steps lagging, she started back toward the house. Head up, steps quickened, eyes glowing, she returned to him.

" Aunt Mary! " she cried, seeing what was afoot.

" Never you mind, an' don't call me your Aunt Mary," snapped the housekeeper. She was busy at Steve's side; Corinna saw the keen-bladed knife hastily brought from the kitchen.

The girl ran to her and caught her hand.

" No! You shall not turn him loose! I—I want to talk with him. And alone, Aunt Mary. Give me that knife! "

"Hmph! Give you the knife? Mos' likely, the pore boy bein' all tangled up like this, you'd cut his throat."

Corinna's eyes began to blaze. The two who watched her were treated to the not altogether novel spectacle of an attractive young woman metamorphosed in a flash into a raging fury.

"Go!" She snatched again at the knife and, catching Aunt Mary helpless in a moment of stupefaction, secured it; the near-miracle attending the act lay in the fact that no one was wounded. "Go into the other room, I tell you. I've got to talk with Steve alone!"

Steve, with that faint ironical smile on his lips, nodded and Aunt Mary departed; at every step she looked back; she merely crossed the threshold into the kitchen; she did not close the door. But neither of the two left behind noticed what she did or where she went.

"I am going to free you," said Corinna. "I am the one who must do it. I hate myself for what I did. I couldn't help it. I wanted to save Tad—to save you —— It seemed the only way."

He said nothing, but the smile left his lips and a curious expression dawned in his eyes. Corinna knelt on the floor and cut the lashings about his ankles.

"You will have to go," she was saying as she worked, her face hidden from him. "I am the one who told that it was you who robbed the stage. But I told only the Judge, and he is a friend of yours, isn't he? I told him, too, that you had not returned the money you took from Tad. You see, they know all these things. You'd have no chance if you stayed. You will know best what other things they know about you ——"

" Tad told you I killed Galloway? " he asked quietly.

The brown head nodded; he could not see her face yet, but somehow he had the suspicion of tears.

" Why are you turning me loose? "

" I have to," she answered miserably. " You must go."

She finished with the bonds about his legs and stood up, going in haste behind him. She winced as she saw how the rope cut into his poor wrists. A faint, stifled exclamation of pity burst from her. She worked feverishly.

" I am sorry ——"

" You, sorry! " he exclaimed bitterly. He rose and stood chafing his wrists. " I hope you'll never know what the word means. To have you turn against me this way—you ——"

" They left your pistol in the other room. I am going to give it back to you." She ran for it and coming back still held it away from him, while she pleaded: " Only promise me you'll never use it unless you have to—to save your own life ——"

Whereas he could, simply enough, have snatched the thing from her, he did not appear to think of that.

" To save my own life," he said, and laughed at her. " And what do you care about the saving of my life? "

" I do care! That was why—it was as much for you as for Tad ——"

He put out his hand and she gave him his weapon. He slid it into his holster and went to where his hat had fallen to the floor.

" I should thank you? For turning me loose? "

" Forgive me! " wept Corinna. And when he went to the door, she stood looking small and frail and pitiful, one over whom the roaring wheels of the great Juggernaut of life were about to go their crushing way. His back was turned; she lifted her arms toward him. " Good-by," she said, in a voice so low that Aunt Mary, all ears, missed it.

But Steve heard. And he whirled and came back to her with long hurrying strides. He caught her hands and stood looking down into her uplifted eyes. He looked very stern, his jaw set, his brows drawn down.

" I love you, Corinna! Love you, do you hear? Love you so that there is nothing else left in life; just you."

He had meant nothing like this; dimly, in some confused, shadow-darkened corner of his brain he knew it for rank disloyalty to her, to Laribee. Laribee, who was fair and square and aboveboard, who did what he did because, in the light he had, it was the right thing. Laribee, who loved her, too; Laribee, whom she loved.

Those were considerations which stood off at the side. The great thing, the compelling thing now was the current which bore him along. He loved her and she had whispered, " Good-by."

No; he had meant nothing like this. He did not even know how it came about. There was something stronger, fiercer than himself dictating now; something to make even fate stand aside with all lesser considerations. He had Corinna in his arms. Corinna! The wonder of it, the glory of it. The terrible agony of it! He abandoned himself to the moment; he crushed her so close to him that he knew he hurt her. When she looked up into his eyes the madness upon him swept on up and up into the greater madness. He kissed her ——

So suddenly did he release her that she almost fell. At the door he said: " Forgiveness? " He went on. He did not say good-by. His voice in the one word he spoke, a word from which he had meant to go on to completion of a thought and did not, rang unpleasantly. Whether it jeered and mocked, whether it broke on the keen edge of despair, none could know. He ran down the steps. There was Laribee's horse; he scarcely marked that it was not his own. He threw himself into the saddle and rode away. Curiously, only when he struck saddle leather, did he remember Vargas.

Corinna did not move; she could not. Aunt Mary came back into the room and she did not know. The hoof beats outside hammered briefly and were gone.

" Steve! " she cried then, and started to the door. " Steve! Come back to me! "

Aunt Mary gathered her tenderly to her deep, motherly bosom.

CHAPTER XXII

IT was for but a few golden moments that the Judge abandoned himself utterly to the long-anticipated ecstasy of riding a horse. During that all too brief time he experienced the richness and fulness of life; he was a man who at last stood on top of the world, which was a way of saying that he was in a saddle that had something else than mule under it. But almost immediately he grew sober and frowningly thoughtful; later he'd revel in horses all he pleased, now he had to respect the high card. It was Vargas who had killed his old friend, and Steve knew and was after him.

He told himself that no doubt hell was poppin' right now, with Steve closing in on Vargas. Well, let 'er pop. Steve could handle the situation. But it was unthinkable that with such an event afoot the old Judge should be out of it.

He headed back to High Town but bent his course a little out of its way in order to pass by the Lee ranch; he'd drop a word there of what was happening and have a message carried on from there to Laribee's ranch; certainly he'd arrange to have someone hurry up to Steve's cabin and lend a hand toward making sure that Spike Freedom didn't come any of his slippery business over the Indian.

He had barely struck into the rough lands of the upper end of the Lee ranch when he caught a glimpse of several riders, hurrying figures swooping down a thinly timbered slope, and waved his hat and whooped at them. When they stopped at his call and seemed to hesitate, like men who are impatient of interference and yet curious, he spurred toward them, waving his hat and shouting for them to hold on. He made out Blue Boy among the other horses and guessed that there rode Steve after Vargas; he could only suppose that somehow Vargas, with his ear always to the ground, had caught a rumor and was making a run for it.

But it was David Laribee; at his back were Grady and some other men and they were plainly in haste and resented even a moment squandered in waiting for him.

" How come you're ridin' Blue Boy? " asked the Judge when he saw his error. " Where's Steve? " His eyes did not tarry with Laribee's face; they flicked across the others, taking swift stock of them; longest they rested, very innocent in the seeming, on Grady. " Hello, Grady," he added casually, quite as though he knew no more of Grady's activities now than he had known two days before.

" We're in a hurry, Judge," said Laribee. " Ride along and I'll tell you what's up."

Under normal circumstances Laribee's tale would have required a deal of explanatory matter which now was passed over; before they had covered a hundred yards the Judge had most of the essential facts: Bird Galloway had been killed, whether by Vargas or by Steve Cody. Dying, Bird had sent them after Spike Freedom; he was at the old stone hut and had something on Vargas ——

" Whoa! " yelled the Judge, and they came to a second

stop. "Spike ain't over yonder a-tall. I jus' come from him.—Wait a shake, boys."

Despite their impatience he forced them to wait what might be accounted several " shakes " while he sought to get his bearings. This was Steve's play, and he did not intend to mess it all up. And then there was Grady to ponder on; Grady, who rode with the hunters and trafficked with the quarry.

" H'm," said the Judge. " Let's see. You say somebody killed Galloway, an' you don't know whether it was Vargas or Steve? How come? "

" We'll go into that later," said Laribee. " We want Spike now before he slides out on us."

" Where's Steve? "

Laribee, obviously finding little joy in the recital, told him in a score of words. The Judge, his face all puckered up, made no comment beyond one involuntary snort.

" I'll tell you boys what we got to do," he said with exasperating deliberation, and the more slowly he spoke the faster did his thoughts race. " Yep; I'll tell you. We got to play this han' right—Spike, now; it's Spike we got to make sure of. That's dead easy. He's up to Steve's cabin, an' he's tied an' there's not much chance of his gettin' away, jus' the same, we got to make sure. We don't need all of us to go chasin' in on him. One man c'n han'le that baby, roped han' an' foot like he is. We other boys hang back a shake an' try to figger things out. Yep; that's her. Now, who'll scoot on ahead an' make sure that Spike don't get away—that he ain't already made a get-away? "

" That's sense! " There spoke Grady for the first time,

hasty and eager. " As the Judge says, he might manage to get loose. I'll ride on ahead and make sure of him. All right, Laribee? "

It was the Judge who answered. He nodded.

" Fine, Grady. You do that. Bring him on down to town. We'll mos' likely be able to han'le the situation then."

Grady hurried away. The Judge watched him well out of ear-shot and then addressed the others much as a testy old schoolmaster might have talked to a flock of boys whom he'd apprehended making the first step toward truancy.

" You darn pack o' bunglin' boobies! Now listen to me an' listen good, 'cause I ain't goin' to say it twice: When you put your rope on Steve Cody you monkeyed with the fines' squares' gent that I know, an' the one and only real sheriff this here county ever had. Got that? Now, listen some more."

And in words which no longer loitered he told them of his visit to Madrone, of the money returned to the district attorney, and of Steve's letter. He told them of Spike and the evidence he could give against Vargas. And, with enthusiasm, he told them of the part Grady had played.

" But you let Grady go to Spike! "

" I give him the chance an' you boys saw how he jumped at it! All he means to do is run a knife over Spike's ropes and somehow make it clear to him he better start for somewhere a long ways off. He thinks we're out of it an' that he's drawin' all the luck. He won't hardly look over his shoulder, in the rush he's in. So now we follow on, huh? We get some dead wood on that jasper, catchin' him red-handed at his dirty work. Come ahead, boys; he's got enough head start."

Laribee alone held back.

" I wish I'd known," he said quietly. " But I guess Steve had to do it his way. So Grady was standing in with Vargas all along?—That poor kid Galloway didn't have a chance! "

" Same as if Grady himself had killed him," muttered the Judge. " He's a damn' accessory, an' that's worse'n bein' the man that pulls the trigger. Well, come ahead, Laribee."

" No. You don't need me; there's enough of you. I'm going on now to the old rock house. Tad Harper's up there, and I've got to talk to him. The kid's all set to get in trouble. I'll tell him about Steve. And then I want to hurry back and get the ropes off Steve—I guess I'll be ashamed of that fool job as long as I live."

" I ought to go along with you," conceded the Judge reluctantly, his eyes strained in the direction Grady had taken. " But I can't take chances. Better be ready for a chance meetin' with Vargas, you know, Dave."

" That's all right. Vargas won't start anything until we do."

So the Judge and the rest of the party left Laribee and rode on after Grady. They rode hard, knowing that Grady would make all haste, and when at last they came in sight of Steve's cabin they saw Grady's horse standing tied at the door. So they made their wide circuit, keeping to the pines, passing behind the barn where they left their horses, and approaching the cabin stealthily on foot.

Grady had encountered his first obstacle when he discovered that Steve's Indian guarded the prisoner. But Grady was desperate; none knew better than he that the old saying that there was honor among thieves sounded well but meant nothing. Let the law clamp down on Vargas, and Vargas would pull down his fellow lawbreakers like Samson wrecking the pillars of the temple. He prevailed on the Indian to let him have a word with the prisoner; was he not Grady of the Glory Girl, a man of importance, a man certainly for a rather bewildered Indian ranch hand to yield to in small matters? But the Indian was stubborn on one point; he would not leave the cabin. Grady shrugged and made the best of it. Later if he said one thing and this shiftless hulk of an Indian said the reverse, whose word would carry the weight?

"You've got to beat it, Spike," he said hurriedly. "I've got a hundred dollars in my pocket; that's yours. Tonight, wherever you say, Vargas will send you ten thousand. I'll bring it myself. You've got to go while the trail's open."

There was some talk back and forth; there were mutterings from Steve's Indian. Grady whirled on him with a snarl and a torrent of abuse.

"You crazy fool," he stormed at him, "I know what I'm doing.—Your boss, Steve Cody, sent me; he's changed his mind. He wants this man to go."

The Judge looked at the men standing by his side; they nodded to each other. A moment later Grady, bending over Spike knife in hand, whipped about to see several forms filing in at the door, the Judge at their head.

"He was trying to get away," cried Grady.

" Yeah," said the Judge. " Well, he won't. Neither will you. You damn' accessory!—All right, boys. Rope him good; then bring the two of 'em along. You don't need me any longer, I reckon, so I'll ride ahead. Pick me up at the Lee place; I'll tell Steve you're comin'." He went to the door as the others closed in on a stupefied Grady. " By the way, boys," he stopped to say, " there's a mule here belongs to Spike. See that he rides it. An' you might try if ol' Heart's-ease will carry double; if so there's room on him for Grady too."

When the Judge rode into the Lee yard Corinna and Aunt Mary came hastening out to him. Somewhere in the back of a brain which was actively given up to graver matters the Judge harbored the queer little flick of realization that neither of them even noted how he was mounted; but then they would not even have remarked upon it had he come galloping to them on a broomstick. At first sight of them he read distress signals in their precipitancy; he accosted them cheerily and reassuringly even before he knew definitely what it was that brought them hurrying to meet him.

" Everything's fine an' the goose hangs high," he told them as he stopped his horse and sat looking down into the two faces raised toward him. " As far's I know the sun an' moon ain't been scraped out'n the sky, an' they say the worl' does go on turnin'.—Where's Steve? "

" Gone," said Corinna. " I turned him loose."

" Good girl! " He leaned out of the saddle and patted her head. " You're one human bein' in this part o' the worl' as has a set o' brains an' uses 'em. Fine."

"No," said Corinna miserably. "I'm not fine. It was I who tricked him so that they could tie him. Oh, I'm ashamed!"

"So's Laribee, I jes' learned," said the Judge drily. "Well, at that, bein' ashamed now an' then don't hurt anybody. Sort o' trues 'em up, I'd say.—Now, what's got you worried? What's put that long look on your pretty face?"

"I am afraid!" She spoke very quietly in a hushed voice, which sounded flat and toneless; the late afternoon was passing into the quiet hour of early dusk, and her face gleamed whitely through the gathering shadows. She went on to tell him of her fears; they were all for Tad—and for Steve. Who knew what was happening up yonder in the woods? Tad meant to stand between Steve and Spike Freedom, and Steve was not the man to let any stand in his way. Then there was Vargas.

"Can't you do something?" she asked, with a first hint of eagerness. She had come to place so much confidence in the old fellow and now, with all life a-tangle, it seemed to her that his hand and his alone might find the right threads and get them clear.

"There's nothin' goin' to happen," he told her. "Tad an' Steve, they'll be all right. Laribee's headed up that-away, too; jes' saw him. He's more'n got there; had time to get there an' back since I met up with him.—Gettin' dark ——"

"It won't be real dark for an hour," she insisted. "Maybe you could do something!"

"Mebbe," said the Judge. "Anyhow, don't you worry; you're worked up an' imaginin' things. It'll come out all right; notice it gen'rally does. Takes a long time, sometimes; I've knowed a thing to go wrong for eight years an' then break right. Yes; I'll poke along an' haze all them young wild uns back home to you, Miss Corinna. You jes' run along in the house an'—— Hello; here comes one of 'em now, ridin' like there was a fire some place. Now we'll get news."

"It's Tad!" cried Corinna, and there was a little catch in her voice as she added, "Oh, thank God, Tad's all right."

"Of course he's all right; didn't I say so?" said the comforting Judge. "Everybody's all right an'—— Hey there; what the devil! Don't ride a man down!"

Even with the dusk coming on there was ample light to see Tad's face; it was deathly white and his eyes were staring blankly. He slid down from the saddle and stood with his rifle grasped in his hands, looking wildly from one to another of them. They waited for him to speak but it seemed that he couldn't find a word to say. Corinna caught him by the arm and began to shake him, knowing now that something was wrong, demanding that he tell her what had happened. Then all of a sudden as he stood looking at her she fell back from him and into her own eyes came a look of horror that duplicated the look in his.

"You—you killed him!" she whispered.

"I killed him," said Tad. "I—— Oh, God!" He seemed to realize for the first time that he still carried his rifle; he hurled it away from him in loathing and put his face in his hands and began to sob.

Corinna shrank still farther away from him; she put up her hands as though to thrust him away, then let them drop heavily to her sides. She looked beyond him into the woods where daylight was dying. Dead. Tad had killed him. It was not only that day was dying now in the forests. The whole world was going dark, eternally dark.

The Judge began shouting at Tad: " What'n hell are you talkin' about? Killed who? Talk, can't you? Who'd you kill? "

" It was at the bridge. I called to him to stop an' he came on. I couldn't hear what he said, the water made so much noise. I saw his horse through the bushes; it was Blue Boy. I thought it was Steve—the sun was down in the cañon——"

" Not Steve! " cried Corinna. " Then——"

" It was Laribee," said Tad with a groan. " Good old Laribee." Tears at last gushed from his eyes and rolled down his face. " I thought it was Steve and that he was going to shoot. I—I shot first——"

The Judge scrambled back into the saddle.

" A man don't always die 'cause he's got a bullet in him," he called back to them and shot his spurs home.

Tad only hid his face in his hands again, saying dully:

" I shot him through the head. I wish to God I was dead."

" Steve isn't dead! " whispered Corinna. For the instant that the realization flashed through her mind nothing else seemed to matter. Emotions came too swiftly; not all could register at once; the greater crowded out the lesser. The golden, glorious thing was that Steve was alive.

But immediately came reaction. Other things did matter. David Laribee, dear old David Laribee—out there where the forest was growing dark. She looked at Tad and shuddered. He was heartbroken; he was being crushed under a grief altogether too poignant, too heavy for any one pair of shoulders. Tad, her brother. He was as much alone as though only he and his guilt, like his shadow, inhabited a universe. She stirred; she must go to Tad. She couldn't. She could only remember David Laribee as he had left her, going to save Tad from getting into trouble.

CHAPTER XXIII

So great a bitterness welled up in Steve Cody that for a little while it jaundiced his whole outlook on life. His vision was blurred and distorted. So hot an anger flared up within him that it was ready to consume all humanity. It was, to begin with, self-anger. It meant far more to him than it would have meant to most men that he had lost all control of himself, for self-control began as a gambler's mainstay and became the backbone of his code. Something had swept him from all his old moorings. It was his part, knowing that Corinna loved elsewhere and was loved in return, to keep his own secret so securely that never a soul in all the world should ever remotely suspect it. Yet, see what he had done!

Riding furiously, he abandoned trails to right and left, taking all the shortcuts he knew. He was grateful for one thing, for one thing only: ahead of him was Vargas. And he strove to clear his mind of all but Vargas.

Yet at first, with his anger flaring up so bright and hot, his mind would, despite all effort, switch back to Corinna and to Laribee. He thought that he had never hated a man as at that moment he hated David Laribee. Why could not the officious fool content himself with his own affairs? Surely he had enough to occupy any man! Was there not Corinna?—Yet, at a supreme hour for Steve Cody, he must come with his rope and his cursed interference, giving Vargas every chance to get his foul house in order. That Laribee had been actuated by all high intentions did not in the least mollify him; that he himself, playing his self-appointed rôle of consort of law-breakers, had misled Laribee made no difference. Laribee was an insufferable, meddlesome ass—and therefore, behold, Corinna loved him! He tried to laugh at that. He tried to call them two of a kind ——

In town, where he had arrived shortly after Galloway died, he had heard only wild, jumbled rumors. But from what he picked up there, from what he had heard at the ranch house from Corinna and from Laribee, from his new understanding of the relationship of Vargas and Spike Freedom, he was in high hope of finding Vargas at the old hut, or of intercepting him.

" It's Vargas I want," he muttered. " The rest go by the board."

But first he came on Laribee. It was when he was riding more warily, only a short way from the river where the old bridge spanned it. He made out through the trees a horse stirring nervously; it was Blue Boy. He had forgotten to find fault with Laribee for helping himself to the horse; now he chose to make a crime of what at another time would have been passed over with a shrug. He spurred closer and his anger which he had fought down burned high again. Then he saw that something was wrong with Laribee. He was down ——

The horse which Steve rode sniffed and took fright; danced and whirled and would not be brought closer. But even before he dismounted Steve caught a fleeting glimpse of a white face with a great smear across it. " Vargas's work again! " was the thought to flash through his brain.

His wariness returned to him; Vargas might be close at hand now, still and watchful behind any tree, steeped in blood lust, a natural killer who would miss no chance to kill. But the woods seemed very still and empty; stare as he would this way and that Steve saw no other horse and no sign of another man than himself and the sprawling figure. He ran forward. Laribee's eyes were open and staring.

It was as though an icy hand closed about Steve's heart, for he thought that Laribee was dead. But instantly he saw that the staring eyes moved; they were clouded and confused and at first could not focus properly. A frown gathered Laribee's brows as he strove to force his eyes to obey his will. Steve understood that he had been stunned and was only now gropingly returning to consciousness.

" Vargas? "

" No," said Laribee heavily. " Not Vargas. I ——"

" Lie still, man! The bullet must have glanced." His fingers began a gentle search for the wound; all he could find was a deep gash across the forehead. And though it had poured forth all that blood to encarnadine Laribee's brow and face, still of itself it was no serious matter, and did not look like a bullet wound at all.

" That's nothing." Laribee seemed stronger, clearer in mind now. " I guess I hit my head on a rock—when I fell, you know."

" You fell? "

Then he saw how one of Laribee's hands fumbled weakly at his side. Steve ripped the shirt away and found the true wound; a rifle ball had cut through Laribee's side.

"Why, man, you're as good as new," he cried in tremendous relief. "Good boy, Dave. Wait a shake; we'll get a sort of bandage around you to keep you from bleeding. I'll have a wagon up here in no time at all. You just lie still." And while he worked with a strip from Laribee's shirt and other strips from his own, he demanded eagerly: "Not Vargas, you say? Who, then?"

"It was —— It was a mistake, Steve. Sure, I'm going to be all right. I'm all right now. It was just the rap I got on the head, pitching out of the saddle, like a fool. The impact, I suppose ——"

"A mistake? That doesn't let anybody out! A man who makes a mistake like this —— Who was it, Dave?"

"Help me up, Steve. I've got to ride back."

Steve talked with him after the fashion which has for some obscure reason long been attributed to a Dutch Uncle. But Laribee, seeming to force new strength into his battered body with every breath he drew, calling upon the last atom of that strength which resides in a man's will, would not hear him. Very wobbly on his feet, leaning on Steve and clutching at a saddle horn, he muttered stubbornly:

"I've got to go to Corinna, you know.—She'll be terribly worried."

Had he said, "Tad shot me," Steve would have understood how that worry might be for someone else than just David Laribee. As it was, he thought that he understood. And, if nothing else was clear, there was no question about what Laribee would do. Looking more dead than alive he was at last in the saddle.

" Good old Dave," thought Steve, looking wistfully after the slowly departing figure. " I was the fool, to find fault with what he did. A man four-square and fine—and deserving of the best. And that's what he's going to get. Another man, in his boots right now, would be lying here, thinking of dying! Not Laribee.—Happy days, old-timer! "

And there, like a puff of smoke vanishing down the wind, went his animosity and all his unreasonable if natural anger. He had even sent Laribee off on Blue Boy. Now, returning to his own duty, he went back to the other horse and hurried on toward the river. As he rode he took down the tie rope from the saddle. Either he or Vargas would soon be at the end of all mundane considerations, or Vargas would ride back with him, both hands tied to the horn of a saddle.

" It's a hunch," he said, profoundly thoughtful. " It's not a question of tomorrow or next day or next week; it's today. Now. I get Vargas or Vargas gets me.—He'll be waiting for me—' At the End of the Road.'—This is the last day for one of us."

Which one?

He dallied with the riddle. Was the thing already decided? Somewhere, where the looms of human destiny busied themselves with all the patterns, bright and dark, was the answer already woven into the fabric, the pattern finished, the archetype done and awaiting its duplication down here on earth where men strove somewhat blindly and fed themselves on the folly of thinking that theirs were the hands that molded fate? A strange mood fastened itself upon him. He began to feel that he was a little weary with life as he found it. It had been full enough and sufficiently meaningful until lately. And now? He shrugged. Full for a man like Laribee who, though sorely wounded, rode eagerly to a pair of arms that awaited him. But for Steve? Once there had been cards, but even these of late had begun to pall, the red of hearts and diamonds no longer the vivid, exhilarating hue of leaping life itself, the black of spades and clubs no longer the intriguing, compelling black of mystery that lured.

Vargas or himself, which?

" Why not both! "

And so to a gambler's " hunch " was welded another. Himself and Vargas.—He was in the thick of the timber which clothed the banks of the gorge. He dismounted and, carrying his rope in his left hand, his revolver in his right, he made his way forward. The rush and roar of the river mounted to his ears and was like the confused throbbing of distant drums all but obliterating the hushed oratorio of some mighty, far-away orchestra. He began to catch glimpses of the river, black with on-coming night.

" I wonder! " said Steve.

There was so much to wonder about. At a moment like this it all swept over a man. At each step approaching his father's murderer, his thoughts, touching everything, turned to his father with the rest. A stern, hard man but, like David Laribee, four-square and fine. There was that day when he had ridden with his son to the mountain ranch, making of it a birthday gift, stocked with horses like Blue Boy. They had jogged elbows that day! There were those other days when a self-willed man and a willful boy clashed. The old Judge had said it all; they were just too much alike, that was all. Yet——

" If it were all to do over again! "

Well, who knew? The black river was winding on into a blacker night now, but the morning would come again, glorious, bright, confident, glad morning, with the river running clear and bright again.

" I'll get him first," said Steve.

A moment later he caught his first glimpse of the bridge. And then he saw Vargas.

Vargas had only now crossed over. Evidently he did not mean to return this way, for he was trying to get his horse across the swollen stream. He stood on the bridge, at its farther end, and with one hand clung to his horse's tie rope, dragging at the animal as it swam and lost footing and struggled again to reach his side. Steve's heart leaped; it was too far to hail Vargas, too far for a shot, so he slid down the steep bank of the ravine, losing sight of Vargas, knowing himself hidden by the brush and trees fringing the river. He found the old trail and hurried on. Only when he stood at one end of the bridge, Vargas at the other, did Vargas see him.

" Got you, Vargas! "

Vargas, who prided himself on an ambidextrous skill with a revolver, fired with his left hand, his right at the moment busied with the rope tied to his horse. It was too close to miss. Steve grunted and the second shot, closer than an echo to the first, added to the roar of the stream a reverberation like machine gun fire. But that second shot had been Steve's. Already hit himself, still he could not miss. His bullet tore through the muscles of Vargas's forearm, and the weapon fell from a paralyzed grip. In haste Vargas stooped to recover it, but no haste was sufficient, for it struck the edge of the bridge and slid off, splashing into the river.

"Got you, Vargas!" said Steve the second time, and started on his way to cross the bridge, crouching curiously yet holding his own weapon steadily enough.

Vargas stood there watching him malevolently, clutching a wounded arm, no longer concerned with his horse which was at last scrambling ashore but a few feet down stream from him. He didn't say anything; he was trying to make out whether his shot had missed altogether. His eyes flashed as he got from Steve's posture the answer to his question. Still he said nothing but stood still and very alert, and presently he in his turn crouched a little; he watched the one last chance he might hope for and was poised in every muscle, set at hair-trigger, as ready to spring as a mountain cat the second before it launches itself on its prey.

But Steve pulled up while still several feet from him.

"Yes—you made a good shot, Vargas," he said coolly. "That's why you've got to mind your step now. I'm not going to lose you. If I feel myself going out before I've got you hog-tied, why then it's your bad luck. I'll drill you."

Vargas grew vehement at that, full of words, naming Steve Cody everything under the sun that was vile and treacherous. Steve, feeling the strength slowly oozing out of his body, striving to keep a queer, light giddiness from usurping the place of determination in his brain, made a quick gesture with his revolver.

" Back up, Vargas. Snappy."

Vargas obeyed, drawing back and still back, the light higher than ever in his eyes as he saw how deathly white the other man's set face was growing. Time was all Vargas needed now, and not much of that!

Steve followed him slowly maintaining that same distance between them, some ten feet, no more, no less. Too far for Vargas to spring upon him, too near to permit of Vargas making a dash for escape. Steve seemed to crouch lower, but his burning eyes were steady and he kept his hands steady, one with its weapon, the other with the rope. In this way in some few paces which were like those of a nightmare they came to the old house of rocks.

" Inside, Vargas. Clear across the room."

Vargas still obeyed. Give him a few minutes longer, that was all he asked. Ten minutes, five perhaps; perhaps even less. There would come a sudden rush of faintness, overpowering, acting like a drug against which its victim has ceased to struggle, and Steve would lunge headlong into unconsciousness. All that was written in the white face.

But all that was denied by Steve's burning eyes. Today was a day for men to hold on to grim purposes taken, and master the whimpering flesh; for sheer manhood to triumph over nature itself. Laribee chose to ride when most men would have lain still and begged for help; Steve elected to make sure of Vargas though the last drop of blood drained out of his body as he completed his task. He tossed the rope to the floor.

"A loop about your right wrist." Vargas, fighting for time, began to argue. Steve snarled at him and Vargas stooped for the rope. Clumsily, for his left hand was useless, he got a loop over his right wrist. "Pull it tight; tighter!—Damn you, Vargas!" There was a metallic click and it was scarcely more metallic than Steve's voice. Yet Vargas, his eyes flashing to the revolver, stiffened. Also he drew the noose tight. "Now a half-hitch. Tight. Tighter!—All right. Now throw the other end of the rope over that beam ——"

Vargas was trapped now and knew it and went mad with the realization. Yet it was a madness which some degree of sanity kept under control. He slavered and gave vent to queer moaning noises of rage; his face was suffused with blood, even his eyes seeming to swim in blood. Steve tensed and awaited the expected spring; nothing was clearer than that Vargas gathered himself to make it. Yet all the while he must have been saying over and over to himself: "A little time; that's all. Any minute may do it. He'll drop."

Vargas, as commanded, threw the free end of the rope over the beam. Steve caught it and drew it tight, jerking Vargas's arm high above his head.

"Got—you ——"

Yes. The thing was done. Steve began to relax; he seemed to hear faint, distant voices saying, "Good enough. Your job's done. You can lie down now. Lie down for a good long rest." He need not fight any longer against the blackness which gathered in his brain. It was done ——

Vargas stirred prematurely. The rope twitched in

Steve's hand. Not done yet? All to be done over? What was it he wanted?

Why, just a something to tie the end of a rope to. He glanced all about him. There was nothing in this bare room that would serve for anchorage. Not so much as a doorknob; the door was gone.

He turned to Vargas as though to ask him what he suggested. He'd best hurry; it was growing dark.

" Got it! " said Steve thickly. " There's always—something to tie to ——"

When every other thing failed a man, there remained himself. He wrapped the end of the rope about his body; he began backing off, turning, winding up the slack. When he pitched forward, at last taking his long dive into the cool dark, his fall still farther tightened the rope. Vargas, on his tiptoes, screamed with the pain of a wrenched arm.

CHAPTER XXIV

STEVE, greatly confused, set himself frowningly to the first task that presented itself. He squeezed his eyes tight shut, then opened them suddenly as though to take the thing by surprise and so make out what it was and perhaps how it came here. Its whiteness had been what had caught his roving eye. A neat little enamelled table, that's what it was. There were objects on it, a glass, a bottle or two, a dish of some sort. A nicely ironed towel, too, serving as a table cover; he could see a big faded blue B.H. embroidered on a corner. He wondered who B.H. was.

" Billy Hill—Bud Hill—Bud Holmes—something like that."

He tried it again, that tight-shutting, swift opening of his eyes. White; everything white; walls and ceiling. A long, cool, quiet white room. Away off yonder was a little white bed, and he rather thought someone, as quiet as everything else here, lay on it. He turned his head and looked the other way; another little table, so close to him that he fancied he could reach it if he made the effort. But it was a far gayer table than the first; no cold glasses and bottles on it but an enormous bunch of roses, the reddest roses a man ever saw.

" Funny," said Steve. Or rather, he thought that he

287

said it. His lips moved but the hush of the room was undisturbed.

After a while he looked again toward the farther end of the room. He wished that he had a good spyglass; he'd make out then whether that was a man sleeping there or just a bundle of bed covers. This time he discovered that someone had moved the table with the red roses, putting it by that other fellow's bed. He frowned again; not only because he was vaguely irritated to think that someone had sneaked in on him this way but also he had rather liked the roses close at hand. He turned his head this way and that, wondering how the roses moved back and forth. Meaning to get at the bottom of the trick, he shut his eyes again and promptly forgot roses, tables, room and all other things.

Later he set himself to work out one of the well-known international and eternal puzzles, meaning to separate the real from the unreal, and of course all that he succeeded in doing was to achieve a still greater muddled confusion. He felt as though life had turned into a queer spotted affair of lights and shadows. He had an impression of the old Judge bending over him, saying something that did not matter in the least; of the Judge not being the Judge at all but Corinna; of himself lying on the broken floor with his head in Corinna's lap. She had kissed him; she had dropped tears into his face; she had said, " I love you! "

And for a space life continued to be a blurry checkerboard affair, and individuals grew into the habit of merging with one another. Dr. Burton, for example, had acquired the trick of changing instantly into a nurse in uniform, and at times into a sallow-faced, hawk-eyed, bulging-foreheaded man in bifocals through which a pair of very keen eyes probed deep into other folks' affairs.

In due course of time Steve and Laribee got acquainted again. For it turned out to be Laribee in that other bed. When first they understood and recognized each other they waved weakly and tried to grin. From that day Dr. Burton and the man in the bifocals agreed that the two men had good fighting chances to get well. If they had the fighting spirit, and it was pretty generally conceded that they did have it, they had something a little better than an even chance to steam along some day under their own power.

They first communicated with each other through the nurse. Laribee said to her, " Tell Steve I'm sorry." She told him he'd better lie still and try to get some sleep, and later on carried the message to Steve. He tried to nod his understanding, but even that was an effort. " Tell him— it's all right. Luck." The nurse did as instructed and on leaving the room advised Dr. Burton that the boys were getting chatty, and she supposed it was time to put them in separate rooms. Thus far, with both taking so little note of what was going on, it had been found convenient to have them in this big, cheery room, but from now on each ought to rest better alone. Two days later they were separated and the result was directly opposite to that expected. They kept looking for each other; they seemed to have felt that they were companions in misery, like two doughboys who had gone over the top together; each began to think that the other had died or was dying; and before night they again shared the long room and tried feebly to wave and grin in a silent way of saying: " Ride him, cowboy! "

Corinna came to see them twice daily, at about the same time every morning and afternoon. They seemed to know in advance when she was coming; for perhaps half an hour before each short visit they did not look at each other nor did they appear to remember each other for some little while after her departure. Of course neither had any memory of her first coming, immediately after Dr. Burton had dressed their wounds and had them put to bed. She had entered silently behind the nurse; she had stood very still, looking from one bed to the other.

" They're both unconscious you know, Miss Lee," whispered the nurse.

Corinna nodded and stood looking from one to the other of the quiet forms; for a little while she seemed to hesitate, not knowing which way to turn. At last she tiptoed to one of the beds, Laribee's. She stooped over him and her lips softly brushed his forehead.

" H'm! " observed the watchful nurse under her breath. " So that's it! "

Back across the long room tiptoed Corinna. At Steve's bedside, looking down at him with eyes which the nurse could not see, of a sudden she went down on her knees and hid her face in her hands against the edge of the bed.

" Oho! " gasped the nurse.

After that day, when the stage brought red roses for one, it brought red roses for the other; when a bowl of violets stood on the table at Steve's bedside a duplicate bowl of violets balanced it at Laribee's; Corinna always arranged them on the back porch and the nurse always brought them in.

Steve's first lucid question was asked of the Judge, who was another daily visitor.

" Where's Vargas? "

The old fellow, under a rather terrifying injunction from the nurse not to disturb either of her patients, came to the point as directly as any man could have done, trimming his recital of all fancy work. He had found Steve unconscious, tied to Vargas by the rope run over the beam; Vargas had fought for freedom, kicking at the fallen man who served as an anchor against his flight. The Judge with all the joy in life had taken Vargas in tow, and had landed him in jail at Madrone. Spike Freedom, in a separate cell, was still being held, though he had told everything he knew to the district attorney. John Bingham, by the way, had read Steve's letter that accompanied the returned money, and had acted on its promptings. Another guest at the local bastile was Grady —— Thus far did the Judge get when the nurse's eye turned on him with such admonition in it that, though he had much more to tell, he grew silent and presently withdrew.

But at the Lee ranch house, where nothing was talked of that did not have to do with Steve or Laribee, and where the Judge made himself very much at home during these days of anxious waiting, there was none to curtail his conversational flow. He lost no time at all in setting them all right as to the sort of man the real Steve Cody was. Corinna's father had returned, hastening his homeward journey on receipt of a telegram from the Judge; and with him had come the keen-eyed man in the bifocals. This was none other than the eminent Dr. Edmund Carew, the surgeon who had operated so successfully on Lee's leg and who, overworked, had carelessly made known to his patient that he was off " to the woods " for a bit of rest. Lee, saying nothing about the two wounded men up here, had tricked Dr. Carew into a visit at the ranch, and had promptly saddled him with two new patients. To these, to Corinna, to a new and very quiet Tad, the Judge told the whole story as he knew it, and certainly the story lost nothing in his telling. He built for Steve Cody a shining reputation that it was going to take a lot of effort to live up to. From the Judge as an able and eloquent broadcasting station there extended over the entire county a brand new conception of the erstwhile gambler who, while lying utterly unconscious of all this, was made into a popular hero. The man who, playing his lone hand, had got Vargas, who had exposed Grady, had taken the first great step toward completion of the job which his father had meant to take on himself.

" I knew! " Corinna confided in Tad when they were alone. " Even when I misjudged him, in my heart I knew. Oh, why didn't I listen to something telling me all the time that he was fine and true and splendid? And now—will he ever forgive me? "

Tad nodded miserably.

" He's a good scout and I'm a damn' fool.—Oh, Corinna, if Dave Laribee only gets well! " He choked up and turned away, an anxious, white-faced boy whose nights were all but sleepless, whose days were endless periods of torment, who started at every step, always in haggard anticipation of the news which he dreaded to hear. What though Laribee, when swaying on his feet, his face bloody, had said first of all when he brought them the visible evidence that Tad was not yet, at least, a murderer, had said: " It was an accident! Tad's not to blame" ? A great gladness then had burst upon them, followed instantly by a fresh tidal wave of fear as Laribee pitched forward into a heavy faint. " I wish it was me, not Dave Laribee," Tad was forever saying.

" He is going to get well, Tad, dear," Corinna told him over and over. And to him as to herself, over and over, she added: " They are both going to get well."

But it was not always comforting news which Dr. Carew brought out to the ranch house.

" It's nip and tuck," he told them in an offhand way that he had. He looked at Lee over the tops of his glasses, his head cocked to one side. " You're a confounded snake-in-the-grass, Lee," he announced. " Getting me up here for a rest, pretending to be doing me a nice little friendly act, then wishing a job like this on a tired business man! Well, at that, I don't know but that I'm glad you did. It's an interesting case. Funny thing; it's just dawned on me that, with two men in the shape those two chaps are in, with just about a fifty-fifty break for both, the betting ought to be on a fifty-fifty compromise. Looks like one of them was going to pull through, and the other ——"

He was not the man to say thumbs down on any patient of his, and let the rest of his meaning go with a shrug.

" I thought ——" began Lee, while neither Corinna

nor Tad could speak a word, but just stared and wanted to ask and were afraid to ask: "Which one?"

"I know," cut in the doctor. "I said yesterday that both ran about the same chances. And I've told you before that we're at a place where no physician on earth can do the corner-turning for those boys. It's largely a question of stick-to-it; of stamina and grit. Of morale; I guess that's it."

"They've both got it," contended Lee.

"Yes. I know it. But somehow I got the notion today that whereas one is set on living, perhaps having something worth living for, the other doesn't seem to take the same interest. And that is going to be the determining factor, if I'm any guesser, and I ought to be after a good many years of this sort of guessing.—Aunt Mary, if I could make coffee like that——"

Corinna's voice, strained and unnatural, asked the question.

"You—you haven't told us. Which one——"

"Mind you," said Dr. Carew, glancing at her and away, and all of a sudden estimating that now he had a clew that might explain this very matter of which he had spoken, "I'm just doing a bit of preliminary surmising. I'll watch for it tomorrow. But it does strike me, Lee, that young Laribee is about ten times more eager to stay alive than Cody.—And they've both got to do a bit of lifting on their own boot straps if we get them up and around again."

Corinna hastily left the table. For an instant she almost hated Dr. Carew. How could he sit there and eat and praise Aunt Mary for her coffee? She went to the window and stood looking out into the fading afternoon, seeing only a bleak hospital room with two little white beds in it, two men lying there so very still, gaunt-faced men whose eyes were always on the door when she came in.

The next morning Dr. Carew, making his report to the Lee household, confirmed his pronouncement of the day before and added to it a bit of news which had for all the direst significance. Steve Cody had made his will; Dr. Carew had been one of its witnesses.

That afternoon it was a desperate Corinna who made her visit to the sick room. She went to Laribee first and had her little visit with him; striving with all her might, she smiled at him and kept her unshed tears from betraying to him how she suffered. Then she went to Steve. Blacker than ever were his eyes now, less than ever did they afford any clew to what his thoughts might be. She brought him a smile, though one of pitifully tremulous lips, and had from him a smile only too patently created for the occasion.

" It's mighty nice of you, Miss Corinna ——"

She lowered her voice so that none but he could hear.

" Steve, dear Steve, do you want to break my heart? " At the first words the slow tears burst forth and began running down her face. She stooped over him and whispered: " You will live—for my sake, Steve. You can if you will. Dr. Carew says so ——"

" That's all right, Miss Corinna," muttered Steve.

Then still lower did she stoop. She was sure that no one would see; the nurse, her back turned, was at Laribee's side now, ministering to him. Her lips came at length to rest on Steve's.

"If you live, we will be so happy! If you won't try to live—I will die, too."

She ran out of the room, dabbing at her eyes; she blundered into a pantry somewhere and there presently the nurse found her crying.

"Look here, Miss Lee; I don't know what you were saying to Mr. Cody, but he seems upset. I won't have you ——"

Corinna burst from the room and ran outside. In her flight she careened full tilt into the Judge's arms and there had her cry out.

Two days later a perturbed and irritable Dr. Carew hurled a new hand grenade into camp.

"Oh, Cody's as good as out of the woods now," he snapped at the old Judge, who had invited himself to lunch. "I was right in all that I said, only I guess I just had the shoe on the wrong foot. It's Laribee now that's worrying me. I don't know what the devil can have come over him, but he seems to have caught the complaint that Cody just threw off. He looks down in the mouth and doesn't seem to give a tinker's dam whether school keeps or not.—I said he'd caught Cody's complaint? Well, he has, down to the last symptom. Made his will today." His eyes stabbed across the room at Corinna. "There's one individual in this neighborhood," he grunted, "who's going to come into a nice bit of property if both those young devils make up their minds it's more fun wearing wings than spurs."

" Made his will, huh? " said the Judge, and fell to scrubbing his head with both hands. " Laribee? Why, he was as perky an' frisky yest'day as a young spring mutton! Made his will, huh? Where the devil's my hat gone to now? "

" Dinner's almost ready, Judge," Lee reminded him.

" Dinner? " exclaimed the Judge. " Well, count me in. I'll be there an' back before the stew's stopped smokin'. I'm ridin' real horses these days, Lee; the best; an' I c'n cover that round dozen miles, yes, an' fix that darn fool Dave Laribee's clock, before you folks can get your elbows planted on the tablecloth. Bought a new three-year-ol' today, Lee ——"

He was still talking as he faded from view; he rode as a man who enjoys the exercise; and in a very short time he was squatting by Laribee's bed, looking mournfully at him.

He brought to Laribee's bedside an expression of countenance which is not as a rule welcomed in a sick room, the sort of face rather which is the conventional thing and quite *de rigueur* at funerals; even the manner of holding his hat was somehow reminiscent of white gloves and formal floral pieces.

" Hello, Dave," he said in a hushed voice. He eased himself down into a chair, taking pains as never before not to make a sound. His lengthened face grew the last degree more lugubrious; he sighed and seemed to make an effort to brace up. " How—how're they comin', Davy boy? "

" I'm all right," said Laribee, with no great enthusiasm. The Judge pulled out his handkerchief and blew his

nose gently; he kept the handkerchief in hand as though
he anticipated using it again.

" I—I hear ——— They tell me you've made your will,
Davy. That so? "

Laribee nodded. The Judge got up and crept to a
window; all Laribee could see of him was his back, all
he could hear was a guarded nose-blowing. Then, walking on quiet tiptoes, the Judge returned. What might have
been decoded as a brave acceptance of the inevitable now
triumphed over the sorrow in his eyes.

" Dave," he said stoutly, deciding it was best not to
overdo that Davy-boy business, " you're about the fines'
man I know. I know you're thinkin' o' her, that little
Corinna Lee; I don't need to ask if that will o' yours
took care o' her. No; you don't have to tell me; I c'n
see it in your eye. An' you save your stren'th, Davy.
Now I come as fas' as I heard about it, an' I want you
to know that as long's I'm still spared to keep on livin',
I'll do all any man could to stan' between her an' sorrow." He expelled a sigh which seemed to have been
dragged up from his boots. " I know what's worryin' you;
you're thinkin' o' what might be done to that no-'count
brother o' hers that shot you. If—if—if anything did
happen to you, Dave, o' course there's goin' to be a lot
o' men that'll mean to make that kid pay to the limit.
That's what's makin' it hard for you, ain't it?—Now,
don't you answer me, Dave; I know. You save your
stren'th.—An' this is all I come to say anyhow; if there
is any way to save her brother from hangin', I'll do it
for your sake. I got influence an' I'll use it; I reckon a
stretch in the pen won't hurt him, huh? An' she c'n go

see him now an' then. It won't kill her; hell no! You jus' quit your worryin', Davy boy. I —— So long, Dave," he ended abruptly, wrung Laribee's hand and hastened away.

He might have capped his climax and done a little more piling of Ossa on Pelion had he not seen the nurse bearing down on him with a look in her eye that there was no misreading. She tracked him down in the hall.

" Judge," she said, her eyes blazing, " you just keep out of that room from now on. Haven't you any sense? You might as well go to work in a sick room with a sledge hammer. I'm going to report you ——"

The Judge turned a beatific smile upon her.

" Ma'am," he told her serenely, " if things get bad again, you jes' send for ol' Jedge William Henery Bull. But they won't. I've fired my volley an' don't you forget it; now you jes' stan' by an' watch D. Laribee snap out of it. So long; got to hurry or I'll be late for dinner."

" Of all the old fools! " gasped the nurse, not yet appreciating him.

But, since she was an open-minded being, appreciation came soon. Laribee did snap out of it. And from that day, though convalescence was slow, both Dr. Carew and Dr. Burton confidently predicted complete recovery for both men.

" Separate them, though," commanded Carew. " Each man in his own room from now on until they're up so that they can ride a wheel chair. I'm beginning to think that there'll be no complications if ——" He thought it over; then concluded gravely: " If each man entertains his visitors alone."

And so, toward the end of convalescence, when the Judge made his longest call on Steve Cody it was in Steve's private room.

" You're a lucky cuss, m' son; that's what I say," said the Judge emphatically. " A man who's been lucky all his life at cards, an' on top of that is lucky in love, he's jus' naturally born under a lucky star."

Steve said curiously: " A lucky star." And then he added thoughtfully and the quick light had dulled in his eyes: " It's going to be hell on Dave, Judge. For a while I thought—I think that poor old Dave thought it, too ——"

" Shucks! " said the Judge. " He'll get over it. Why, I was a young feller once myse'f." He chuckled reminiscently, yet somehow to Steve's critical ear there was something spurious about the chuckle; it should have been a sigh but the Judge would have none of that. " Yeah; I was young an' there was a girl that would make this here Corinna Lee party look like a pug-faced high contender in the ugly girls' competition. Don't know's I ever tol' you? Well, it worked out so your dad got her, an' she was your mother, Steve, ol' tarantula. An' at that, me an' your ol' man got along firs' rate, all things considered." He got up and twirled his hat on a horny forefinger. " Well, so long, ol' he-goat; keep a-ridin'. It's a funny ol' world but, I dunno. Things works out, give 'em time. An' it's kind o' lucky, come to think of it, that time's one thing there's a lot of! Adios, potato bug."

CHAPTER XXV

WHETHER or not Laribee " got over it " as the Judge so confidently predicted, at least it is certain that he did not add another long face to the lugubrious visages already regarding life in sufficient numbers. He picked up the old threads, all but one, where he had laid them down, and no man ever got a hint from him that he mourned over the one thread dropped as the single one of gold. He was man enough to regard life with a kindly smile, full of courage; though it was not fated that he should have the great dream come true, at least he felt himself enriched by what had been granted him, by what was still to come to him through the deep affection of friends.

He remained the chief factor of the Forty which continued for some months to function. He saw Vargas forced to take the slow yet inescapable steps to a full retribution; saw Vargas's Place closed, empty, a padlock on the door; saw Grady moving on into the shadow of those chill gray walls wherein men paid for their crimes with long years of their lives; and came to feel day by day a cleaner air blowing through High Town. Vargas's men fell away from their fallen leader, loitered for a brief period of vacillating indecision, and melted away.

For Laribee old friendships strengthened. He and the Judge became almost inseparable. Perhaps the old fellow, in a mellow reminiscent mood, had confided in Laribee his own love story? Surely some bond existed which drew them very close together. And there was Tad; the boy who was forever carrying his young enthusiastic worship to some idol or another, made of Laribee the most heroic of all those figures which from time to time had filled his horizon. Tad became Laribee's general foreman and right-hand man, and was some degrees prouder than any youngster with a new pair of red boots.

"I been thinkin', D. Laribee," said the Judge one day, "o' makin' you a proposition."

"It's a go," laughed Laribee, and ran an arm, like a son's, about the Judge's shoulders. "Whatever you say, clicks with me."

"What I'm a-thinkin'," the Judge rambled on, "is like this: There's big doin's comin' up, an' I'm all frisky to spread m'se'f. What I need's a pardner. Now, like I rec'lec' tellin' Steve's ol' man one time, this neck o' the woods has sort o' run wild a spell, but like a man it sort o' settles down after the wildness peters out. It's come alive an' there's money blowed in an' stuck, an' there's bound to be what lan' sharks calls development. Get a few gents together that's got land, money an' mebbe a spoonful o' brains between 'em, let 'em sort o' spread out an' pick up a section o' land here an' one there an' another over yonder, let 'em grab onto all the water rights that's runnin' free right now an' cook up what you might call a Water an' Power an' Irrigation Projec', an'—— There you are, m' son!"

"I'd have thought you'd have gone to Steve with a thing like this," said Laribee.

"It's kind o' hard gettin' any sense drove in on Steve right now," returned the Judge. "Later on, why not? Me an' you an' Steve Cody! Whew!—How'd you like that, Dave?" He bent a penetrating eye on his companion, adding briskly: "Me an' you an' Steve, pardners!"

"Why, there's nothing on earth I'd like so well," said Laribee. "A close corporation——"

"The closes' on earth! Jus' three frien's, huh, boy?"

During these days Laribee saw both Steve and Corinna often, and on the surface of things there was only a placid happiness and a sincere sympathetic understanding. Yet now and then the shadow of a shadow dimmed the glory of the sunshine which springtime was bringing back into the mountains. Well, what piece of smooth amber does not have its tiny bubble?

"No," said Laribee doggedly. "There's to be no flaw in it; it's too fine a thing."

And so he sent a little note down to Corinna. He asked quite simply if she would come up to his ranch on the following day, and if she would arrange to arrive just at dusk.

In the fading afternoon he sat on his porch and looked out across the slowly darkening fields rippling away into the greater dark of the timber-clad slopes which in turn extended into the higher and more broken uplands of the mountains, which still caught the sunlight on their rocky summits. He sat long without stirring, scarcely seeming to breathe. Then he heard horses' hoofs in the distance and stiffened to listen. From the clatter, even when he first heard it faint and far-off, he realized that there were two riders, and he had counted on Corinna alone. Well, at this late hour, it was but natural that she would want someone with her.

Laribee stood up. The hush of twilight was all about him. He looked out across his little valley catching the night shadows in its bowl, and beyond to a noble, rugged old giant of mountains shouldering up into the sky, still catching the full sunshine; a fine old mountain, staunch and enduring and, somehow, friendly. A sturdy old optimist, thought Laribee, who was first to look upon each sunrise, who clothed himself in purple and was serene above the darkness gathering down below.

"A man ought to learn from you, old boy. To stand straight, never minding the shadows—keeping his head up—and when night comes, seeing the stars ——"

The hoof beats grew louder, ceased suddenly, were quiet for a minute or two, then came on again. But with a difference. It was just one horse now. And Laribee, understanding, kept his eyes on the mountain-top.

"You are good to come," he said and ran down the steps to Corinna. He helped her down and for a moment held her hands very gently. "You were good to come."

"David! You know that I would do anything ——"

"Of course I know, my dear. Now you are going to come with me and stand on my old porch for just about as long as a man could count a hundred."

He ran lightly back up his steps and waited for her at the top, smiling down on her as, wondering, Corinna slowly mounted to his side. He lifted his hand and pointed.

She saw the little valley running away in ripples,

catching the dark so very tenderly, and beyond it the
mountains enwrapping themselves like kings in purples.
Purple above, too, slowly deepening while they watched
it. And then:

"Look!" said Laribee. "The star."

Corinna looked where he looked and felt something of
the emotion which he experienced; a faint shivery sigh
escaped her and she withdrew her eyes to fix them,
shining through the dusk, upon him. His own, meeting
hers frankly, had that same kindly smile in them.

"I want you to be happy, Corinna; perfectly happy.
Oh, I know; but there has been that tiny fleck in the
sunshine. It will be gone after tonight. I have told you
before, haven't I, how I love these old mountains? And
how no day is perfect for me that does not bring me at
its close out here to sit and take it all in? And I want
you to know that as I love what I can see of God's
world here, just so do I love you. It's in the same, same
way, my dear. Am I unhappy because I do not own that
old mountain? Or that star? Unhappy because I cannot
call them mine?" He shook his head, still smiling. "I
am very, very happy; more than that, I am a contented
man. Do you understand?"

"David!" she cried impulsively, close to tears. "You
are so ——"

"Sh!" said Laribee, and laughed softly. "Now run
along, will you, Corinna? That was all. You don't mind
having come, do you, just to humor me this once? Good
night, my dear, and thank you; and God bless you."

He watched her out of sight; presently he heard horses
galloping again, a diminishing sound, fading away in the

distance, lingering faintly, at last lost in the great hush of evening.

" It's a great old world," said Laribee. He extended his arms as though to draw it and himself close together, breast to breast. But the gesture was hardly completed; he let his arms drop to his sides. Some things were too big, too vast, too mighty to be encompassed by a man's arms and must be embraced by a limitless soul.

Far away, all unheard by Laribee, swifter and swifter grew the hoof-beats as two horses raced through the shadows pounding out the gayest of gay rhythms. Then after a little while when the night sprinkled the first handful of stars across the sky, and that first burst of speed was over, slower and slower went the hoof-beats— so slow that they seemed about to stop.

Corinna made a perfectly atrocious pun. Yet Steve seemed to like it!

" You are my starry knight! "

" You are my star! "

" I love you."

" I love you."

The horses rubbed noses, moving more slowly than ever, closer together. With a laugh Steve put his arm about Corinna and lifted her to his saddle; like one of her knights from Malory, riding with his damsel no longer in the slightest distress, he carried her home.